# TRIGGER CITY

Also by Sean Chercover

*Big City, Bad Blood*

# TRIGGER CITY

# SEAN CHERCOVER

*wm*

WILLIAM MORROW

*An Imprint of* HarperCollins*Publishers*

Grateful acknowledgment is made to reprint the excerpt from "Onions" from *Blue Daffodils and Other Poems,* copyright © 2007 by Bryan Owen.

HarperCollins books may be purchased for educational, business, or sales promotional use. For information please write: Special Markets Department, HarperCollins Publishers, 10 East 53rd Street, New York, NY 10022.

FIRST EDITION

*Designed by Renata DiBiase*

---

Library of Congress Cataloging-in-Publication Data

Chercover, Sean.
    Trigger city / Sean Chercover. —1st ed.
        p. cm.
    ISBN 978-0-06-112869-1
    1. Private investigators—Illinois—Chicago—Fiction.  2. Middle-aged women—Crimes against—Fiction. 3. Schizophrenics—Fiction. 4. Murder—Investigation—Fiction.  5. Chicago (Ill.)—Fiction.  I. Title.

    PS3603.H47T75  2008
    813'.6.—dc22                                              2008018164

---

08 09 10 11 12   OV/RRD   10 9 8 7 6 5 4 3 2 1

*To Barbara and Murray Chercover,*
*who gave me a running start, picked me up*
*when I fell, and loved me anyway*

*And to my sister, Holly,*
*with more love than*
*I can say*

# ACKNOWLEDGMENTS

**I owe many thanks to many people.**

To Barbara and Murray Chercover, for being exceptional parents, friends, and first readers.

To my agents, Denise Marcil and Michael Congdon, for their ongoing belief and guidance.

To my editor, Lyssa Keusch, for her terrific editorial insight, and to Tom Egner, Amy Halperin, Danielle Bartlett, Buzzy Porter, Johnathan Wilber, May Chen, and the entire team at William Morrow/Harper-Collins.

To Lt. Robert Biebel, Sgt. Eugene Mullins, Kristina Schuler, Monique Bond, and Pat Camden at the Chicago Police Department.

To Special Agents Frank Bochte and Ross Rice at the FBI.

To Manic Dave, Grits, L.J., and especially Maddoggie for pulling back the curtain and offering me a glimpse inside the world of the modern mercenary.

To Jon Jordan, Ruth Jordan, and Jennifer Jordan (Sly & the Family Jordan) . . . for so many kindnesses, too extensive to cover in this space.

To Ken Bruen for massive doses of public support and private encouragement, and for keeping me at least partially sane. Partially. *Whoa . . . pot, kettle, black.*

To Dianne Bazos, Judy Bobalik, Jake Burns, Holly Chercover, Eric Cherry, Lee Child, Jane Cornett, Crimespree Magazine, The Real Ray Dudgeon, Barry Eisler, Russell H. Ewert, Paul Guyot, Libby Hellmann, Jane and Knut Holmsen, Alison Janssen, Eugene Jarecki, Rick Kogan, Joe Konrath, Ben LeRoy, Deborah Liebow, Paul Magder, Eric Murphy, Annie Neyfakh, Sara Paretsky, Doug Patteson, Otto Penzler, Todd Robinson, Sandra Ruttan, Marcus Sakey, Gordon and Heather and Jessica Schmidt, Michael D. Sullivan, Terry Young, Stella and Rocky Z.

To the end-of-the-bar gang at Jake's Pub—next round's on me.

To Marian Misters and JD Singh, Richard Katz, Robin and Jamie Agnew, Jim Huang, Augie Aleksy, Mike Bursaw, Pat Frovarp and Gary Schulze, CPL Commissioner Mary Dempsey, Annie Tully, Penny Halle, Linda Schehl, and the many other booksellers and librarians who've been so kind to me on my travels.

To my very good friends and fellow bloggers at www.theoutfit collective.com—Barbara D'Amato, Michael Allen Dymmoch, Libby Fischer Hellmann, Kevin Guilfoile, Sara Paretsky, and Marcus Sakey . . . and my friends at www.killeryear.com . . . and the many good folks at rec.arts.mystery.

And finally (but most importantly) to Martine . . . gorilla my dreams.

# PROLOGUE

Searching for the truth the way God designed it,
The truth is I might drown before I find it.

Bob Dylan, "Need a Woman"

**F**acts are not truth. Listen carefully, this is important.

Facts can point to truth, or can be manipulated to point away from it. You search for the facts that support the goal of your client. Could be a civil litigator pressing a defendant to settle out of court. A defense attorney manufacturing some reasonable doubt for some guilty-as-hell client. An insurance company looking to deny a claim that may or may not be fraudulent. Doesn't really matter. You uncover facts until your client is satisfied, send a bill, and move on.

That's the job. That's your goal. Because if your goal is truth, you'll go both broke and crazy.

And if your client's goal is truth, run away screaming, fast as you can.

* * *

Joan Richmond died just after 2:00 P.M. on a sunny Saturday in mid-August. She was in the middle of a telephone conversation with her father, discussing where to meet for dinner that evening, when the doorbell rang. She was not expecting company and told her dad she'd call him right back.

"Probably Jehovah's Witnesses or something," she said.

She was wrong.

Joan Richmond's condo was on the ground floor of a converted Lincoln Park three-flat. Through the cut-glass window of her front door, she could see Steven Zhang, a colleague from work.

Did she smile as she unlocked the door? In my mind she smiled, but there's no way to know. I'm pretty certain that she didn't see the gun in his right hand. But again, that's speculation, not established fact. Maybe his hand was in his pocket.

This much is certain: Joan Richmond opened the door and Steven Zhang shot her in the face. He put three more bullets between her breasts as she lay on the Spanish tile of her foyer. Dropped a signed confession on the floor and walked away as her brain, no longer receiving a fresh supply of oxygen, began to die.

Steven Zhang drove straight home to his town house in the University Village neighborhood, near the UIC campus. He locked the door, poured a few ounces of Talisker over ice, and phoned his wife at her mother's Chinatown apartment. Or maybe he phoned her first, then poured the scotch. Anyway, he told her that he had done something terrible and that he was sorry and that he loved her. He hung up before she could respond.

Steven Zhang put *ABBA's Greatest Hits* on the stereo, turned it up to full volume. He drank the scotch. He put the barrel of the gun in his mouth, pulled the trigger, and decorated the wall with his brains.

These are the known facts surrounding the death of Joan Richmond. The truth? Shit, I already warned you about that . . .

# PART I

A nation of sheep will beget a government of wolves.

—Edward R. Murrow

# CHAPTER ONE

**F**orty-four is too young for a woman to die." Isaac Richmond sipped black coffee from a U.S. Army mug, then fixed his ice-blue eyes on the framed photograph in his other hand. He rested the mug on the coffee table. "You don't agree."

"It's only right for you to feel that way, Colonel Richmond," I said. "But no, I don't think there's such a thing as 'too young to die.'" I drank some coffee. It was instant, but I like instant. Guilty pleasure.

Isaac Richmond had been retired from the army for twenty years, but a cursory examination of his study told me a lot. There were photos of Richmond in full dress uniform receiving medals and commendations, shaking hands with generals. In other photos he wore green camouflage BDUs—boarding a transport plane, standing in a mess hall, sitting in a jeep on a downtown Saigon street. There was the framed degree from West Point. And the coffee mugs. Not one thing gave testimony to the two decades of Richmond's life since he retired his commission.

And then there was the man himself. He was harder at seventy-four than I was, still (if barely) a year shy of forty. He held himself in perfect posture and even his silver hair stood at attention, trimmed just slightly longer than a standard-issue crew cut. Clearly this was a man who defined himself by his military service, so I addressed him by rank and he didn't correct me.

"You have children, Mr. Dudgeon?"

"No, sir."

"Believe me, there *is* such a thing as 'too young to die.' If you ever have kids, you'll understand." He cleared his throat and handed me the photograph. "My daughter. Joan."

Joan Richmond looked remarkably like her father—the same erect posture, the same blue eyes, the same compact features. Sharp chin, sharper nose, thin lips. On Isaac Richmond, the features conspired to make him look like a hard-ass, whereas on Joan the overall impression was that of a shy librarian. Proper, but not a prude. Not beautiful, but pleasant to look at. Friendlier than her father. And fragile.

Before coming to Richmond's house in Dearborn Park, I'd read over the newspaper coverage of his daughter's murder, six weeks earlier. Joan Richmond was single, lived alone. She was the head of payroll for HM Nichols, a midsize department store chain. The man who killed her, Steven Zhang, was a naturalized American citizen who'd come from China thirteen years earlier. He was a freelance IT consultant Joan had hired to update the employee payroll system and optimize the database. After shooting Joan to death, he'd gone home and killed himself, leaving behind a wife and young daughter. And a written confession that sounded all kinds of crazy. The cops investigated and collected the results of various forensic tests and cleared the case within two weeks.

So why had Mike Angelo sent Richmond my way?

"Colonel Richmond, I am sorry for your loss but I'm not sure what I can do for you. Do you think the police got it wrong?" I set the photograph on the coffee table between us. Isaac Richmond's mouth tightened, twitched once.

"This is a very intimate business between us, Mr. Dudgeon, and I am not accustomed to discussing my personal life with strangers."

His mouth tightened again and, although I hadn't noticed any room for improvement, his posture got even straighter. "I'm sorry," he said, "that's not fair. I called you, you didn't call me."

I reached into my briefcase and withdrew a form, signed it, and handed it to him. "Standard nondisclosure agreement. I'm not in the habit of spreading the details of my clients' personal lives around the schoolyard, Colonel."

"No, I'm sure . . . I didn't mean to imply." He put the form on the table, next to the photo of his dead daughter. "It just goes against my nature to discuss such things. I spent twenty-six years in military intelligence. Our division motto was *Learn All, Say Nothing.* I've been living by that motto since I was a very young man. It made me a somewhat distant husband and father, I'm sorry to say. My wife—Joan's mother—died when Joan was only seven years old. Bad heart . . . genetic. Joan grew up on military bases all over the world, raised really by a succession of army matrons, and I was not there very often. She was like an orphan with a wide assortment of kindly aunts, but we were redeployed regularly and even those relationships never had the time to deepen."

He sat for a minute saying nothing. The look on his face suggested that he was back in time, on army bases in Germany and Korea and who knows where else.

"I'm sorry, where was I? Yes, right. I was absent for much of Joan's upbringing. She developed into an exceedingly intelligent young woman but very inward, quiet, not as socially confident as she should have been. Eventually she moved stateside, matriculated from Northwestern—double major: Economics and Accounting. Summa cum laude." He drank down the rest of his coffee, which had long since gone cold. "She could've done so much. But she was a whiz at math and I suppose a career in accounting shielded her from having to deal with people, to some extent. And she was good at it.

"My parental failings notwithstanding, Joan welcomed me into her life when I eventually settled in Chicago and we managed to build a friendly relationship. A good relationship. There were boundaries I could not cross—she was not going to pretend that we had much history and I was not invited to offer fatherly guidance. And she insisted on calling me Isaac, never Dad or Father. But we spoke on the phone almost daily, and we dined together every Saturday. I suggested that we make it a weekday—Saturday is prime dating time for young working people—but Joan didn't seem interested in dating. I don't think she was a lesbian, and even if she were, one presumes she would still go out on dates. She just seemed uncomfortable with the idea of romantic relationships of any kind. No doubt a result of her upbringing. Collateral damage of my service, I'm afraid." Richmond shook it off with a rueful chuckle. "Listen to me. An old man wallowing in his regrets, while you sit nodding politely and wondering what the hell any of this has to do with you."

I gave him an accommodating smile. "I've been wondering where I fit in."

"Put simply, I want you to bring me the truth of Joan's death. In answer to your question, I do not think that the police got it wrong. Joan was killed by a mentally unbalanced employee. I can accept that. But I need more. They say that he was schizophrenic. Fine. But what triggered him to go off his meds? And why did he focus on Joan? Were they friends? Was he in love with her? Were they having an affair? I know I said she wasn't interested in romantic relationships but the truth is I didn't know her that well. She must have had needs, even if she didn't want a relationship, so perhaps they were . . . involved. He came to her house—how did he know her address? Had he been there before? I ask myself these questions . . . constantly. They wake me in the middle of the night. They never subside. I need you to bring me answers."

Isaac Richmond stood and got a checkbook from his desk drawer, ripped the top check free, handed it to me. It was payable to Ray Dudgeon in the amount of $50,000. My jaw must've bounced off my chest.

"It's a lot of money, Mr. Dudgeon, but here's what I want from you: I want the next sixty days of your life. I want you to work on this case exclusively. No other clients, no vacations. You may take one day a week for yourself. And you will have to cover your own expenses, within reason, out of that money.

"I do not want written reports but I do require biweekly verbal reports. All that you've learned. All. You are not to protect me from any unpleasantness. Joan was my daughter and I loved her but I don't put her on a pedestal. I need to know whatever you learn about her, about her killer, about whatever relationship they had—personal or professional. I want the truth."

Isaac Richmond didn't really want me to bring him the truth of his daughter's death; he wanted me to bring him the truth of his daughter's life. He wanted me to make up for a relationship they'd never had, and there was no way I could fill that emptiness. Whatever I learned, it wouldn't be enough. It wouldn't be what he really needed.

But what I really needed was money. In the previous months, I'd been x-rayed and arthrogrammed and MRIed and cortisone injected. I'd learned terms like *ruptured supraspinatus* and *neural foraminal stenosis* and *acute osteophyma*. It was Greek to me.

Bottom line: I needed surgery to fix the damage. My crappy health insurance plan only ensured that I could plan on personal bankruptcy if I went ahead with the surgery, so I'd been putting it off. But the shoulder was getting worse and I'd have to do something soon. The previous week I'd asked Sasha Klukoff to find a buyer for my '68 Shelby. The car had been a gift, and it was worth a bundle. It easily constituted over 80 percent of my net worth. I could barely afford the insurance on it.

And now I held a check for $50,000. All I had to do is take a case that had zero chance of success. A case I should turn down cold.

"Colonel Richmond, I understand that grieving is not easy. But my poking around in the residue of your daughter's life is not going to bring her back. And it's not going to bring her closer to you. You had the relationship you had. I think you need to make peace with that." I held the check out to him.

He didn't take it. Instead, he put a set of keys on the table in front of me. Attached to the key ring was a little LED flashlight with the HM Nichols logo printed on the side.

"Joan's apartment keys. Don't refuse me, I can think of no better use for the money. I have cash in the bank, investments, a pension, and no heirs." His right hand moved in a sweeping gesture, taking in the room. "I bought this house for $600,000. It is now worth more than two point four million. After my service, I did extremely well as a consultant and I have more than I could ever spend. So take the money, I won't miss it." He fixed me with a steady look. "And I know you need it."

"Oh?"

Isaac Richmond smiled, said, "Even with the recommendation of a CPD lieutenant, you don't think I'd hire you without some due diligence. I'm an old army spook—I don't go into anything without a little recon. Your reputation is one of honesty and persistence, to a fault."

"Perhaps to a major fault," I said.

"Yes, you were quite the newsmaker a little while back. I do admire the way you handled yourself, but you made trouble for powerful people and I know your business has suffered as a result."

"A little slow for a while but I'm doing fine now. Thanks for your concern."

"No need for sarcasm, Mr. Dudgeon, I meant no offense." Isaac Richmond stood and motioned toward the door. "Please sleep on it tonight, decide in the morning. Take the check home with you. And the keys. If you decide not to help me, return them here. You can do that much for an old man."


I awoke to the sound of my own voice screaming, felt my body shaking from the adrenaline surge.

*Fuck. Not again . . .*

I rolled onto my back and took a few deep breaths to bring my heart rate down, pressed my palms against my chest to stop the shaking. Then came the tears. I let myself cry for a minute or two, then cut it off. I tried to push the images from my mind, but some images push easier than others.

And this particular memory slideshow was insistent. I was tied to a chair while a couple of very bad cops wearing very bad aftershave did very bad things to me. To call them cops is really an insult to cops. More like sadistic crooks with badges. They'd whipped me with an electrical cord, pried off a fingernail, knocked out a couple of teeth. And then they'd dislocated my shoulder and stomped on it.

That was almost ten months ago. They were both dead. But the images remained.

*Get over it, Dudgeon.*

I got up and stripped the sweat-soaked sheet off the futon. It had become such a common occurrence that I kept a fresh sheet and pillowcase on a nearby chair. The bedside clock read 3:23 A.M.

The nightmare had been triggered by rolling over in my sleep, onto my right side. Onto my shoulder, which now felt like someone had sunk a hot ice pick deep into the joint. I left the bedsheet in a heap on the floor, went to the bathroom mirror, and opened my mouth. No blood. I didn't expect blood, knew that the taste of it was just a sense memory, but I always checked anyway.

The taste of blood, sudden sweats, and flashback images sometimes happened when I was wide awake. Sometimes triggered by pain in the shoulder or neck, sometimes by the smell of diesel fuel or Aqua Velva. And sometimes I couldn't identify the trigger. The episodes had diminished during the months I'd spent with my grandfather down in Georgia but when I came back to Chicago they were right here waiting for me.

Chicago was full of triggers. Chicago was Trigger City.

I swallowed a couple of Percocet and took a cool shower. My doctor had insisted that painkillers were not a long-term solution and warned that my supraspinatus tendon was at risk and the shoulder would continue to deteriorate until I got the surgery. But I already knew. I'd read the MRI report—it was a mess in there.

I toweled off and put the new sheet on the bed, thinking *You can't live like this much longer, it's just too exhausting. Get the surgery. Take Richmond's money. He's a grown-up. He said it himself, he's got loads of money and he won't miss it and you gave him fair warning besides. If the case is a loser, so be it.*

So be it.

# CHAPTER TWO

Lieutenant Mike Angelo, commanding officer of the Area 4 Homicide Section, leaned back in his squeaky chair and patted his belly, which threatened to pop the buttons of his polyester shirt. "You take the gig?"

I slid a book across the desk to him. *The Guards,* by Ken Bruen. "Brought you something," I said. "An Irish detective novel. Great book, you'll like it. Full of bent cops, very realistic. Present company excepted, of course."

A gentle tease, and I wouldn't even go that far with any other cop I knew. But Mike Angelo and I had built a good working relationship based upon earned respect. To call us personal friends would be a stretch, but I knew Mike was good people and I'd like to think he'd say the same about me.

Mike sent me a deadeye cop stare. "Cops make convenient punching bags the world over, why should Ireland be any different?" He picked up the book and flipped the pages and his eyes grew wide. I'd inserted his finder's fee, spread throughout the book. Hundred-dollar bills. Twenty-five of them.

"Thanks for the referral," I said. "Richmond wants eight weeks, exclusive."

"No shit?"

"Even paid in advance."

"I figure two weeks at most to confirm everything we already know," Mike said. "What the hell you gonna do with the next six?"

"It's not like that. Richmond says he doesn't doubt the CPD."

"So what does he want?"

"I think he wants to know his daughter better. He wants me to bring him the *capital-T* truth of her death, beyond the pertinent facts."

"Oh Christ."

"I know. I tried to turn him down but he wasn't having any."

Mike shrugged, "Ah, what the hell, he's rich. Bring him a few tidbits that he didn't know about his daughter, make him happy and spend the money with a clear conscience."

"Nothing's gonna make him happy," I said. "His daughter will still be dead and he still won't know her any better."

"Not your problem." Mike plucked a black three-ring binder off the stack on his gray metal desk and dropped it in front of me. "Joan Richmond's *deceased file*. Just about as open and shut as I've ever seen."

"Anything bother you?"

"Read the file, you'll see. Steven Zhang was a paranoid headcase who killed his boss. Case closed." He stood, picked up the book I'd given him, and headed for the door. "I'm gonna make dinner reservations for Susan and me at Anna Maria's. God bless her, she prefers great food to fancy."

"You're a lucky man."

"Back in twenty. Happy reading."

The binder wasn't as thick as most. Not surprising, given the circumstances. The cops had responded to a 911 gunshot call. They found Joan Richmond, dead of multiple gunshot wounds, in the foyer of her condo. A signed confession lay next to the body, written on *Zhang IT Consulting* letterhead. Naturally, the cops headed for the address on the letterhead. On the way there, the radio dispatcher announced a gunshot at the same address. The cops found Steven Zhang dead of a self-inflicted gunshot from the same caliber gun that had killed Joan Richmond. Ballistics later confirmed that it was the same gun. And the handwriting on the confession matched Zhang's.

Steven's wife, Amy Zhang, arrived on the scene in a state of panic. She told of Steven's strange phone call, and phone records later confirmed it. Understandably, she had a meltdown when she saw what was left of her husband and she wasn't much use to the police. But they came back a couple days later for a follow-up and she confirmed that Steven had recently been acting secretive and paranoid and had been launching into verbal diatribes that made no sense. She'd begged him to see a doctor but he had insisted that the doctors were all part of a conspiracy to poison him.

The detectives interviewed Joan Richmond's boss and subordinates at HM Nichols. Joan was well liked but no one professed to know her very well. She had hired Zhang on contract and for the first couple of months all went well and she was happy with his job performance. She and Zhang often lunched together and coworkers said they seemed to be friends. None thought there was anything sexual between them. In the couple of weeks prior to the murder, Zhang started to display erratic behavior, acting fearful of his coworkers, not combing his hair or shaving his face, holding loud arguments with voices that seemed to exist only in his head. For the last week of his life Zhang wore the same clothes every day. When a coworker commented on it, he explained that someone was putting poison in his laundry soap, to control his mind.

The written confession gave further evidence of these same delusions. Apparently Zhang came to believe that Joan Richmond had been co-opted into the vast conspiracy against him. The tasks she assigned demanded that he read computer code that was designed to reprogram his brain so that he wouldn't be able to carry out his "vital mission, imperative to saving American democracy." Having been infected by the computer code, Zhang now received auditory instructions from

"Them"—instructions that arrived as Joan Richmond's voice, even when she was nowhere near. Killing her was the only way to silence the instructions, so he could carry out his mission.

The detectives interviewed Joan Richmond's neighbors, none of whom recognized a photograph of Steven Zhang. Similarly, none of Zhang's neighbors recognized a photo of Joan Richmond. They interviewed Isaac Richmond but he knew nothing about Zhang, had never heard of him.

I examined the crime scene photographs taken at Joan Richmond's condo. Joan lay on her back. Her legs, slightly bent at the knees, lay to the right, crossed above the ankle. Her right arm was down by her side, while her left went straight out from her shoulder, like she was signaling a left turn. She wore blue jeans and a turquoise T-shirt. The first bullet had entered through her left cheekbone, and the tissue above the bullet hole was enlarged. There were three more entry wounds in the center of her chest. She'd been shot right in the heart, so there wasn't a lot of blood. Her eyes were open, but there was nobody home.

Next came the photos from Steven Zhang's town house. Zhang sat on a blue sofa, legs spread out in front of him, arms down by his sides, hands palm up. His head lay back to one side and his mouth hung wide open, like some drunken dinner guest, passed out and snoring in the middle of your party and making everyone uncomfortable.

He'd put the barrel in his mouth, shot up through the soft palate. That doesn't slow a bullet very much and it had exited out the back of his head and splattered blood and brains and skull fragments all over the cream-colored wall behind him.

Mike Angelo returned just as I was closing my notebook.

"Get your fill?" He sat and his chair squeaked.

"And then some," I said.

I picked up two beef sandwiches at Al's #1 Italian and took them back to my office on Wabash. Vince Cosimo was sitting in my chair when I entered.

"Just test-driving it," he said.

"Yeah yeah. Other side, rookie." Vince squeezed his muscular frame into one of my client chairs while I grabbed two bottles of Capital Wisconsin Amber from the little bar fridge. I gave him a sandwich and he dug into it like the next day was Lent. Gave him one of the bottles, sat at my desk, and took a swig of beer.

Vince Cosimo had earned his blue card that summer and was working for me part-time. At first there wasn't any work to give him. Isaac Richmond had been right—after the big ruckus and my four-month exile, I'd returned to Chicago to find that most of my clients had purged my name from their Rolodexes. Hard to blame them, really. They had to think of their own safety, and that of their families.

So it was strictly B-list gigs for a while. Process serving and petty insurance fraud and a couple of divorces to get me over. But I stuck with it and eventually word got around that I'd managed a truce with Chris Amodeo, and some A-list clients returned, followed by a surge of new clients. My pseudo-celebrity status was a hell of a draw, once everyone knew they could hire me without running afoul of the Outfit.

So now I often had work for Vince, but he lacked experience. I was bringing him along as fast as was prudent. I'd recommended him to an agency that specialized in serving subpoenas and they gave him about twenty hours a week. I gave him another twenty, but almost half of it was unpaid, since more than half of the time he was just observing how the job was done. I was trying to be a nice guy but I wasn't looking to put Santa Claus out of business. Anyway, Vince made enough to get by while learning the trade. And Mary had left him, which significantly reduced his living expenses.

Vince wiped beef drippings from his chin, said, "How'd the job interview go?"

"It wasn't a job interview," I said. "It was a meeting with a prospective client."

"Yeah, how'd it go? Any work for me?"

"Probably not. Too early to say." I moved the second half of my sandwich to the paper in front of Vince. "Anyway I've already got you on a paying gig."

"I'm still on that?"

"Did I tell you to stop?" I held Vince's eyes until he looked away. "Then you're still on it."

"Yeah, but Ray . . ."

"I don't want to hear it, Vince. Really." I took another bite of my half sandwich and chewed, not tasting it. Washed it down with some beer. "Look, in a perfect world none of us would ever have to do divorce work. But I promise you, if you're gonna make a career out of this, there will be ups and downs and you'll have to do them."

"This isn't even a divorce."

"Extended surveillance. One subject. Working solo. It's the same profile as 90 percent of domestic surveillance jobs and most workman's comp, too. It's good experience for you."

"Okay, but Ray . . ."

"What? You want to continue to apprentice under my license, or not?" I put the beer bottle on the desk a little harder than intended, which sent my Ernie Banks bobble head doll into a spasm of bobbling.

"You're a bastard today." Vince stopped eating and picked up his beer. We drank in silence for a minute and I made the executive decision to light a cigarette. I was mostly nonsmoking now but the time seemed right. I drew smoke into my lungs and felt the way you feel when you slip into that favorite sweatshirt you've had since college. Vince opened his mouth to speak, closed it, tried again and said, "I'll do the job until you say it's over."

"Good."

"But I'm your friend, so I gotta say what I gotta say. If you fire me, you fire me."

I couldn't deny him that. "Go ahead, unload. But I don't want to have this conversation every week. Hit me with your best shot and then we're done with it."

Vince swallowed some beer. "It's a little creepy, Ray."

"A little creepy? That's your best shot?"

"More than a little creepy. Paying me to spy on your ex-girlfriend? Solidly creepy."

"Whoa. Did I not specifically instruct you to terminate surveillance *any* time Jill shows up?"

"Yeah but—"

"Then I'm not spying on her."

"Spying on her boyfriend then. Still creepy."

"I just want to be sure Dr. Feelgood isn't bad for her," I said. "Once I'm reasonably confident he's a straight-up guy, I'll pull you off the job and leave them to their blissful coexistence. But if he *does* turn out to be a bad guy, then I'll warn Jill. And I know that doesn't mean we'll get back together. I just want her to be safe."

"You're rationalizing and you don't even know how lame that sounds," Vince said. "You gotta move on and forget about her."

Actually, I was keenly aware of how lame I sounded. But I wasn't just rationalizing, I was in rationalization overdrive, and I just didn't care. It just didn't matter.

"Thanks for sharing," I said. "Hope you feel better."

"Well that's how I feel about it," Vince shrugged. "I've had my say, do what you want."

I stubbed out my half-smoked cigarette. "You can pick him up at Rush tonight. His shift ends at six."

"I know when his shift ends," said Vince.

"Good for you," I said.

# CHAPTER THREE

**J**oan Richmond's blood had been mopped up six weeks ago, but between sand-colored floor tiles, the grout bore dark stains where her body had lain. I stood for a minute, making mental comparisons between the hallway and my memory of the crime scene photographs.

Then I worked my way through the apartment, room by room, assembling an impression of the woman who had lived here. Earth tones predominated and the decor was tastefully generic and fairly gender neutral. It looked like the catalog photos for a midpriced furniture store. Clean, orderly, coordinated, and completely soulless.

There was still food in the fridge, some of the leftovers moldy. It was clear that Joan's father had simply locked up the place after her death and had not returned to deal with the fact that she wasn't coming back. The freezer held a bag of frozen peas, a pint of chocolate ice cream, and five microwavable low-calorie meals. And two blue bottles of Skyy vodka. I pulled the bottles out and now saw that one was three-quarters empty, the other waiting on deck. Most people would wait until the first bottle was empty before putting the next in the freezer. Hell, most people probably wouldn't even *buy* the next bottle until the first one was empty. Joan Richmond was a drinker and, from the absence of appropriate mixers, I guessed she took her vodka straight. The five ice cube trays suggested she liked it to stay cold in the glass.

The bedroom was forest green with natural oak trim. Mission-style furniture. A masculine room, but for the duvet cover and pillowcases, which boasted a fiercely cheerful floral print by Liberty. Joan Richmond favored the right side of the bed, the side nearest the door.

The bedside table offered *Accounting Today, Vanity Fair, The Economist.* In the drawer, a pen, a notebook, and a pair of reading glasses. The notebook contained innocuous "to-do" lists—the sort of things jotted down to clear a busy mind at the end of the day and make room for sleep.

The matching table on the other side of the bed was vacant. No magazines, empty drawer. Like it was waiting for someone to move in and put his (or her) personal stamp on the place.

The bathroom contained all the requisite unctions, ointments, and creams that women employ as weapons in their foredoomed battle against nature and time. And the usual over-the-counter drugs. And sleeping pills. Consult your doctor, use as directed, for occasional use only . . .

*For use when vodka isn't enough to dull the loneliness.*

In one corner of the living room, a computer on a small desk. There was a television, a stereo . . . and music. Like lonely people everywhere, Joan Richmond owned a lot of music. A woman after my own heart.

The Stones, Stevie Wonder, Neil Young, and James Taylor . . . Carole King, Joni Mitchell, Emmylou Harris, Bonnie Raitt, and Sheryl Crow . . . Aretha Franklin and Tina Turner . . . a large collection of Bowie . . . Pink Floyd, early Genesis . . . The Clash, The Psychedelic Furs, The Replacements . . . Blondie, The Cars, and Cheap Trick.

A few disco and Europop albums, which seemed out of place for a woman who listened to prog-rock and punk and new wave. But we all have a few albums we keep for an occasional nostalgia trip, even though we know better. Disco had arrived when Joan Richmond was a teenager and those are prime years for midlife nostalgia trips.

I decided to select something that I'd never heard before. Something of her life, but not of mine. When I opened the stereo's CD tray, there was already a disc loaded. *The Cure.* The first time around, I'd dismissed them as a *makeup and hair* band. Then in college, my friend Terry Green had insisted that I give them a fair listen and I'd had to admit they were good. But their latest album was virgin territory for me. And this was probably the last music Joan Richmond had listened to before her death. I pressed Play.

I filled a glass with ice, poured cold vodka over the ice. I was listening to the woman's music . . . I might as well drink her booze.

I called Vince Cosimo at home. I knew he was on surveillance and I could've called his cell but it's easier to apologize to an answering machine.

I waited for the beep and said, "Vince . . . Ray. I, um, I know you're not having fun on this gig but I appreciate you doing it for me and I want you to stay focused. You're learning important skills . . . and I'll have some better work for you pretty soon. Okay? Thanks. See you tomorrow."

Some apology.

Vince was probably right—I should forget about Jill and move on with my life. But I'd never let anyone get as close, never told anyone as much as I'd told Jill. I'd even allowed myself to envision spending the rest of our lives together, and I liked the view.

But she ended it. As much as I'd told her, it was far less than what normal people share of themselves and she said she needed me to trust her. But that wasn't the only problem. Jill couldn't get comfortable with what I do for a living.

We met in the hospital, just after I'd taken a beating. I convinced her that the job was not usually like that and she agreed to go out with me. It was intense. It was love. But she was uncomfortable with the gun, so I started going around without one. I got into the habit of leaving my gun locked in the office and only wearing it when I thought I might need it.

But the thing is, you never know where and when you'll need your gun. If you did know, you'd simply arrange to be somewhere else at the appointed time. And then you wouldn't need a gun at all.

In my effort to ease Jill's concerns, I ignored that logic. And it cost me another beating.

Having learned that lesson the hard way, I now carried all the time. I didn't know how or if Jill would ever be comfortable with it, but I wanted the opportunity to try to get past her fears. I'd returned to Chicago in May but it took a month to work up the courage to call her. Whereupon she informed me that she was involved with someone.

No use rehashing it. I picked up the phone and called Terry Green at the *Chicago Chronicle*. I figured to get his voice mail but he was working late so I got him on the line. I asked him to search the archives for anything on Joan Richmond and Steven Zhang.

"There a story in it?" he said.

"Nope. But next time we go drinking it's on me and I'll throw in a couple good cigars."

"I'll do it," he said, "if you come for dinner on Thursday. Angela hasn't seen you in ages and you're becoming a hermit."

"I'm not a hermit," I said, "I just haven't been socializing."

"Which is the definition of a hermit," said Terry. "Thursday, our place, dinner, seven o'clock."

I poured another vodka and turned up the volume. Robert Smith seemed furious with the state of the world and his place in it, and the music matched. Great album, on first listen. I wondered what it had meant to Joan Richmond. It was in her current rotation, so I assumed it spoke to her. But I may have been looking for too much meaning in it, as I sometimes do. Maybe it was just the latest album from a band she really liked. Maybe there was no deep meaning here.

I sat at her desk and booted up her computer. It all looked pretty straightforward. No password-protected partitions or files, no cryptic file names.

The Excel files of Joan Richmond's personal finances told of a successful single woman in her forties. As the head of payroll for HM

Nichols, Joan made $96,000 a year. She'd bought the condo five years ago for $328,000, minus a 25 percent down payment. Mortgage companies were offering huge loans with little or no down, but Joan was an accountant and didn't fall for that con. She took on a mortgage she could afford, had premium quality health insurance, drove a Toyota Corolla, and put money away for retirement. The picture of fiscal responsibility.

I launched Thunderbird and went into her e-mails, found nothing unusual. The computer was new and the e-mails only went back six months, so not a lot to search through. She'd kept in occasional contact with a handful of girlfriends from college, sending congratulations on new husbands, new babies. The e-mails she received were a little more restrained. There was no new husband, no new baby, and there didn't seem to be a lot of congratulations. She did her job, lived her life alone, and put on a brave face for the rest of the world.

I searched for Steven Zhang's name. She'd contacted him six weeks before he came to work at HM Nichols, saying she might have a gig for him. The e-mails were informal and she did not ask for credentials or references, and I got the impression that she'd used his services before. And she asked him to give her best regards to Amy, so she at least knew of his wife. Zhang's replies were sane enough—he seemed eager to take the gig and appreciative of her offer.

I went into her Firefox history file and browsed the cookies on her system. No unusual surfing habits, no fetish porn or online gambling sites. She was a regular visitor at the *Chicago Tribune, New York Times, Wall Street Journal*.

Nothing in Joan Richmond's computer suggested a double life, or any reason for Steven Zhang to kill her.

The music ended. I looked for something to change my perspective. Something I knew and loved, something equally righteous but less angry. She had a little reggae. A very little. Black Uhuru, Jimmy Cliff, and of course some Bob Marley. I put *Exodus* on the stereo.

I refreshed my vodka, wrapped the bag of frozen peas in a dishtowel. My shoulder had started barking around noon and I'd ignored it since. The vodka helped some, but not enough. I popped a couple of Percocet.

I sat in the living room, holding a bag of frozen peas to my shoulder, drinking cold vodka and waiting for the Percs to kick in. Thinking about the dead woman whose life I'd invaded.

The computer told me little, the music a little more. But what had I really learned about her? The apartment itself didn't say much. And maybe that said a lot. Generic decor, no evidence of guests, lonely bedroom.

No personal photos on display. Which reminded me of my own apartment, but was definitely not normal. I searched for a photo album, found none.

The bookshelves held some literary fiction and thrillers, but mostly biographies and current events. Almost a dozen books on 9/11 and the war in Iraq. Not wing-nut conspiracy stuff, all mainstream, but all critical of the administration. The top two shelves held books she'd kept from her college days.

I pulled Albert Camus's *The Myth of Sisyphus* off the shelf and took it back to the couch. The book had meant a lot to me, years ago. It had helped me make sense of things at a time when nothing made any sense, helped me navigate the bumpy transition from adolescence to adulthood. Most of all, it had enabled me to intellectualize the worst experience of my life, giving me the emotional distance I desperately needed.

Maybe Camus could help me again. I opened the book and read:

*There is but one truly serious philosophical problem and that is suicide.*

Maybe not. I closed the book, dropped it on the coffee table, and listened to Bob Marley sing about the movement of Jah people. The Percs had gone to work inside my brain and the pain was now dull and distant. When the music ended, I tossed the peas back in the freezer and brushed my teeth. I didn't think Joan would mind me using her toothbrush, given our increasing intimacy.

I stripped off my clothes, climbed into bed on the side opposite where Joan had slept. I lay on my back and stared at the motionless ceiling fan. And was immediately gripped by a sense of dread. Thinking *Just look under the bed. What's so hard about that? Just look.*

I looked under the bed. And there it was. I pulled it out and opened the leather cover, recognized Joan Richmond's handwriting on the lined pages.

Anger coursed through my veins and my face burned. I tossed the book aside, thinking *What is it with diaries kept under the bed, a fucking rite of womanhood? Goddamnit.*

I knew it was totally irrational, but I was livid with Joan Richmond for keeping a diary under her bed. For making me feel like the thirteen-year-old boy who found his mother's cold body naked on top of the sheets, an empty pill bottle beside her, a half-empty bottle of Sambuca on the nightstand. For making me feel like the thirteen-year-old boy who crawled under his mother's bed, squeezed his eyes tight and stayed there an hour, pleading with a nonexistent God: *I'll do anything . . . Please, just make her wake up . . . I'll never do anything bad again . . . I'll do anything you want . . . Please . . . Kill me instead.*

The thirteen-year-old boy who found his dead mother's diary under the bed.

# CHAPTER FOUR

**It took a couple of days to get a meeting** with HM Nichols's CFO, Douglas Hill, but at least he'd been straight about it, saying matter-of-factly that he needed to check up on me first. I'd given him the numbers for Isaac Richmond and Mike Angelo and I guess they said the right things and now I sat across from Hill at this uncluttered desk in the HM Nichols head office in a Skokie industrial park.

Tall and slim, Hill wore a brown three-piece suit, rimless glasses, and a wedding band. His fingernails were chewed beyond short. His slicked-down comb-over wasn't fooling anybody and, like all comb-overs, actually drew more attention to his impending baldness. He wasted the first five minutes of our meeting telling me about what a busy man he was and how he couldn't spare a lot of time. As he wrapped up his opening monologue, I reached into my briefcase and, bypassing Joan Richmond's diary, pulled out my notebook.

"I won't take a lot of your time."

"I mean, there really isn't much to say, Mr. Dungeon."

"Dudgeon," I said. "But call me Ray if that's easier."

"Yes, well, not much to say. Joan was our payroll manager. She hired Mr. Zhang on a three-month contract. Two months into the contract, he went crazy and killed her."

"Were there other bidders on the contract? How did she come to choose Zhang?"

Hill made a steepling gesture at me. If there's a gesture that better conveys superiority, I haven't seen it. "Mr. *Dudgeon,* I do not micromanage my managers. Joan had my trust and confidence, she didn't have to clear a short-term freelance contract through my office."

"Do you think she might have used his services before she came to HM Nichols?"

"I have no idea."

"There must have been something on paper—an application, a résumé—something I could look at."

"All of our records on Joan Richmond and Steven Zhang now reside with the Chicago Police Department. Perhaps they will let you look at them."

"You gave the originals to the police? Usually they just take photocopies."

Hill's smile was designed to look apologetic but it failed to look sincere. "You must understand," he said, "we were all very upset around here after . . . well, after what happened. Joan was well liked and I suppose we were in shock. Of course we should've made copies for the police, but we gave them our originals."

"So HM Nichols kept absolutely no paper whatsoever on Joan Richmond or Steven Zhang," I said.

"That's correct. It's *all* with the police." Hill's words sounded like a door closing. He took a long look at his watch.

"How long did Joan work here?" I asked.

"Just over eight months."

"Previous employer?"

"I can't recall." Hill's thumb started rubbing back and forth against the nail of his index finger and he pressed his lips together. I stared at him and let the silence become uncomfortable until he said, "I'm sorry, I just . . . I really can't recall." Another smile of false apology. "I'm an accountant, I have a head for figures."

"But not for company names."

"I guess not. But you can check with the police, that information will be in her file." He glanced at his watch again. "I really must get back to work."

"Sure, thanks for your time, Mr. Hill. One more question—did you observe any of Steven Zhang's erratic behavior?"

Hill's head jerked side to side like he was trying to shake the question from his ears. "I really didn't know the man. Our paths rarely crossed. The payroll department is on the third floor and, as I said, I'm not a micromanager. But I've arranged for you to see Joan's former assistant, Kate Weinstein. She knew Mr. Zhang." Hill looked again at his watch, as if the time might've changed radically in the past thirty seconds. His eyes moved to the computer screen on his desktop without meeting mine along the way. "I'll ask you to please take as little of her time as possible."

"Time is money," I said.

"That is a fact," he said without looking up.

Meeting over.

I didn't mind. Further questioning would've only yielded further lies.

Kate Weinstein told me everything I'd already read from her police interview transcript, but also this: Joan never talked about the job she had before coming to HM Nichols. Never. Any time the subject of work history came up, Joan checked out of the conversation. The topic seemed to make her nervous. Steven Zhang came to HM Nichols at Joan's invitation. There were no other applicants for the contract and Joan had not advertised the position; she simply brought Zhang in. Kate overheard conversation between Joan and Zhang that gave her the impression they'd worked together before. When Kate asked,

Joan denied it, said that Zhang came on the recommendation of a friend's husband. Kate thought Joan was lying.

"Why didn't you mention any of this to the police?" I asked.

"Oh, I did. I told them all about it."

"You sure?"

"Absolutely. The detective even wrote it down in his little notebook."

I believed her, which meant the cops deliberately left it out of the interview notes for the case file. I said, "How long before the murder did you notice a change in behavior by Mr. Zhang?"

Kate Weinstein twirled her wavy hair with an index finger while she thought about it. "It was three weeks, almost. See, it was a Monday when he first started acting all crazy. I remember because at first I just thought he was being grumpy and I tried to make a joke of it and said, 'You must've had a big weekend, maybe you should've called in hungover,' and he just looked at me really strange and said, 'They can make people disappear. They control everything,' and then he just kept staring at me. I thought he was kidding and I started to ask who *they* were, but he put his hands over his ears and made a strange moaning sound and turned away and left the room. It was weird."

"That would definitely qualify as weird," I said.

Kate laughed and said, "Tell me about it. And he just kept getting weirder and then three weeks later, he killed Joan." She reached a hand out and touched my arm. "And the sad thing is, she was really worried about him. I mean we all were, but mostly we were just creeped out. Joan was talking about putting him on sick leave or something and making him see a doctor. She was the only one of us who really wanted to help him . . . and she was the one he killed. Don't you think that's sad?"

I agreed that it was sad, handed her a card and asked that she call me, should anything else come to mind.

"Like what?" she said.

"If it comes to mind, you'll recognize it."

*Daddy doesn't love me. He wants to, but he doesn't know how. I think he's waiting for me to open up and reveal myself. We both must know, on some level, that it can't happen that way. I wish . . .*

*I wish we could go back in time. Does he even know how much it hurts? Does he know? Sometimes I think he does, but then he says something that makes me realize we're on different planets and it makes my stomach hurt. He can't know. But sometimes when I look at him, I go back in time, to the day I lost him.*

*"Be a good soldier," he said. He wiped a tear off my cheek with a rough finger, turned and walked away from me and went back to work. I didn't see him again for six months.*

*Be a good soldier?! Daddy— I'm just a little girl. Mom is gone. I'm all alone. Don't leave me. I'm seven years old, Daddy! If you loved me, you'd stay. It's just not fair. If you loved me, you'd stay.*

*From that day on, I ripped up your letters without reading them. If you only knew.*

I sat in my office, reading Joan Richmond's diary and not liking it much. I put the diary aside and refilled my coffee mug from the half-empty pot. Or half full, if you're an optimist. I took my coffee back to the desk and, for the third time, turned my attention to Vince's surveillance reports on Dr. Feelgood.

Dr. Feelgood had a real name—Dr. Andrew Glassman. The night before last, Glassman left Rush Medical Center and drove his Mercedes east on Harrison to the Printer's Row neighborhood. He had dinner at Custom House with a colleague from work—Dr. Sam Martell—during which they talked shop. He then headed up Lake Shore Drive, exited at Fullerton. He spent two hours visiting his mother at a fancy nursing home, like a good son should. Then he retired for the evening to his Gold Coast condo, arriving just before eleven o'clock. Probably drank himself to sleep with a warm glass of milk.

As fervently as I might have wished him to be, Dr. Andrew Glass-man was not Public Enemy Number One. I'd had Vince on him al-most a month and the guy hadn't so much as changed lanes without signaling.

I flipped to the next report. Last evening, the good doctor left work, bought a single red rose at the hospital flower shop, and drove to Lakeview. Jill's neighborhood. He parked at a meter on Halsted and took a table at Erwin Café, an upscale American bistro. He sipped a glass of white wine and read a novel called *The Book of Ralph,* until his date arrived fifteen minutes later. Of course his date was Jill. Vince terminated surveillance, according to my instructions.

The last item on Vince's report: "Subject closed his book, stood and presented the rose to Ms. Browning. They kissed."

# CHAPTER FIVE

**S**urprise!"

Terry and Angela Green stood on the other side of their front door, both wearing huge smiles. Their greeting confused me at first. Then I looked down and saw the bump. Angela was pregnant. I almost dropped the wine.

"Congratulations," I said, because what the hell else was I going to say? Big hugs ensued as the happy couple drew me into their home. I handed the wine to Terry and said to Angela, "How far along?"

"Five months. We didn't want to tell anyone right away because, well, you never know."

I held her at arm's length and looked her over. She was always a thin woman and hadn't really filled out yet, cheekbones still prominent on her chestnut brown face. But she seemed to be gaining weight where it mattered. She had the bump and was a little fuller in the hips and backside. I judged that she was now a C-cup, the inappropriateness of such an observation notwithstanding. I'd always had a secret thing for Angela.

I let go of her shoulders and said, "You look great," in a tone purely platonic. Turned to Terry and asked, "Boy or girl?" Terry was a reporter—I knew he wouldn't wait to be surprised with the pertinent information readily available.

"Boy," said Terry.

Angela said, "His name is Chester, after Chester Himes. And if it's okay with you, we'd like his middle name to be Ray, after Terry's best friend."

It hit me like a bucket of cold water. Why would anyone want to name a kid after me? I said, "Sure, it's okay with me."

"Try to contain your enthusiasm," said Terry.

"No, I didn't . . . I didn't mean it that way. I think it's great. Thanks."

Angela laughed and waved us off. "You boys go out on the balcony, smoke your cigars. I've got dinner to make."

"Cheers, man." I clinked my glass against Terry's and we sipped his scotch and smoked my cigars. "I'm happy for you guys."

"Thanks. It's not a done deal but all the tests are normal so far. I think this one's gonna take, knock on wood."

"You'll make a great dad." And I meant it. But on another level, I wasn't happy for Terry at all.

More accurately, I wasn't happy for me.

Truth is, I felt the end of an era approaching. Terry and Angela were moving on. Soon their life would be all about little Chester Ray Green. They'd be obsessed with first teeth and bowel movements, things I do not find fascinating. And they'd have new friends. Friends with babies. Friends similarly obsessed with first teeth and bowel movements.

Terry stood and went into the house. A minute later, music came piping through the balcony speakers. Hound Dog Taylor, *Natural Boogie*. I'd given this album to Terry for his nineteenth birthday, when we were journalism students at Columbia College. Terry turned me on to bands like The Cure and XTC, while I turned him on to Hound Dog Taylor and Son Seals. Terry is black and I'm white. Neither of us was unaware of the potential for irony but I think we were both pleased that it was about the music and didn't have to be about race.

We met as J-school freshmen and quickly bonded by comparing idols. The names you'd expect—Mark Twain, H. L. Mencken, Studs Terkel, David Halberstam. Hunter S. Thompson was massive for both of us, as he was for most American teenagers who aimed at a career in journalism and many who didn't. Mike Royko and Clarence Page were our current local heroes.

And then there was Woodstein. Bob Woodward and Carl Bernstein. Between us, we'd read *All the President's Men* probably a dozen times and we spent many nights in Terry's studio apartment, drinking bargain beer and eating white cheddar popcorn and playing the movie over and over again. We knew it by heart and would often say our favorite lines along with Redford and Hoffman, Balsam and Robards. Sometimes we'd talk right over the film, debating the investigative techniques and journalistic ethics portrayed on the screen.

The editor of the school paper affectionately dubbed us Woodward and Bernstein, and we sometimes still used the nicknames, twenty years later.

Christ, twenty years. Terry hadn't brought down any crooked presidents but he'd built a solid career, married a lovely woman, and was now about to become a dad. I'd given up on journalism and wasn't entirely sure what I had become, or what I was building.

Terry returned to the balcony and said, "Still love this album."

"Tempus fugit," I said. Looking for safer ground, I steered the conversation to Joan Richmond and Steven Zhang.

He pulled out his notebook. "Thought you said there wasn't a story in this."

"Far as I know, there isn't."

"You may change your mind. If there is a story, I want it."

"Goes without saying," I said.

He flipped some pages. "Joan Richmond. Murdered by Steven Zhang on August 13. Worked at HM Nichols . . ."

"I'm up on current events," I said. "I'm looking for red flags in the background. Previous employer may be a lead."

"Damn right it is," said Terry. "You've heard of Hawk River."

"Military contractors. Got a lot of security guys in Iraq and Afghanistan."

"And at least fifteen other countries," said Terry, "including ours. Since the geniuses in Washington sent our National Guard to the Middle East, we've even got these guys in New Orleans and Mississippi."

"Politics aside—"

"Politics is never aside," said Terry. He'd finished his scotch and refilled his glass, topped mine up. "Dude, we're talking about some powerful motherfuckers. And there are whispers . . . assassinations, sabotage jobs, you name it. Word is, if you want a civil war started in some Fourth World country, these are your guys."

"And Joan Richmond used to work for them."

"And Joan Richmond used to work for them. Six years, head of payroll. She quit ten months ago." Terry drew on his cigar, blew out a stream of fragrant smoke. "But it gets better . . . or worse. The congressional Oversight and Government Reform committee is looking into Hawk River's billing practices. Care to guess what comes next?"

"Joan Richmond was scheduled to testify?"

Terry shot me with his finger. "Bull's-eye. She was scheduled to testify this month, in a closed-door hearing. But now she's been murdered."

"People get murdered all the time," I said.

"Which brings us to Steven Zhang," said Terry. "Not much on him, but once I knew about Joan Richmond and Hawk River, my curiosity was piqued. Checked Zhang's tax records."

"And he worked for Joan at Hawk River," I guessed.

"Don't know if she was his boss, but he worked at Hawk River. Seventeen weeks."

"Odd number," I said. "He was an IT guy. Contracts are usually three months, six months, one year. Seventeen weeks?"

Terry shrugged, "Maybe he was hired for six months, but he was efficient. Or three months but he was slow. Or maybe he quit or got fired. His tax records showed seventeen weeks. Anyway, it would seem that his contract ended, however it ended, about a month before Joan

Richmond quit. Point is, he worked there when your victim worked there and he killed her just in time to keep her from testifying before Congress. And you know how I hate coincidences."

I hated them, too.

As my cigar burned down to the band, I heard the doorbell ring inside the apartment. Terry said, "Oh yeah, Angela invited a friend from work. Diane. She's great, you'll like her."

I left my cigar to die in the ashtray. "You have got to be shitting me. A blind date?"

"Relax, you'll like her—"

"You already said that. What I don't like is being ambushed."

"It's no big deal."

"To me it is. And I don't appreciate it."

"Just come inside and be nice." Terry stood up. "It's not a blind date. It's just Angela and me, each inviting a friend for dinner."

"A couple of single, heterosexual friends of the opposite sex. That's what we call a blind date." I fished a pack of cigarettes from my pocket and lit one.

"Fine, call it a blind date if you want. I'm not asking you to propose marriage to the girl. Angela had her heart set on introducing you, and—"

The balcony door swung open and a perky brunette stepped out, pulling a pack of Dunhill Lights from her purse. As I stood, she flashed a mouthful of perfect teeth at me and extended her hand and said, "Oh, you smoke! Me, too!"

"We've got that in common," I said. "Wanna get married?" I went for dry humor, barely suppressed the sarcasm. It could've been taken either way.

And that pretty much set the tone for the evening.

I wasn't rudeness personified but I put little effort into hiding my disinterest and my humor was more caustic than usual. And throughout dinner, I seemed to find ways of turning conversation into debate. I tried not to notice the uncomfortable glances between Diane and Angela, Angela and Terry.

Suffice it to say, I acted like an ass and by 9:30 we all suddenly re-membered that we had early starts in the morning and we'd better pass on coffee and call it a night. I told Diane that it had been a pleasure meeting her, reiterated my joy over Angela's pregnancy, thanked every-one for a lovely evening, and got the hell out of there.

# CHAPTER SIX

**I**t was warm for late September and the sky was clear and I felt like walking. Terry and Angela lived in Andersonville, a hip, recently gentrified neighborhood on the north side. I walked the clean, tree-lined streets and counted the FOR SALE signs until I lost count. Most of the rentals had gone condo. Which was happening all over Chicago, including my neighborhood south of the Loop.

The week before, I'd gotten another letter from my landlord—just a friendly reminder that time was running out. The building was going condo. After renovations it would be called the Burnham Park Lofts. Which was funny because it was about fifteen blocks south of Burnham Park, and funnier still because Burnham Park was a fake name given by developers to the neighborhood properly known as the South Loop.

The "Burnham Park Lofts" would boast modern kitchens with Sub-Zero refrigerators and trash compactors. Jacuzzi tubs in the bathrooms. A communal workout room and a roof deck complete with hot tub. All this can be yours, starting at $395,000. My unit was a two-bedroom. The second bedroom had served as a workout room, and although I still used the recumbent bike, the punching bags had hung silent since my injuries. My apartment was priced at an even $439,900. Plus about $600 a month in maintenance fees and taxes.

I couldn't afford it, and my lease was up at the end of October.

Terry and Angela loved Andersonville and it looked like a nice place to live, but I couldn't see myself living there. It was becoming a family neighborhood.

I walked south into Uptown, which seemed more like my kind of neighborhood. Uptown had been trying for years to gentrify, but all the surrounding neighborhoods had beaten it to the punch and there was nowhere nearby for the poor folks to go. So it was holding on to its shabby charm. I slid over to Broadway and took in the neon glow of tattoo parlors, the homemade signs in the windows of army surplus shops and Jamaican grocers and used bookstores, and the warm aroma of Mexican take-out joints.

When I got to Lawrence I stopped in at the Green Mill. Thursday is swing music night, but the big band was on a break between sets and the place was mercifully quiet. I took a stool at the bar and signaled the bartender with a nod. The bartender came over with a generous pour of Appleton Estate twelve-year-old over ice and put it in front of me, water back. I hadn't set foot in the place in at least a month. I like bars where they remember your poison.

I swiveled on my barstool to face the booth that had been Al Capone's, back in the day. From Capone's booth, you could keep an eye on both entrances, and you were five steps from the bar. Behind the bar there was a trapdoor in the floor that led to a system of subterranean tunnels, and you could emerge a block away.

Capone's booth was now full of young urban professionals, who knew nothing of the tunnels and who didn't have the sense to keep an eye on either entrance. There were four of them. Double dates, I figured. They were too young and frivolous to be married. They drank Cosmopolitans and Bullshit-Tinis and wore Versace suits and carried Prada purses, and everything anybody said was hilarious, judging by the recurrent spasms of too-loud laughter that erupted from the booth.

I hated them. Then I hated myself for hating them. I finished my drink, dropped enough money on the bar, and resumed my walk.

I meandered down to Wrigleyville, over to Clark and Addison, and stopped across the street from Mecca.

Wrigley Field.

Yeah yeah, I know. I've heard it all before, so save your breath. Sometimes it sucks being a Cubs fan.

I stood for a minute and admired the oldest ballpark in the National League. A beautiful ballpark, where some truly ugly baseball had been played this year.

I continued my walk south. I could've hailed a cab or hopped the Red Line down to Roosevelt. But I knew that I would do neither. Since leaving the Green Mill I'd been fingering the HM Nichols keychain in my pocket and Joan Richmond's apartment was within walking distance. I wouldn't be going home tonight.

I crossed Belmont, well aware that if I turned east and walked a few blocks, I'd be standing in front of Jill's yellow brick apartment building. But I didn't turn. A few blocks south of Belmont, I stopped at Jake's Pub for a pint of Guinness. Jake's is a friendly place that caters to neighborhood regulars and has a very good jukebox, but I didn't stop in for the music.

When Jill and I were an item, we'd spent a few evenings at Jake's and I knew she sometimes met friends there for drinks after work. I didn't know what the hell I'd say if I bumped into her. Vince was almost definitely right—I should forget about her and move on with my life. But I still had it bad and I didn't know how to let go. I did a circuit of the long barroom, nodded at a few familiar faces.

Jill was not there.

By midnight I was lying in Joan Richmond's bed, reading her diary.

Joan Richmond did not catalog the daily events in her life, so much as her emotional state. She'd write about how upset she was about some annoyance and how she shouldn't allow such things to bother her so, without ever being specific about what had triggered the upset.

A feeling of isolation prevailed throughout the diary and Joan often wrote about feeling "different" and "disconnected" from the people at work, in bars, on the bus. She wished that she could be "like everyone else."

As if everyone else were alike.

But then this flash of insight:

*Took the El today, fifteen stops and wanting to scream the whole way. A hundred people in the car, all crammed together, all far apart. Parallel universes. What's it like in yours? The same, I think. Why can't we talk? Why can't we look at each other, smile at each other, even acknowledge each other's existence? Why can't we say, "I know you. You're me." We don't have to be alone, we're standing right next to each other. But we can't even look at each other.*

*And then I saw a man, and he saw me. He was a black man, very dark skin, very thick hands. We looked at each other and, I swear, we saw ourselves reflected. And we had to look away. Frightened. And that's how it will always be.*

*Sometimes I just hate the world.*

Not a light read. I skimmed some, looking for anything related to Hawk River. Found it, although she never wrote down the company name.

Joan worried about her decision to quit her job without ever saying what led to the decision. She worried about how *Daddy* would react, and her fear of disappointing him was palpable. Then she would chastise herself for caring what he thought and that would lead to a new round of reliving the trauma of her childhood abandonment by a mother who died and a father who was never there.

And then I noticed the alteration. About a dozen pages had been removed from the diary. They'd been cut out cleanly, right at the binding, so it was easy to miss. It looked like a professional job, not just someone tearing pages out. With the pages removed so carefully, I knew there wouldn't be fingerprints. Anyway, it could've been Joan who removed the pages. Maybe she'd written something that she later regretted saying. Maybe she'd cut them out carefully so that she wouldn't be reminded of it when she flipped through the diary.

Or maybe it was someone else.

Joan had been an irregular diarist. Sometimes six entries in one week, other times weeks would go by between entries. She was always careful to record the date in the top right corner of the page, whenever she started a new entry. Terry had said she quit her job at Hawk River ten months ago. Douglas Hill said she began work at HM Nichols eight months ago.

The missing pages fell right in between.

# CHAPTER SEVEN

**Many people believe houses can hold** the emotional residue of a terrible event that took place within. They say they can feel the lingering vibrations. I don't buy it. I think, once we learn that a place has a tragic history, we project our own sadness onto it. But sitting in my car across the street from Amy Zhang's town house, the feeling was strong. So strong that, had I been the superstitious type, I'd have thought I was picking up paranormal vibes. Since I'm not, I didn't.

The sky was a solid sheet of gunmetal gray right down to the horizon and had been making ominous threats of rain since morning. In the small front lawn, a FOR SALE sign swayed back and forth with the wind. The grass was brown in patches and needed cutting and the flowerboxes displayed dying dwarf dahlias in differing degrees of decay. Put all that together with the knowledge that a man shot himself inside this house, leaving his wife and daughter behind . . . easy to conjure a feeling of sadness without any vibrations from the spirit world.

Amy Zhang had arrived about twenty minutes earlier. I figured she'd had time to settle in, so I left my car and crossed the street and rang the doorbell.

"Very sorry to bother you, Mrs. Zhang," I said. "I have just a few quick questions by way of follow-up on the investigation." As I spoke, I withdrew my badge wallet from my breast pocket but didn't actually open it. Her eyes darted to the wallet and as they left the wallet and returned to my face, I flipped the badge open and shut and returned it to my pocket. "If your daughter is home, we can do this tomorrow during school hours."

Amy Zhang sighed. "Come in and remove your shoes." Her accent was soft but noticeable. I took off my shoes and followed her to the living room. She said, "I just made a pot of tea, Detective . . . ?"

"Dudgeon. Call me Ray. Thank you, tea would be nice." Amy Zhang slipped into the kitchen and I slipped out of my raincoat and sat. There was a new couch and a freshly painted wall where Steven Zhang had blown his brains out. The wall was blue, a dark enough shade to keep the bloodstains from showing through. Amy Zhang returned and put a teacup in front of me and sat on the couch.

She was a small woman—about five-two and slender—and pretty, with a heart-shaped face and deep brown eyes and raven hair cut in a pageboy. A pretty face, but the eyes were tired and dark circles under them spoke of nights without sleep and days filled with worry. She said, "I don't remember meeting you . . . you weren't one of the detectives from before."

"No," I put a business card on the coffee table between us, "I'm not with the police—I'm a private detective, working for Joan Richmond's father."

"But I thought—"

"I know you did."

"You tricked me."

"I allowed you to make the wrong assumption."

Amy Zhang's eyes moved to the right, then back to me. She said, "You *helped* me make the wrong assumption."

"It was the surest way of getting inside. But I don't want to mislead you. You don't have to talk to me."

She sat and looked at me for almost a full minute. Finally she leaned forward, put her cup on the table, and said, "Are you really working for Joan Richmond's father?"

"Yes. Mr. Richmond is having trouble coming to terms with Joan's death. He feels that he might be able to accept it if he had a better understanding of how and why things happened the way they did." Thinking *Dudgeon, you are such a scumbag. If you were a human being, you'd just walk out of here and leave this woman alone.*

Again Amy Zhang examined me for a long time before speaking. "I will try. I owe him that. I don't expect forgiveness, but please tell him how deeply sorry I am."

"He doesn't blame you."

"With a thing this terrible there's blame for everyone. I'm sure he has some for me. And not without reason. I misjudged how fast Steven's condition was . . . deteriorating." She said it like her words had no meaning, but she'd probably gone over it twenty times with the cops. "I should have called emergency and had him committed by force . . . for evaluation. I should not have waited." She picked up her cup, put it down again without drinking any tea.

She seemed more frightened than grief-stricken. Her delicate hands came up and thin fingers hooked her hair behind her ears. With her ears showing, she looked ten years younger. She pulled a Kleenex from her pocket, dabbed at her eyes, and smiled a shy apology.

"Your English is perfect," I said.

"It has to be. I work as a translator."

"At the consulate?"

"I would *never* work for them. I work at the university, helping Chinese students with their English. And at the UIC Medical Center, translating for Chinese patients."

"Was Steven's English as good as yours?"

"No, he was—" She stopped herself, formulated a new answer. "His English was fine. His accent was more pronounced and his vocabulary limited, but he was fluent."

I said, "The police file indicates that Steven did not have a history of mental illness."

"That's correct. Nothing until about a month before . . ."

"Do you have any idea what might have triggered it?"

"No."

"Was he on any medications? Prescription, over-the-counter, recreational?"

"None. Nothing."

"Any idea why he focused on Joan Richmond?"

"No, and I doubt that there was a reason. He was ill."

"Did you know Joan? Were you friends?"

"We never met."

"Reason I ask, I was reading through her old e-mails, and she asked Steven to give you her best regards."

"Well, I, um . . . we spoke on the phone a few times, when she called for Steven."

"Did that happen often?"

"Just a few times. Steven often brought his work home with him."

"You mean his work at HM Nichols, or when they worked together at Hawk River?"

Her eyes darted away. "I don't know what you mean." There was a tremor in her voice.

"Steven worked on contract for Joan at a company called Hawk River, about a year ago. This doesn't ring a bell?"

She didn't answer me, just stood up and disappeared into the kitchen again. She was gone for a few minutes and then returned with a small glass of what looked like sherry.

"I understand this is a very bad time for you and your daughter—"

"My daughter cannot even *step* inside this house anymore. She barely eats, suffers nightmares. . . . Sometimes I don't think she'll ever smile again. So do not pretend to understand. You may be able to come in here and ask me questions I've already answered, but do not talk about my daughter."

Amy Zhang's attitude had changed, but it had changed before I mentioned her daughter and my *spidey senses* were now tingling. Yes, she was frightened and maybe I was a scumbag for inserting myself into her life while her grief was so fresh. But there was something wrong about her. Something very wrong.

"So you never heard of Hawk River? That's odd. Your husband worked there for seventeen weeks."

"I know very little about computers. Steven and I did not talk about his work. He was self-employed. I don't know the names of the companies he worked for."

She was lying. And she was scared. I let the silence build. Her hands were clasped together in front of her chest and she squeezed them together so tight that I thought her fingers might snap like twigs.

"Please," she said, "what do you want me to say? I said everything right."

*Said everything right?*

"What the hell does that mean?"

"It . . . it's nothing. It, I just . . . I said everything right. I told you, I told you everything I know." Her hands unclasped, clasped again. She couldn't look at me. Her performance was falling apart and she knew it. "I told you everything I know," she repeated. "If it's not good enough, I can't help that."

"Are you in some kind of trouble, Mrs. Zhang?"

"You mean besides the fact that my husband killed a woman and then committed suicide?" she snapped. Before I could formulate an answer, she stood and gestured to the front door. "Just go. I'm tired, I have a headache, and I don't like being tested." She turned and ran upstairs and I heard a door slam.

I saw myself out.

# CHAPTER EIGHT

**M**ike Angelo said he'd let me buy him lunch but he didn't want to see me at Area 4 HQ. I suggested Lou Mitchell's, mainly because you can't get any privacy there. That Mike didn't want me in his office was a red flag—or at least an orange flag—and if he rejected Lou Mitchell's and suggested some place more obscure, then I'd know there was real trouble on the way. But Mike agreed and we met at eleven-thirty and sat side by side at the long counter.

We made it through lunch on the Bears' impressive defense and weak offense and Rex Grossman's latest injury. The waiter cleared our dishes and refilled our coffee mugs. I brought out my notebook.

"Not here," said Mike Angelo. "Meet you outside." He stood and left the restaurant without waiting for a reply.

I paid for our lunch and found Mike in front of the building, smoking in the warmth of the midday sun. It had rained overnight and the sky was clear and blue and reflected bright against the Sears Tower and the rest of Chicago's skyscraper skyline.

The sunlight landed heavy, a physical force touching my skin, warming my face. I always loved that feeling.

Mike held a pack of Marlboro Lights out to me. I shook my head and he stuffed the pack into the patch pocket of his brown blazer.

"You got that fancy little car around here someplace?" said Mike.

"Left it at the office," I said.

Cops tend to be more aware of their environmental conditions than civilians but as we walked west on Jackson, it seemed Mike was casing the surroundings with even greater than normal care. His eyes never settling, always scanning, like he halfway expected to discover that we were under surveillance.

I had enough paranoia of my own these days. I said, "You want to tell me what's going on?"

He stopped walking and hit me with the patented cop stare. They give them out with the badges, but thirty years of police work had seasoned Mike's to concrete perfection. He tossed his cigarette butt in the gutter, started walking again. We turned north on Jefferson, walked a block, and came to his car, parked in a tow-away zone. No ticket. The car was an unmarked blue Chevy Impala. Unmarked, but obvious.

"Get in," he said.

I did.


"Tell me what you've learned about Daddy's little dead girl." Mike Angelo piloted the car east on Lake Street, over the Chicago River, and hung a sharp left onto Wacker Drive. He drove like a maniac, even by Chicago standards. Most cops do. I avoided looking at the speedometer. Steering with one hand, he cracked open the side window and lit a cigarette, and now I wanted one.

I flipped open my notebook. "Joan Richmond's boss says her employment records, and those of Steven Zhang, were turned over to the CPD. But they weren't in the Deceased file you showed me. Nor was there any notation that they ever had been. Also, Joan's assistant made statements to the detectives, which seem to have been redacted out of her interview transcript."

"Sloppy police work," said Mike with a smile just shy of sardonic. "Next?"

"The missing statements and employment records point in the same direction: Richmond and Zhang worked together last year at Hawk River."

"That a fact?"

"It is. And there's more."

"Of course there is." Mike swerved a right turn onto Wabash and headed south, under the El tracks. "Shoot."

"For Hawk River, the timing of Joan Richmond's death was extremely fortuitous."

"You don't mean fortuitous," said Mike. He slammed the brakes and screeched to a stop for a red light and raised his voice to compensate for a passing train that rumble-rattled over our heads. "Fortuitous just means *by chance,* it doesn't necessarily imply a positive development. You mean fortunate, or maybe even serendipitous, but not fortuitous." He flicked ash through the opening in the side window and said, "Why was it fortunate for Hawk River that Richmond was murdered last month?"

"You don't know?" Mike didn't answer. "Joan Richmond was supposed to testify before Congress. The Oversight and Government Reform committee is looking at the billing practices of military contractors, and Joan would be answering their questions right now if she weren't dead."

Mike tossed the rest of his cigarette out the window and made a sucking sound through his front teeth—this was news to him. Car horns blared behind us. The light had changed to green. Mike glared at the rearview mirror and shouted, "Go pound sand up your ass!" and waited another ten seconds before stepping on the accelerator, just to make a point.

"Go pound sand up your ass? A minute ago you sounded like you'd swallowed a dictionary."

Mike shrugged, "I can go either way." We crossed the intersection and he pulled to the curb half a block down, across the street from my office building. He put the car in Park.

I nodded across the street. "Got beer in my office." Mike just lowered his window, lit a new cigarette. This time, I took one. "If you don't want to come up, we could do this in a bar. I'm buying."

Mike reached between the seat and the center armrest, pulled out a stainless steel flask. He twisted the top loose and took a swig, handed the flask to me. This was not what I had in mind. The fact that Mike didn't want to have this conversation in public, or even be seen visiting my office, bothered me more than a little bit. I took a swig from the flask. Vodka. Cops who drink on duty tend to prefer vodka because it doesn't announce itself on your breath as strongly as any other spirit. The taste reminded me of Joan Richmond's lonely and incomplete diary. I handed the flask back to him and he put it out of sight and said, "Cut to the chase, I gotta get back."

"Okay, check this out: Joan's boss lied to me, pretended not to remember Joan's previous employer, and emphasized that HM Nichols gave *all* their original paperwork on Richmond and Zhang to your detectives. He said if I wanted to learn about their previous employers, I'd have to ask the CPD. And he seemed nervous."

"So?"

"So I find out that your detectives removed everything relating to Hawk River from the binder—"

"Or never put it in, in the first place," said Mike. "You're making assumptions."

"Either way, there's a lot missing."

"None of which would change the identity of Joan Richmond's killer."

"No, but you've got the, uh, *serendipitous* timing of her death, and now the fact that every mention of Hawk River is missing from the case file. Taken together, it's suggestive."

The flask came out again and Mike took a swig and handed it to me. I took a swig and handed it back and it disappeared again. We smoked and said nothing as a couple of trains shrieked their brakes above.

When the trains had passed, Mike said, "You know what percentage of murders we clear?"

"Slightly less than half?"

"Slightly more, 53 percent, last year. The Richmond murder puts us one to the good. Why would I want to fuck with that? You're not telling me that someone other than Steven Zhang pulled the trigger."

"But there may be more to it," I said.

"So what? Zhang killed her, killed himself, and the case has been cleared. I've got the other 47 percent of murder victims and their families crying out for justice—which they'll probably never get—and you want me to reallocate my detectives' time stirring shit in a cleared case? Even if there is more to it, Zhang is dead. And without him our chances of getting anywhere go from slim to none."

"That doesn't explain actively tailoring the case file to cover up any connection to Hawk River."

Mike took a deep drag on his cigarette, blew it out. He said, "That's a heavy accusation and if I were you I wouldn't make it in public. Think about it. They find a dead woman with a signed confession by her killer who then killed himself. Ballistics match, nice and neat. They go through the routine to dot and cross the appropriate letters, and witnesses confirm the guy was crazy. Even the guy's wife agrees. So maybe they aren't too careful preserving all the paperwork, since the case was closed and cleared from day one."

"Detectives under your watch just aren't that sloppy, Mike. I've known you too long for that line."

Mike Angelo's façade cracked and now he just looked tired. "You get to play Lone Ranger but I gotta work within a system."

"That's what worries me. The system. Did an order come down from on high, to bury the connection to Hawk River?"

Mike tossed his cigarette butt out the window and I did the same with mine and he rolled the windows up. "'Course not," he said, "they're not that stupid."

"Then what?"

He didn't offer the flask this time. Just took a swig for himself and put it away again. We sat in silence for about a year, me staring at Mike and Mike staring out the front windshield at nothing in particular. Finally he said, "God, I hate this job sometimes. Fucking politics." He glanced my way, then stared back out the window again. "What I say now goes no further than this car."

"Yeah, and if I ever said anything, you'd call me a liar and never speak to me again. I know."

He looked at me hard. "You ever say anything, I'll do a hell of a lot worse than that. We clear?"

Mike had never threatened me like that before. He'd threatened our relationship a few times and he'd threatened my license more times than I could recall, but this was something else. I knew what he was saying, and I knew he meant it.

"We're very clear, Mike," I said.

"Okay. I tell you this, and then I'm out of it. The case looked like a no-brainer from the get-go. My dicks didn't need me holding their dicks for them, you know?"

"Everybody's careful not to micromanage nowadays," I said.

"Yeah, whatever. It was an easy case, a smoking gun. Nothing to it, open and shut. Then during a briefing, one of my dicks says he's not so sure, maybe there's more to it. I tell him to bring me the Deceased file the next day and we'll talk it through. That night, I get a call at home."

"Who?"

"I'm not giving you names. Let's say, someone far above my pay grade. Wants to know exactly what I know about the case. I tell him the truth—I don't know anything yet but I'm having a meeting with my guys in the morning and I'll let him know what I think after the meeting." Mike reached into his pocket, fired up another cigarette, but kept the windows rolled up. "Fuck it, I'll be a chain-smoker. Want one?"

"I'll just breathe your exhaust," I said. "So the next day . . ."

"Next day, the two dicks working the Richmond-Zhang case are nowhere to be found. I'm told that they were summoned to headquarters and they took the deceased file with them. I call down to Thirty-fifth, get bounced around to nowhere. Ten minutes later I get a call from an asshole assistant state's attorney telling me to hang tight and I'll be briefed soon enough. I tell him to go fuck himself and give me back my men. An hour after that I get a visit—a heavy suit from the governor's office. Tells me there are federal implications but won't say anything more. Couple hours later, my dicks show up along with a CPD lawyer *and* the asshole ASA. Lawyer tells me they've been reassigned to Area 3, effective immediately, and the case goes with them. My guys clean out their desks and off they go. Can't even look me in the eye. And the case was cleared the next fucking day."

"But you showed me the file," I said.

"They sent me a copy for records, since it was our case for a while. But I tell ya, my binder is about half as thick as the original. And here's the kicker: both detectives made sergeant a week later."

"Damn, Mike."

He put the car in Drive, kept his foot on the brake. "Seems to me you've got a choice to make. This can still be a simple gig and you can make some easy money. Or you can make it complicated. You go that way, I wish you good luck. But I cannot help you, not even a little bit. I won't brainstorm it with you, I won't vouch for you . . . and if you break the law this time, I sure as shit won't cover for you. I mean it."

I didn't know what to say to that. I said, "I paid a visit to Amy Zhang yesterday. She acted like she'd never heard of Hawk River but she's a lousy actress. And she's scared to death."

"Somebody threatens her, she can go to her local district station and file a complaint, like any other citizen."

"At some point during my visit, she decided I wasn't really working for Isaac Richmond. She was petrified. We're way past someone threatening her."

"Sorry. Nothing I can do about it."

"Well I can't just leave her to twist in the wind," I said.

Mike said, "She's not your client, Ray."

"Duly noted." I got out of the car and slammed the door.

The passenger window lowered and Mike said, "Don't call me again about this case."

The window went back up and the Impala screeched off down Wabash.

# CHAPTER NINE

**M**y office door was unlocked, but Vince was not sitting behind my desk. I drew my pistol and flattened against the wall. I scanned the room. The percolator on top of the little bar fridge was making burbling noises. Beneath the coffee aroma I caught the smell of Aqua Velva and my head started swimming and the room began to slip away from me and I felt like throwing up. The taste of blood flooded my mouth and a wave of heat rolled over me and my skin broke into a clammy sweat.

*You killed the guy. He's not here. It's just in your head . . .*

I forced a long deep breath and fought against the surging flashback images and managed to stay out of the torture chair. After a minute of deep breathing, I was relatively normal again.

The office was obviously empty and the only thing I was sure of was that I was losing my mind. I got a beer from the fridge and sat in my desk chair and put the gun on the desk. I swallowed half the beer and lit a smoke. Vince came into the office, started for the coffeemaker, saw me and said, "Hey, you want some coffee? Just made a fresh pot."

"How many times am I going to tell you to lock the door?"

"I had to drain the main vein," he said. "I was just down the hall."

"You leave the office, even to go to the can, you lock the door. Next time I find it unlocked, I dock twenty bucks from your pay. Got it?"

"All right, okay. Sorry." Vince poured coffee into a mug and planted himself across the desk from me. "You okay?"

"Your aftershave smells like Aqua Velva." I pulled a wad of bills out of my pocket.

"It isn't. It's a new one, called—"

"It smells *similar* to Aqua Velva." I tossed three twenties across the desk. "Go buy some good cologne. Nothing from the drugstore, go to Field's."

Vince picked up the money with a confused look on his face. "Thought you were mad at Field's 'cause they're selling out to Macy's."

"I don't care where you go, just get something that smells better."

Vince shoved the money in his pocket with a shrug. "Thanks, I guess."

"Don't guess. It'll improve your love life. And don't thank me, I'm doing it to improve the atmosphere around here."

I got another beer from the fridge and Vince gave me a verbal report on his recent surveillance of Dr. Boyfriend. While half my brain listened to Vince, I considered the implications of what Mike Angelo had told me and how it related to what I'd learned from Terry and Kate Weinstein and Douglas Hill. And how it related to Amy Zhang's fear and Isaac Richmond's grief.

I wanted to toss it around verbally, as I would've with Mike if he hadn't so elegantly recused himself. I liked Vince and he was smarter than most people realized, but he was still too green to offer any useful advice and, anyway, our relationship hadn't developed far enough for me to lay this on him. I pushed it out of my mind and refocused on what Vince was saying.

Andrew Glassman had continued to be a good doctor and son since the last report. He and Jill had not gotten together but she'd switched to the night shift, so they probably wouldn't see a lot of each other until she went back on days two weeks from now.

Vince flipped the page of his notebook. "So the subject had coffee with another doctor in the cafeteria at Rush and I sat at the next table . . ."

"I hope you didn't get made."

"Not a chance," said Vince with some pride. "I was careful. And doctors are too full of themselves to notice civilians, anyway. Hey, I heard two nurses talking and one told a great doctor joke: Most doctors think they're God, but God thinks he's an invasive cardiologist. Funny, huh?"

"A riot," I said. Thinking *Maybe it's time to give it up, Dudgeon. You're starting to look pathetic.*

"Well I thought it was funny," said Vince. "Anyway, so our subject is having coffee with this other guy and he's talking about Jill. Saying how he thinks Jill is the one and maybe he's ready to make a commitment . . ."

It felt like a punch in the gut. I wanted to tell Vince to stop right there. But I just said, "Oh yeah?" I swallowed some more beer, lit a new cigarette with the butt of the old one.

"Thought you were quitting." Vince caught my look, went back to his notes. "Anyway, he says he's got some concerns. First he says they've been fighting a bit because she won't stop smoking." Vince conceded the obvious with a smirk in my direction. "Then he says he wouldn't want the mother of his children to work outside the home and he isn't sure how she'd react to that, 'cause she loves being a nurse. Finally he says that, at the end of the day, all relationships are about who has the power, and this worries him because he thinks he loves Jill more than she loves him, so the balance of power will always be in her favor."

For the first time I was hearing things about Andrew Glassman that made me dislike him. And call me shallow, but it offered new hope. I said, "That's a terrible way to look at love."

"I think he was just talking, I don't think it bothers him that much."

Vince closed his notebook. "The way their conversation ended, I think he's getting ready to propose."

So much for new hope. "Okay. Thanks," I said.

"Yeah. Sorry."

Vince left to go serve some court papers for his other employer and I switched from beer to coffee. I called a flower shop and had a "bright and cheery mixed tulip bouquet" sent to Angela Green. The woman on the phone asked what I wanted on the card. I opened my notepad and read aloud what I'd written there earlier:

> Very sorry about Thursday night. I'll do better next time. Please give Diane my apologies and tell her I had a migraine. She's very nice. Congratulations again on Chester. I'm very happy for you guys.
>
> Ray

Then I called Terry at work and got his voice mail, on which I left a full and unabridged apology complete with offers of self-immolation.

*What do you want me to say?* Amy Zhang had pleaded. *I said everything right.* And then, *I don't like being tested.*

Given what I'd learned from Mike Angelo, it was easy enough to conceive that Amy Zhang might be under pressure to stick with some official version of events . . . to *say everything right*. She came to believe that I'd been sent to test her, to make sure she could still sell that official version. That now seemed obvious. And the way she said it suggested that it wasn't the first time she'd been tested. And it scared the hell out of her.

The pressure may have been applied by a bent cop or other government official involved in the cover-up of whatever the hell it was they were covering up. But Amy Zhang wasn't frightened at the front door, when she thought I was a cop. More likely, she thought I'd been sent by Hawk River. I had no evidence that Hawk River was behind it, but the company was at the very least a cobeneficiary of the cover-up, along with some part of the government.

*If . . . If* Joan Richmond knew anything damaging to Hawk River, and *if* she was willing to testify about her knowledge before the congressional Oversight and Government Reform committee. And *if* they knew she knew. And *if* they knew she was gonna spill to Congress.

That's a lot of ifs.

After a half hour of research online, I picked up the phone, dialed Hawk River's head office, and asked to speak with Joseph Grant. Grant was the CEO and I knew I wouldn't get him on the line, but the CEO's secretary is one of the true power positions in any company.

I told Grant's secretary who I was and who my client was and explained that I was on a fool's errand to collect information about Joan Richmond so that her father could come to terms with her death. I asked if Mr. Grant could spare me a few minutes, just to tell me what he remembered of Joan.

The secretary assured me that she would relay my request and asked me to please call back in an hour.

I spent the hour surfing the Net, reading what I could about Hawk River and its place in the world of government contracting, and about the congressional hearings into military contractors and their alleged billing abuses. It looked like a rat's nest but Washington had been a rat's nest for a long time now. Maybe it was ever thus. And besides, you can't always believe what you read in the papers.

I called back and the secretary told me that Mr. Grant would be happy to give me fifteen minutes at three o'clock tomorrow, if that was a convenient time for me. I assured her that three o'clock was perfect for me and thanked her for her help and hung up with a sour taste in my mouth.

*Fifteen minutes.* Joseph Grant ran a company with private soldiers servicing hundreds of government contracts in at least fifteen countries. Although most of the business was with Uncle Sam, some contracts were with other sovereign states. Plus dozens of contracts with several multinational corporations. All together Hawk River was billing three-quarters of a billion dollars, give or take a few bucks. Billion, with a *b*. And Joseph Grant can give me fifteen minutes of his time? He shouldn't have fifteen *seconds* for me. Some half-assed gumshoe taking $800 a day from a grieving father? Grant should've had his secretary pass me off to a public relations lackey with instructions to shine me on.

But Grant had time for me, so obviously he saw things differently. Perhaps he saw a gumshoe asking questions about Hawk River's former head of payroll who was murdered just in time to stop her from testifying before that congressional committee. The murdered former head of payroll whose every connection to Hawk River was quietly scrubbed from the CPD's case file by the concerted effort of several Chicago cops, a police department lawyer, an assistant state's attorney, and a lawyer from the governor's office.

I unplugged the percolator and put on my jacket, thinking *Don't wander too far down Speculation Alley, Dudgeon. Even if Hawk River is a beneficiary of some cover-up, you don't know that Grant even* knows *of it. Stay within sight of the established facts.*

I left the office. And locked the door behind me.


Back at my apartment, I changed into my sweats and did an hour on the recumbent bike with the stereo blasting Stiff Little Fingers. You don't get much better than SLF, and the music kept me motivated on the bike. I toweled the sweat off my face and got down on the floor. I lay on my left side, with a three-pound dumbbell in my right hand, and struggled through the exercises prescribed by my physical therapist, isolating muscles and feeling them tremble under the strain of such incredible weight.

Nothing so humbling as a contest lost to three pounds.

Having just barely survived the workout, I shaved and showered and put on jeans and a Columbia College sweatshirt. Padded barefoot into the kitchen and swallowed two Percocet and a pint of water, opened a can of Beefaroni and ate it right out of the can, *cowboy style*. Poured three fingers of Mount Gay Extra Old over ice. Added a splash of water. Took my drink to the living room and faced the stereo.

Over half my music collection was jazz but for the last nine months I hadn't been able to listen to it. Jazz had been my musical anchor since I was sixteen. But now, every time I tried, it just made me angry. I hoped that I'd be able to return to it someday.

But not yet.

I put on Lurrie Bell's *Blues Had a Baby*. To my ears Bell had the most soulful voice and inventive guitar on the Chicago blues scene. And that's saying a lot.

I drank the rum slowly and let the music wash over me and waited for the Percs to kick in. My shoulder hurt like a bastard, and it took some effort to stay in the present tense. The pain was a houseguest you never invited, who doesn't know when to leave and insists on retelling the story of how you met, over and over. A trip down a specific memory lane that I'd just as soon never take again.

The thing about being tortured is, there comes a point where you just want to die. You don't care anymore. You just don't give a fuck. All that exists is pain and self-hatred and the only way to make it stop is to tell them what they want to know. Or die.

So you want to die. You want it more than you want to tell them what they want to know, or you'd have told them by now. You want it more than you've ever wanted anything in your life. The desire for death actually strengthens you, buys you a few more minutes of resistance. You know you're going to break soon, and you beg death to come sooner.

It's sick, I know, but that's how it is.

Talk about ultimate tough guy credentials. That's what you'd think, right? You made it through that and you never told them a goddamn thing. But here you are almost ten months later, still waking up crying in the middle of the night like a small child with night terrors. Or freaking out because you catch a whiff of cheap aftershave.

Some tough guy.

I finished the rum in my glass and poured another and returned to the stereo.

Next up, Dylan's *Blood on the Tracks*.

The pain was dull enough that I could use my arm again, so I started packing books into cardboard boxes while listening to Bob get tangled up in blue. I hadn't been in complete denial about my upcoming move and I'd actually bought packing boxes. But only a few were packed. I had less than six weeks to find a new place to live and I hadn't even started looking in earnest.

As I looked around the apartment, I realized that this place was part of the problem. My belongings were part of the problem. The back of the couch had loose threads where my cat used to sharpen his claws. The cat died seven years ago. And the old battered piano bench that served as a coffee table? I'd had that thing since college. I'd bought the big reading chair as a gift to myself, to mark my second year working as an investigative reporter at the *Chicago Chronicle*.

They were relics of a closed chapter of my life—life before torture. Constant reminders of the man I used to be, and of what had been taken from me. I decided right then that I would make a clean break, leave all the relics behind and start from scratch in the new place. All I needed to pack were my books and CDs, my electronics, clothes, exercise equipment, and kitchen gear. Everything else could go in the Dumpster.

Hell, moving would be a cinch.

Feeling liberated by my decision, I went to the bedroom and packed a small suitcase and left the apartment. I walked a few blocks over to the Red Line and hopped on the northbound El, headed for a dead woman's apartment where so far I'd been able to sleep without nightmares.

# CHAPTER TEN

**E**xcuse me, Mr. Dudgeon?"

The man closed my office door behind him and strode toward my desk and stuck out his hand. "I'm Tim Dellitt. I'd like to hire you." I stood and shook his hand and gestured to one of the client chairs and he sat and so did I.

I guessed him in his early or midthirties. His blond hair was cut close to the scalp and he wore a precision-trimmed goatee and mustache. His suit was expensive.

"I hate to turn away business, Mr. Dellitt, but I'm on an exclusive case and I won't be available for another seven weeks. If you can wait that long—"

"No, I really can't."

"Well, I am sorry." I reached for my Rolodex. "I'd be happy to recommend another detective agency . . ."

Tim Dellitt held up a hand. "Just out of curiosity then, what are your rates?"

"Depends on the job. Eighty-five dollars an hour, it's billed that way. Eight hundred is my daily rate."

"And I suppose you charge a premium for an exclusive assignment, like the one you're on now, so I'm guessing you're set to rake in . . . almost fifty, sixty grand in the next seven weeks." He smiled and backed it up with a manly wink. "Am I right?"

Subtlety was not this guy's strong suit. I didn't want to know what was.

"Mr. Dellitt, I think you'd better find yourself another detective—"

"Wait, hear me out. Now what if I told you I'm willing to go *double* what you're making now. A hundred grand. All you gotta do is drop the case you're on and work exclusively on *my* case for the next seven weeks instead." He made it sound nice and friendly. "No wait, scratch that. I think I'll need you for eight full weeks. But I'll bump it up to one-twenty." Big smile.

"Mr. Dellitt—"

"You didn't even think about it."

"I don't need to think about it, I already have a client."

Dellitt shrugged. "So your client will be upset. With a hundred and twenty thousand dollars staring you in the face, who cares? You can refund what he's paid you so far and still come out way ahead."

We were approaching the tipping point. *This thing might deteriorate rapidly, Dudgeon.* I hit the foot switch under my desk, activating a video camera hidden in my bookshelf.

"How do you know my client is a 'he'?" I said.

"He, she, it. Whichever applies. Look, I'm making you a generous offer."

"Very generous," I said. "And I'm turning it down, with thanks."

"It's not just the money. The job I'm offering is very safe. Just a research project, no risk at all." His tone remained cordial. "The job you're on now, maybe it isn't as safe."

*He didn't really just say that, did he? Fuck, he really did just say that.* The muscles in my neck threatened to go into spasm.

I gave him my version of the deadeye, said, "You didn't have to take it that far, Mr. Dellitt. I got your point a while ago. You've made your offer and I've turned it down."

Without losing the affable smile, Dellitt said, "Gee, I'm really disappointed to hear you say that."

"You may go now."

"Really disappointed," he repeated. Then he stood and left my office without saying good-bye.

I hit the foot switch under my desk again, to turn the camera off.

I lit a cigarette.

I said some bad words.


The thirty-five-mile drive from Chicago to Aurora was unmarred by road construction delays. I considered calling the Vatican to report a miracle, but decided against it.

The pope wasn't from Chicago; he'd never understand.

The newscaster on WGN told me another public corruption scandal was breaking. In recent years they'd become as frequent as Cubs losses and revised Iraq war strategies.

Most recently we had the big Outfit Scandal, which snared a bunch of corrupt public servants and cost some lives and made me into a slightly damaged semicelebrity. That was but one of many, and not even the biggest one. We had the Minority Contracting Scandal, the Hired Trucks Scandal, The Riverboat Casino Scandal (successfully suppressed before it could really blossom), the CPD Chief of Detectives Jewel Thief Scandal, the CPD Jon Burge Torture Scandal, the CPD Drug Dealing Scandal . . .

It had been a bad few years for the Chicago Police Department. Cops had been arrested for sexual assault, extortion, forgery, financial exploitation of the elderly, bribery, solicitation to commit murder for hire . . .

The new scandal was more bad news for the CPD. Yet again, a convicted murderer had been proved innocent by DNA testing. Another young black man, convicted with no physical evidence against him. Convicted solely on a false confession that had been tortured out of him by cops.

A few years earlier, Governor George Ryan placed a moratorium on the death penalty after a group called the Innocence Project cleared thirteen Illinois death-row inmates through DNA testing. That was just the beginning. New cases came along regularly, and by now more than twenty-five wrongful convictions had been voided, with more on the way.

Ex-Governor Ryan was now on the verge of being convicted himself, on federal corruption charges, but at least he'd done something decent before leaving office. Meanwhile, Washington politicians and media pundits were furiously defending torture as a necessity in the "war on terror." Their most eloquent opponent was Republican senator John McCain, who knew a lot more about it than they did. He spoke of what engaging in torture makes us as a nation, as a people. And they accused him of being a closet liberal and insisted that torture was "a practical necessity in the post–9/11 world." Regardless of what kind of people it made us, or what kind of nation we were becoming.

Despite the latest news (or because of it), I felt sorry for the cops. Not those involved in the scandals, but the vast majority of Chicago cops who are generally straight up. And I'd had some friends on the force. Not close friends but definitely more than friendly acquaintances. I'd lost most of them when I helped put some bad cops in prison but that had more to do with peer pressure than anything else. A few of them even thanked me privately, before shunning me publicly.

I needed to approach Hawk River with a different mind-set. I switched from the radio to the CD player and loaded a disc. *Back on the Right Track,* by Sly & the Family Stone.

I cranked the volume and sang along.

I needed the distraction. It was hard not to think about Tim Dellitt's attempt to buy me off the case. Dellitt could've been sent by Hawk River, or he may have been sent by one of the other interested parties. It was too early to say.

And I didn't even know who the other interested parties were.

# CHAPTER ELEVEN

I don't know that I can be of much help, but Isaac Richmond deserves any peace you can get for him." Joseph Grant was unsmiling but not unfriendly. From a high spot on the wall above his head, President Bush compensated with a grin wide enough for both of them. Grant's office was modern and expensive and confidently masculine.

"You know Mr. Richmond?" I asked.

"We've met a few times. I haven't seen him in years, but he knew my father and Dad always spoke highly of him." Before taking over Hawk River from his father twelve years earlier, Joseph Grant had been a Navy SEAL and he still looked fit. Lean and tanned, he was in his early fifties but I'd have probably guessed midforties. His dark brown hair showed just a little silver at the temples. He said, "And Joan was one of the finest people I've ever known. We were all very sorry to see her go."

For a second I thought Grant was referring to her death, but of course he wasn't. I said, "Mr. Richmond told me she was an excellent accountant."

"That too. It was a shame to lose her."

"Did she leave on good terms?"

"It's always a little awkward when someone quits. We pay well and try to make our employees feel valued, and there's a temptation to see it as a criticism."

I took a look around the office. "I'm sure you pay very well." He could take that as a veiled reference to Tim Dellitt's offer, if he'd sent Dellitt. And if not, the comment was innocuous enough.

Grant let out a very small smile. "We believe in sharing the wealth. But Joan did the right thing by leaving."

"Why?"

"Her issues had nothing to do with how she was treated as an em-ployee—they were much bigger than that—and we really couldn't have done anything to make her happy, had she stayed. It's unfortunate. But as our head of payroll, Joan not only cut checks to our men, she also oversaw the disbursement of death benefits to their families. She took it very badly when there were no WMD in Iraq. She was skeptical about the war from the beginning, I think, and that really hit her hard. She felt our men were dying for nothing."

"How did you feel?"

"We're a for-profit corporation. Our men die for money." Grant finally let out a full smile. "Does that sound cold to you?"

"It sure doesn't sound like a line to toss out at your next press con-ference," I said.

Grant laughed. "That's very good. Mind if I use that?"

"Be my guest," I said. "I got a thousand of 'em."

"Seriously though . . ."

"Seriously? Yeah, it sounds a little cold," I said. "But honest."

"It is honest. But it's only half the story. We make money, and I'm not ashamed of that. More importantly, we support our men and women in uniform and help further American interests around the world. I take great pride in what we do. We really provide a public service."

Most active-duty military personnel—the real soldiers—didn't share Grant's sunny assessment of Hawk River's public service, but saying so would do me no good. So I said, "How about the other PMCs?" just to see if he'd jump on it.

He did.

"Let me stop you right there, Mr. Dudgeon. Hawk River is a private *security* corporation, not a private *military* corporation. We protect equipment, facilities, and VIPs. We never fire first and, when attacked, we only fight until our VIP is off-the-X, until the threat has ended. Despite the sexy image in the press, we're basically security guards . . . albeit very well-armed and exceptionally well-trained security guards."

"Yeah, mercenary sounds way sexier than security guard," I said without attitude.

"You got that right. We are not mercenaries but you know how the press is—after all, you used to be one of them," said Grant, telling me that he'd been briefed on my background. "Anyway, the distinction is essential but was not sufficient for Joan, and she couldn't in good conscience continue to work here. I disagreed with her, but I respected her decision to leave and wished her well. I didn't see her again after she left, but I'd like to think we parted as friends."

"And what about Steven Zhang?" I said.

"What about him?"

"Did you part as friends?"

Grant laughed easily. He was a pro. "I don't have a lot of contact with people working below the level of *department head*. I'd like to be friends with everybody here but there are only so many hours in the day."

I waited a few seconds, but Grant didn't expand upon his answer. Clearly I would have to tell some of what I knew but I wanted to avoid setting off alarm bells in Grant's head.

I said, "Steven Zhang worked under Joan, left here about a month before she quit. Worked for her again at HM Nichols and eventually killed her."

Grant offered an indulgent smile, "What can I tell you about him?"

"Mr. Richmond wants to have a better understanding of why his daughter died, so any insight you can give me about her killer would be helpful."

Grant leaned back in his chair and thought about it. After an uncomfortable thirty seconds, he sat forward and said, "From what I read in the papers, Steven Zhang went crazy. That's why Joan died. I'm afraid I don't have any insight into his particular mental illness."

"I understand. I'm not asking you for a medical opinion, just any recollection you may have of the man."

The office door opened behind me. Joseph Grant's head turned slightly and nodded, as if controlled by servos. "Blake. Join us."

An Aryan-looking man dropped a thin file folder on the edge of Grant's desk and squeezed himself into the chair next to me. His eyes were set too close together, like he'd been designed to attack a single goal undistracted by peripheral concerns. Like anything coming from the periphery would just bounce off of him.

He said, "Blake Sten," and held out his hand and I gave him mine and he made me wish I hadn't. He stopped short of breaking metacarpals but it took some effort not to say *Ouch*.

Grant said, "Blake is our vice president of corporate security."

It was a title perfect for a company thug, and Sten fit the profile. Bald by choice and muscled in a way that made me doubt he'd pass a urine test, he was an impressive sight. A puckered burn scar covered the left side of his face and neck. He looked angry about it.

"Desert Storm, '91," said Blake Sten, in answer to the unasked question in my mind.

"Blake pulled four men from a burning Humvee," added Grant. "Earned a Bronze Star."

"Should've been silver," said Blake Sten, "but great soldiers don't make good politicians and I'd pissed off the wrong major."

"Well, thanks for your service," I said, just to be saying something.

Joseph Grant said, "A man in my position cannot, and in fact should not, know the details of everything that happens during day-to-day operations. We terminated Steven Zhang's contract early—fired him, essentially—but Blake will have to brief you on the details."

He stood and held out his hand and I shook it.

"Thanks very much for your time, Mr. Grant."

"It was a pleasure meeting you," he lied. "Good luck with your case."

We stood side by side in the wood-paneled elevator. Blake Sten pushed the Lobby button and said, "Let's do this outside. I want a smoke." As we descended, he tapped the file folder absently against his leg, with no discernible sense of rhythm.

The doors opened and we passed through an airy glass lobby, which was dominated by a giant Hawk River logo set into the vast marble floor. A black silhouette of a hawk, with three wavy lines (red, white, and blue) beneath, in the middle of a shield. It was nothing if not literal.

Next to the visitor parking lot, there were a few picnic tables on the lawn. We stopped and sat. In the afternoon sun, Sten's burn scar looked even more impressive. He was wearing a white shirt and blue tie but no jacket, and as he reached for the cigarettes in his shirt pocket, his bicep flexed and strained against the tight sleeve and a tattoo of the Hawk River logo showed through the thin white cotton.

Sten got the cigarette going, snapped the lid of his brass Zippo shut, and said, "Steven Zhang was a traitor and I fired him for cause." He blew smoke out his nostrils, flipped the lighter open again, spun the wheel and watched the flame dance in the breeze, then snapped it shut again. "I'm a poker player. I play the 5/10 tables at Honest Abe's. You know the place?"

"Not intimately," I said. Honest Abe's was one of the newer riverboat casinos that were popping up all over the state.

"But you know of it."

"Sure," I said.

"Okay, well I was playing there a year ago and I saw Steven Zhang at the blackjack tables. It was pure chance that we were in the place at the same time. I usually only play on weekends, but just happened to be there on a Thursday. Zhang didn't see me. He was focused on his game, betting $10 a hand and losing. After a while he upped his bets to $25, chasing his losses, losing even more." Sten took a drag on his smoke. "Later, he went to one of the ATMs and took $500 out using a credit card. Lost that, too. He looked like a problem gambler to me. And that's a security risk." Sten went through the *flip-spin-snap* routine with the Zippo again. "Anybody gets deep enough in debt, becomes vulnerable to outside influence, right?"

"Sure," I said.

"Right. So I put a guy on him, kept him under surveillance. I mean, he was working for Joan on the payroll computers—he had access to every employee's Social Security number, home address, bank account numbers for those who take direct deposit. You know, he could sell all that." *Flip-spin-snap* went the Zippo.

"Sure," I said.

"Right. So my guy follows him and he visits the casino once or twice a week, always losing." Sten pulled an eight-by-ten photograph from the file folder and turned it toward me. "And then this."

In the photograph Steven Zhang sat in a Caribou coffeehouse, drinking coffee with another Chinese man. Zhang was dressed casually, the other man in a suit.

I said, "You fired Steven Zhang for drinking coffee?"

Sten laughed smoke through his nose. "Funny. The other man is Jia Lun, a television reporter from Hong Kong, on semipermanent assignment to Chicago. Been here three years, reporting on politics, the financial markets, big business." *Flip-spin-snap.* "But that's just his cover. He's a case officer for China's Ministry of State Security."

"No kidding?"

"No kidding. We picked up audio on their conversation, had it translated. Zhang was trying to sell our employee records; Jia Lun wasn't interested. He wanted Zhang to access our deployment records instead."

"Jesus. Could Zhang do that?"

"He'd have to hack through a few layers of passwords and I'm not sure he was that talented. But I wasn't gonna wait to find out." *Flip-spin-snap.* "I fired his ass and passed everything to the FBI."

"Why didn't the FBI set up a sting?"

"I'm sure they would have. That's why I fired Zhang first, before approaching them. We've got a business to run here, and business is very brisk these days. We don't have time to do the FBI's job for them."

Public service. Clearly, public service was Hawk River's *raison d'être.*

Blake Sten's cell phone rang and he flipped it open and said, "Yes . . . right. Okay, I guess you're done. . . . He's got what? No, I don't want it. Break it. And leave it there." He closed the phone. "Sorry about that." He put his cigarette butt down in the grass and ground it under his heel. "Now I've just shared some sensitive information with you. And I don't mind if you pass it along to Joan's father. Isaac Richmond has our trust. But I'm asking you to be discreet with it." *Flip-spin-snap.* "None of it is a secret, as far as Hawk River is concerned—in fact, I think it shows the strength of our internal security. But our *biggest client* doesn't want to bring public attention to the fact that the Chinese government is interested in our deployment records."

"That's understandable," I said. "What happened with the FBI's investigation of Zhang?"

"No idea," said Sten. "Once I passed it on to them, it was out of my hair. Zhang was not a threat to us anymore, so I moved on." *Flip-spin-snap.* "I sincerely hope that, once you pass all this to Mr. Richmond, he can move on, too."

It sounded like a warning but I decided not to notice. I smiled. "I hope so, too." Sten nodded, did the Zippo dance again. I said, "Your lighter fluid bills must be astronomical."

"You ever been burned?" He rubbed the closed Zippo against the puckered skin on his face.

"Not seriously."

"Most people haven't. I've been stabbed, shot, fragged, and burned.

And I'll tell ya, burned is the worst." *Flip-spin*. But no *snap*. Sten watched the flame burn, said, "Fire is the most powerful weapon there is, bar none. Know why?"

"No."

"Because it scares people the most."

"If your yardstick is what scares people the most, then public speaking is the most powerful weapon there is," I said.

*Snap*. Sten looked at me, laughed through his nose again. "Funny." He stood and put the lighter in his pocket. We walked to my car and shook hands and this time he took it easy on me. I opened the door and got in, rolled down the window, and turned the ignition over.

"Nice wheels," said Sten.

"Thanks."

"Cubs fan, huh?" He lit a new cigarette. "Your car, white with blue stripes. Cubs colors. Mr. Cub, Ernie Banks," he added.

"My favorite," I said.

"Mine, too. Ernie Banks."

Our obligatory professional sports team bonding successfully accomplished, Sten gave me a short wave and turned back toward the building.

# CHAPTER TWELVE

**I**saac Richmond opened his front door and looked at me for a full five seconds before speaking.

"I wasn't expecting you until next week," he said.

"We need to talk," I said.

"I suppose you'd better come in then." Richmond led me inside but instead of turning toward his study, he opened a door under the staircase. I followed him down carpeted stairs into a finished basement that must have been twice the length of the structure above ground. The front room looked like any upscale basement den, and through a door I could see what looked like a darkened workshop in back.

"Runs all the way to the back of the property," said Richmond. "I bought during the development phase, before construction began, and I had the developer alter the plans to include all this." Richmond opened a door to our left and flicked a wall switch. Pot lights illuminated the long room. "This is my personal recreation center."

There were two fully functioning bowling lanes, complete with electronic pinsetters, scoring system, and automatic ball return. Immediately before us was a scoring table and chairs. It looked just like

what you'd find in a real bowling alley, minus the beer bellies and cigarette smoke.

Next to the two bowling lanes was a two-lane gun range with elec-
tric clothesline mechanisms for sending out paper targets and bringing
them back. On a side bench sat a stack of paper silhouettes, hearing protectors, and eye protectors. A Fort Knox gun safe stood in the
corner.

"I was just bowling a few frames," said Richmond. "Helps to
clear my mind." He picked up a ball, set his fingers in the holes, and
executed a perfect strike. "Some people meditate, I bowl. Care to
join me?"

"I don't bowl."

"Never too late to learn."

"I can't bowl, Colonel Richmond. I have a shoulder injury."

He looked at me with what I thought might be mild skepticism. "I
didn't know that," he said.

"I guess your intel was lacking."

Richmond seemed to finally pick up on my anger. "Get you a
drink?" But it wasn't really a question and he was already walking
back to the den.

He gestured to a leather couch and I sat and he went upstairs and
came back with two bottles of Wisconsin Amber, the same beer that
was currently stocked in my office bar fridge. He handed me a bottle
and sat in a leather wingchair and we both drank.

I said, "A year ago Steven Zhang worked with your daughter at
Hawk River."

"Yes."

"Why didn't you tell me that when you hired me?"

"To be frank, I wanted to see how long it would take you to learn
it on your own. I thought if you came to me after two weeks for our
first briefing and you still didn't know, then you were the wrong man
for the job."

"I assume you also know that Joan was killed just before she could
testify before Congress."

"You *do* work fast."

"So why don't you tell me why you really hired me, Colonel? Because it sure as hell wasn't to help you come to terms with Joan's death."

Isaac Richmond looked down at the floor, then to the label on his beer bottle, which depicted the largest granite dome in the world. His back was still ramrod straight, but his perfect posture now seemed more defensive than proud. "I admit, I was not completely forthcoming at our first meeting. But I wasn't insincere. I really do believe that Steven Zhang was mentally unstable, and that he killed Joan."

"But . . . ?"

"And I really do need to come to terms with her death. But I can't help but have questions. Suspicions, if you like. Put yourself in my shoes, knowing what you now know. If she were your daughter, someone you loved . . . wouldn't you have questions?"

I knew far more than Richmond realized, and I had plenty of questions. Big, ugly questions. The thing is, I wasn't sure how far I wanted to pursue them or what the cost would be if I did.

"Why didn't you just level with me from the start?"

"I didn't know if I was being paranoid," he said. "Another occupational hazard, with the career I've had. I was fully aware that, as a father, I wanted to believe Joan died for a reason. I mean a more tangible reason than the fact that her attacker was crazy. A reason that made more sense, in the big picture. A reason that provided meaning to her death." He said it as if it were a shameful admission.

"That's perfectly normal," I said.

Isaac Richmond's eyes glistened and he shook his head and took a swig of beer. I figured that was as close as he came to crying. He said, "I thought the police had the right man, but they concluded the investigation so quickly. Joan never told me that she'd been called to testify before Congress, and there wasn't a lot of media coverage because they were closed-door hearings, so the issue wasn't even on my radar. And I didn't know that Steven Zhang had worked at Hawk River." He made eye contact, held it. "I really didn't know—I want you to believe me. It wasn't until after the police closed the case so quickly that I became suspicious. Something didn't seem right, so I made a few calls, and I learned these things. Then I visited the police lieutenant and he recommended you. I thought, if you came up with the same information and it also made you suspicious, then maybe I wasn't just an old man refusing to accept that his daughter's death was senseless."

I felt sorry for him, but I didn't much like being tested. And that made me think of Amy Zhang, who also didn't like being tested.

Isaac Richmond said, "You're right, I should have leveled with you from the start. Now I have. Please don't turn your back on me."

If I hadn't met Amy Zhang, I would've quit the case right there and refunded the rest of his money. But I had met her and the deeper I got into this case, the more I became convinced that her life was in danger. I suspected, perhaps more than Richmond, that Joan had died for a very good reason and it was the same reason that Amy lived in fear.

And I wanted to do something about it.

"All right," I said. "I'll stay on the case for now."

"Thank you," said Isaac Richmond.

I reached into my briefcase and withdrew Joan's diary, handed it to him. He opened the cover and saw Joan's handwriting on the first page and dropped the book on the table like it might be coated in anthrax.

"It's Joan's diary," I said.

"No, I-I know." Richmond's mouth twitched three times in quick succession. "I don't want that."

"You said you wanted to know everything I learned about her."

"Well, I do. But I can't . . ." He swallowed some beer. "You can just brief me on it, tell me what it says."

"It says a lot. Maybe it would be best if you didn't know. That's your call. But I'm not giving you a book report on your daughter's private thoughts. Especially her thoughts about your relationship."

Isaac Richmond stared at the diary for a long time and when he looked up at me, his eyes were wet and his face no longer seemed young for its age. "Just tell me this," he said. "Was she happy?"

"No, sir, she wasn't."

# CHAPTER THIRTEEN

**I**❚ **powered up my cell phone** and there was a voice-mail message waiting. It was Terry. Apparently my bad behavior was forgiven and he wanted to meet later and compare notes on the Richmond case. I called him back and we agreed to meet at the Billy Goat at midnight.

Then I called the local FBI headquarters and asked for Special Agent Holborn. He was not in the office, so I told his voice mail that I needed to see him and left my cell number.

I considered calling Gravedigger Peace. Gravedigger was the head groundskeeper at Mount Pleasant Cemetery, and a very old friend. He was also a former soldier for hire and he might be able to steer me in the right direction on this thing. But I decided to put that off for now and approach him later, with as complete a picture as I could.

I arrived at my office just after 7:00. I unlocked the door and entered, flicked the lights on and picked up the mail, and took off my jacket. It wasn't until I dropped the mail on my desk that I saw it.

For a moment I didn't know what I was looking at. A random pattern of shapes, brown and black, scattered on my desk blotter. A metal spiral. Below the spiral . . . a little Cubs uniform?

The Cubs logo snapped me out of my cognitive hiccup and now I saw what I was looking at. Saw it clearly.

Ernie Banks lay on his back on the desk blotter. Ernie's bobble head had been smashed into about a half-dozen pieces scattered around the spring that served as his neck.

And then I remembered what Blake Sten had said, when he took that phone call.

*Break it. And leave it there.*

And later, in the parking lot: *Mr. Cub, Ernie Banks.*

I looked away from Ernie Banks and saw something even more disturbing—my gun was in my hand. I couldn't remember drawing it from the holster.

I reholstered my gun. *Get a grip, Dudgeon. Exercise control . . .*

I dumped the remnants of Ernie Banks into the wastepaper basket and took quick inventory of my office. They'd gone through my filing cabinet but all the files were there. Desk drawers, closet, even the cupboards in the kitchenette. All searched but nothing taken. I went around the place shifting items ever so slightly, returning everything to its proper position. But I still couldn't get comfortable. Even sitting at my desk, I felt the presence of the intruder who'd sat there as he combed through my computer only hours earlier.

I went back to the closet and brought out a black, hard-shell case, took it to my desk. I snapped open the clasps, lifted the lid, and pulled out my bug detector. I spent the next twenty minutes sweeping the place for listening devices. Checked everywhere that could be checked.

Nothing.

I put the apparatus back in the case, pulled out the tap detector, and took my time checking the phone and fax lines.

Nothing there, either. I put the machine back in the case, snapped it shut, and stowed it back in the closet.

I opened a beer and set fire to a cigarette, sat at my desk. I went online and did a search for "Jia Lun Hong Kong journalist" and found a photo easily enough. It was the same guy who'd been photographed drinking coffee with Steven Zhang. Didn't find anything online to suggest Jia Lun was an MSS agent, but didn't expect to. When the second beer bottle was empty, I got up and put on my coat and headed for the door.

I didn't want to be in my office anymore.

I locked the door, despite the obviously limited value of such a gesture. Shunned the elevators, took the stairs down thirteen stories to burn off a little of the residual adrenaline that had leaked into my system when I'd discovered the violation of my office. Walked over to State Street and up two blocks to the Borders bookstore at Randolph, where I found a copy of *The Book of Ralph*.

Sometimes after a few fastballs, life throws you an unexpected changeup. I was headed to the cash registers when I saw Jill in the poetry section. My heart raced and I took a step backward and watched her. She was dying her hair a darker shade and the cut was a little shorter, revealing her long elegant neck. She was standing in that familiar pose, weight on one leg, the swell of her left hip showing through her tan raincoat, and in that instant I felt the cumulative ache of the nine months we'd been apart. In that instant, I missed her more than I'd have thought it possible to miss anyone. She closed the book she was reading and took it to the checkout line, passing so close that I could smell her perfume. *Amarige.* I almost passed out.

I caught my breath and got in line directly behind her. She didn't turn around. I stood three feet behind her and imagined taking her by the shoulders and kissing the back of her neck. The fantasy made me light-headed and I pushed it from my mind.

Jill walked forward and paid for her book, and I paid for mine two cash registers down the line, but she didn't look over. We were both environmentally friendly consumers and both declined a plastic bag for our books.

Outside, Jill walked around the corner and stopped in front of a North Community Bank ATM machine. I stopped beside the row of newspaper boxes barely ten feet away. She still hadn't noticed me, and it bothered me that she was so unaware of her surroundings.

She seemed particularly oblivious, seemed lost in thought. Dangerous for anyone—man or woman—navigating the streets of the big city. Human predators smell unawareness like dogs smell fear. It's the smell of easy prey.

She withdrew some money from the machine and stuffed the money and her bankcard into a wallet and stuffed the wallet into her purse. Crumpled the receipt and tossed it into a full garbage can as she walked away. I plucked the receipt off the top of the trash and stuck it in my pocket.

She walked back to State Street and toward the stairs that led down to Washington Station. I opened my mouth and said, "Jill," but I didn't say it loud enough and she kept walking and started down the stairs.

"Jill," I said, louder. Too loud. She spun around. "Sorry, didn't mean to startle you," I said. "I saw you in the bookstore." I held up my book as if that explained everything.

"Hello, Ray." The same English accent I remembered. "How've you been keeping?" An awkward smile.

I smiled back, hoping mine looked more comfortable. "Well, I'd be a lot better if you'd have a drink with me."

I held my breath for about an hour until Jill said, "All right, but one is my limit. Work overbooked and they sent me home but I'm still on call."

We walked around the corner to the Elephant & Castle. Along the way I asked about her work. She said things about it never being dull in the ER and about how she might stop taking night shifts even though they pay better than days. We walked side by side and I felt the proximity of our bodies like the collision of two energy fields, wanted to reach out for her hand. Of course I didn't do it.

"What about you?" said Jill. "How's the *Mike Hammer* business these days?" I wasn't deaf to the undercurrent of hurt in her mild sarcasm.

"Oh, you know how it is, dollface," I said, "another day, another gunfight. But if I don't save the world, who will?"

"Sorry," she said, "I didn't intend for it to sound so sharp." She stopped walking, ran fingers through her hair, said, "Look, maybe this isn't such a terrific idea . . ."

"Hey, it's just a drink," I used as lighthearted a tone as I could muster. "You can even tease me about my job." I turned to walk and gently placed my hand in the small of her back and she came along.

We found a relatively quiet booth in the back corner of the pub, took off our coats, and sat. Jill was wearing a burgundy turtleneck. Outside the sweater a silver chain hung around her neck and a rose pendant lay against her chest just above the swell of her breasts. I didn't remember ever seeing the necklace when we were a couple and I wondered if it was a courtship present from the good doctor.

I ordered a pint of Guinness and Jill ordered a gin and tonic and after the waitress left Jill pointed at my book, on the table across from hers. "A friend of mine is reading the same book. She says it's excellent." *She.* Jill didn't want to say "he." I took that as a positive sign.

"It's really good to see you, Jill," I said. Thinking *You idiot—It's really good to see you? That is so lame.*

She didn't answer, just stared into my eyes. Then her hand inched forward and came to rest on mine and *zing* went the strings of my heart. After a few seconds her hand retreated and she looked away and said, "What am I doing here?"

But she said it quietly, really to herself, and our drinks arrived at the same time so I pretended not to hear it. I knew I should respect her pullback, not force things. I tried to think of another subject. Took the bank machine receipt from my pocket, slid it across the table. "You should be more careful at bank machines," I said. Jill read the receipt, recognized it.

"You were following me."

"Yeah, I was right behind you at the ATM. You never noticed me. If I were a mugger, I'd have watched you punch in your PIN number." I gestured at the receipt. "And I'd know how much you'd withdrawn and your bank balance. You need to pay attention to your surroundings."

Jill didn't seem to appreciate the advice. She scowled as she sipped her drink. "Did you follow me from work to the bookstore?"

"No. No, I just—"

"Because this is starting to get creepy."

"No, Jill. I swear, it was just coincidence. I saw you in the bookstore and wanted to ask you for a drink."

"So you could offer me personal safety tips."

"No. Okay, forget about the bank machine. I was just trying to be helpful."

After a moment, Jill's face softened. "All right, I suppose I got the wrong impression for a second. I thought perhaps you were, you know, following me."

I forced a smile, said, "Relax, I'm not a stalker." Thinking *No, you just hire Vince to do your stalking by proxy.*

It was time to change the subject again. I read the title of her book upside down: *Blue Daffodils and Other Poems.* I said, "I never knew you were into poetry."

Jill forced a smile of her own. "I'm broadening my horizons."

"Any good?"

"Don't know yet. I bought it because of the one poem I read in the store."

"Can I see?"

Jill's hand reflexively covered the book. "I'd rather not."

Another extended silence. Jill rummaged in her purse and brought out a pack of cigarettes. I reached into my pocket and grabbed my Zippo, lit her cigarette, then one for myself. We smoked and sipped our drinks and I scrambled for something to say.

*Lay it on the line, Dudgeon. You've got nothing to lose.*

I said, "Let's just cut through the bullshit for a minute. I miss you and I think you feel the same. Now, I know you were unhappy with my job—"

"For good reason. You almost got yourself killed."

"I understand. But I've been careful with the cases I've taken since then. Hell, I haven't had a concussion all year," I said with a smile.

"That's good to hear."

"I still love you. Let's give it another shot."

"Ray . . . I'm seeing someone. I told you that when you called in June."

"That's still going on, huh?" Like I didn't know.

"Yes, it is. And it's serious."

"But you came with me for a drink." I reached across the table and took her hand in mine. "And your eyes are full of tears. Come on, Jill. You don't feel the same way about him."

She pulled her hand away. "You're not being fair. Whether or not I love you is completely beside the point."

"Then what is the point?"

"Nothing's changed, don't you see? We'd have the same problems . . . if I still have feelings for you—that just makes it worse." She picked up her book. "I can't— I . . . this is wrong, I shouldn't even be here with you."

Jill scooped up her purse and stood and grabbed her coat and left me sitting there with half a pint of stout and a knot in my gut.

# CHAPTER FOURTEEN

**Terry sat with some regulars** in Wise Guys Corner at the Billy Goat. Wise Guys Corner was a spot at the end of the bar where eminent newspapermen had congregated for decades, from Mike Royko to Rick Kogan . . . and now Terry Green. In addition to newspapermen, it was also the favorite perch of local political operatives, union bosses, advertising executives, and other hustlers. One of the last great water-cooler spots for people plugged into Real Chicago.

As I looked down from the doorway, it struck me that Terry was Alpha Dog tonight. If Kogan or John Kass had been there, that wouldn't have been true. But they weren't, so it was. Terry was Alpha Reporter and for a second I felt a twinge of envy and wondered what might have been had I not abandoned my newspaper career.

Then I remembered the compromises Terry had to make along the way. How he'd seen legitimate stories—sometimes his own—spiked by clout, and how he'd seen other stories tailored and trimmed to protect the powerful and corrupt.

*The business of the newspaper is to comfort the afflicted and afflict the comfortable,* wrote Finley Peter Dunne. Or words to that effect. Anyway, I don't know how Terry lived with the compromise, but he did.

My old editor at the *Chronicle,* Colm Stanwell, once tried to help me with his gruff brand of fatherly advice. I'd just been pulled off a good story and I was sitting in my newsroom cubicle eating my spleen about it. Stanwell walked by and without pausing said, "Welcome to the world, Ray. If you don't bend, you break. Get used to it."

I couldn't.

There were about two dozen people in the Goat tonight. It was after midnight so there wouldn't be any more tour bus invasions that evening, although we were sure to get some drunk college kids if we stayed long enough. Terry saw me coming down the stairs, picked up his drink, and nodded me over to the "VIP Room" at the back. I stopped at the bar and got a couple mugs of dark from Nick the bartender, took them to our table. Terry and I were alone back there, surrounded by framed and faded Royko columns and photos of ballplayers and famous Chicagoans and infamous Chicago goats.

I lit a smoke and briefed Terry on recent events.

We agreed that Blake Sten had given me a plausible accounting of Zhang's firing. Unusual? Yes. Unexpected? Hell yes. But plausible nevertheless, and we agreed to look into the identity of Jia Lun. We also agreed that Dellitt was working for Hawk River.

"But Sten threw in a little friendly menace of his own," I said. "So why'd he tell Dellitt to smash Ernie Banks? Seems like overkill."

"Yeah, but you're not an idiot," said Terry. "Maybe they're taking no chances, in case you are."

"Always good to be underestimated," I said. "That way I never disappoint. Still, it doesn't sit right. Dellitt's search wasn't meticulous. They knew I'd notice the place had been searched. They didn't have to smash Ernie Banks."

"Then maybe Blake Sten is humping you," said Terry.

"Beg your pardon?"

"You know, like dogs in the park. Showing dominance. What's so funny?"

"Nothing," I said, "I was just thinking about Alpha Dogs a few minutes ago. But without the humping imagery."

"The humping imagery is important," said Terry. "A lot of Alphas need to express their dominance, so they hump until they get a display of submission. But some keep on humping, even after the Beta Dog has submitted. Giving the order to smash Ernie Banks was overkill, you're right. So maybe Blake Sten is the second type of Alpha."

"Maybe I should roll over and expose my belly and find out."

"Not your natural posture." Terry finished his beer and picked up my empty mug. He left the table and returned a few minutes later with a couple of rocks glasses filled with something amber over ice, handed me one. I swirled the ice around and took a sip. Jameson.

"Sláinte," I said.

Terry raised his glass in reply, swallowed some whiskey, and said, "You know, there's a major flaw in the working hypothesis here."

"Good. I didn't like the idea of being humped by Blake Sten."

"Not that. The hypothesis that Hawk River engineered Joan Richmond's death to stop her from testifying. Given the specifics of the murder, it's all a little too *Manchurian Candidate* for my liking."

"Ever hear of MK-ULTRA?" I said.

"Yeah, it was a failure," said Terry. "Proves the point. The poor bastards were completely unreliable."

"Unless you count Sirhan Sirhan."

"Oh, come on. You don't believe his bullshit."

I dragged on my cigarette. "Maybe not, but I don't believe the official version, either. Anyway, you're assuming that my hypothesis includes Hawk River causing and managing Steven Zhang's psychosis. I'm saying, maybe he wasn't crazy at all. Maybe they got him to fake it."

"Still too unreliable. These guys don't leave anything to chance, and they couldn't count on him doing a perfect impression of a paranoid schizophrenic."

"Didn't have to be perfect," I said. "Just good enough to fool his coworkers. His act wouldn't be scrutinized by a psychiatrist until after his arrest. My bet is, if he hadn't killed himself, he'd have been shivved in jail before he could undergo a psych evaluation. That's easy enough to arrange."

"The more obvious explanation is that Steven Zhang was crazy," said Terry.

I pulled out my notebook. "So everyone thinks Steven Zhang was crazier than a shithouse rat. Paranoid schizophrenic."

"Looks like it."

"Looks *exactly* like it," I flipped a few pages. "The confession," I said. "It's got everything. Paranoia? Check. Messianic complex? Check. Vast conspiracy? Check. Auditory hallucinations? Check. It's like Zhang was serving up a psychiatric diagnosis on a platter, when any two of the symptoms would've been enough to lead the cops to the same conclusion. Like he was making absolutely sure."

"It could just as easily mean he really was a paranoid schizophrenic. In essence, you're saying he was so crazy that you don't believe he was crazy. Both his wife and coworkers confirmed behavior consistent with the disease."

"His coworkers aren't qualified to judge and I think his wife is just saying what she's been told to say. And there's this: With the overwhelming majority of schizophrenics, initial onset of symptoms occurs in their teens. Sometimes in their early twenties. But Zhang was thirty-seven when this suddenly started. That would be extremely unusual."

"Unusual but not unheard of," said Terry. "What else you got?"

"Okay, he kills Joan, leaves the confession, goes home. According to the confession, he killed her so he could 'carry out his mission.' But when he gets home, he's no longer crazy, is he? He calls his wife and tells her he's done something terrible, then kills himself. Both reasonable things to do if you've just killed an innocent woman. But not if you've just foiled an evil conspiracy that was trying to stop you from saving American democracy."

Terry nodded, "That's better, but still not enough to outweigh the more reasonable premise that he went crazy. I think if you do some research you'll find that they can occasionally snap out of it for moments at a time."

"Hold on." I took a drink and told myself not to be frustrated by Terry's resistance. He was a good reporter doing his job as a skeptic, poking holes where holes could be poked. I said, "Here's the final piece that takes it from suggestive to conclusive: Amy Zhang made a mistake during our interview. She said that Steven's English wasn't as good as hers. Said he had a limited vocabulary." I read from Zhang's confession, "'I must carry out my vital mission, imperative to saving American democracy.' That sound like a guy with a limited vocabulary? If my theory is right, Blake Sten somehow convinced Zhang to put on a crazy act and kill Joan."

"You and Joan are on a first-name basis now?"

"Don't," I said.

"You're getting emotionally involved in this case, Ray. That's not good."

"Can we please get back to my theory? Sten convinces Zhang to act crazy, but he's not gonna take any chances with the confession so he writes it himself. He wants the note to read like it was written by a paranoid schizophrenic but he's a little overzealous about it, makes sure every damn symptom is present and accounted. He gets Zhang to transcribe it in his own handwriting. But the confession doesn't read like it was written by an English-as-a-Second-Language guy with a limited vocabulary. Instead, it uses words that are second nature to a guy like Sten. Any military man has heard the words *vital* and *imperative* about a zillion times in the service. Hell, Zhang even spelled imperative correctly. I always want to put two *r*'s in it. And I am fluent."

"That's debatable," said Terry.

"But you concede my point."

"I concede that you *have* a point, and I think it takes us from suggestive to highly suggestive, but not all the way to conclusive. And it doesn't promote your hypothesis to theory. You may end up being right, but you're way ahead of yourself in the certainty department. And that's dangerous."

"Now you're just being intractable," I said.

"Ooh, I guess you *are* fluent, after all," said Terry.

"Thank you," I said.

"Look, I'm telling you, you're losing your objectivity on this case. You can't afford that. Not with these guys."

Back between the floral-print sheets of Joan Richmond's bed, I lay waiting for sleep. I'd taken my last two Percocets with some cold vodka and the pain was receding and I could feel sleep nearby, making a tentative approach. But Terry's warning still rang in my ears, keeping the sandman at bay.

Maybe Terry was right. Maybe I was getting too emotionally involved in this case.

*Maybe? You're sleeping in the woman's bed, man. This is not a "maybe" situation.*

Okay, so I was definitely getting too emotionally involved in this case.

The operative question was—why? It wasn't about Isaac Richmond's grief. That wasn't even close to it. It was about Joan, who lived alone and died alone and whose life and death meant nothing to the rest of the world, but who died for a reason. And it was about Amy Zhang, who was scared for the same damn reason.

Amy Zhang, who had been effectively thrown to the sharks by the police and who needed someone's help.

Jill had once suggested that I became a private detective as a way to save people—as a way to fulfill an *unconscious* desire to go back in time and save my mother. Or maybe she said *subconscious*—I can never keep the psychobabble terminology straight. I didn't care much for her amateur psychoanalysis and I thought the mother angle was a stretch. But I realized she was right about the desire to save people. I'd spent my whole life watching the strong roll over the weak, and if I could occasionally win one for the underdog, that seemed a worthy goal.

As a young man, I thought I'd be able to do it as a journalist. That hadn't worked out so well. But as a private detective, I'd gotten an innocent man off a murder charge, I'd helped a prostitute get out of the life, and I'd found a few runaways. I'd helped get insurance settlements for people who deserved them, while catching a bunch of others who were trying to defraud the system. And of course I'd bagged a bunch of corrupt public servants in the big Outfit scandal.

I hadn't changed the world, but I'd made a difference in the lives of a handful of society's underdogs.

And sure, I'd also worked a hell of a lot of crap cases, digging through people's garbage and poking around in their private marital woes and generally feeling like a scumbag. But a man's gotta eat, and it was worth it for the few cases that meant something. Right or wrong, working as a private detective was the only job I'd ever had where I didn't feel like I should be doing something else. And the only job that purged the internal pressure of simmering rage.

Jill was wrong. I wasn't trying to save my mother by saving other people.

I was trying to save myself.

# CHAPTER FIFTEEN

Dear Amy:

    I know you don't trust me, and I can't give you a good reason to. I do not work for the government, nor do I work for Hawk River, but there's no way for me to prove either of those things to you.

    I also know you're frightened, but I'm not sure exactly why. Although you have no reason to trust me, I suspect that you have no one else to turn to. If your situation is such that you need help, I'm available.

    I hope you will believe that I have no interest in bringing harm to you or your daughter. Just the opposite.

Best regards,

Ray Dudgeon

It was perhaps the stupidest letter I'd ever written. But my visit to Hawk River was chum in the water and the sharks were now circling, as evidenced by the assault on Ernie Banks.

Until I started poking around, it was better for them to coerce Amy Zhang's cooperation than to kill her. Joan Richmond's murder had been successfully put to bed, and Amy Zhang served to corroborate the official version of events. Another death would only bring unwanted attention, perhaps fresh scrutiny. But my involvement had obviously set off alarms and now it might be worth the risk to tie off loose ends.

So if they killed her, wouldn't I bear some responsibility?

I signed the letter, added my cell phone number under my signature, and sealed it in an envelope. Drove to her town house, parked in front, and rang the doorbell.

The door opened a few inches, secured by a chain lock that a twelve-year-old could snap with a hard kick at the door. Behind the chain, a pair of frightened eyes.

"I can't talk to you," said Amy Zhang. "Go away."

My foot prevented the door from closing and I stuck the envelope through the narrow space.

"Just read it," I said and flicked the envelope past her onto the floor.

I pulled my foot away and the door slammed shut. I heard the dead bolt slide into the door frame.


I'd slept on my right shoulder again. No nightmare, thankfully. But shifting up through the gears now generated intense stabbing, and it was hard to shift. I was out of Percocet and had neither the time nor inclination to make a doctor's appointment, just to get a new prescription and yet another stern lecture about putting off the surgery.

I opened my cell phone and scrolled down the list of stored numbers to the entry that said D, pressed the call button.

"Hey, Jimbo," said Darnell Livingstone. Darnell's frame of reference for a PI was *The Rockford Files,* and he always insisted on calling me Jimbo. And I let him. He was not a man with whom you want to argue over trivial stuff.

"You gonna be there?" I said.

"Come around midnight." The phone went dead in my ear. Not a man for long good-byes, either.

I parked just north of Fiftieth Street and glanced at the luminous hands of my Submariner: 12:05. I rang the brownstone's front doorbell and when the lock buzzed, I pushed the door open and walked down the hallway to the ground-floor apartment. This was not a neighborhood where you'd normally leave a '68 Shelby parked on the street—day or night—but *nobody* messed with a car parked in front of Darnell Livingston's crib. There wasn't a safer parking spot in the city.

I didn't have to knock. If Darnell hadn't recognized me on his video monitor when I rang the bell outside, he wouldn't have buzzed me in. He didn't have to worry about an upstairs tenant buzzing a stranger in—he owned the building and the two floors above were unoccupied. I opened the apartment door and was greeted by the sweet smell of reefer and the heavy bass notes of hip-hop. I crossed the threshold into the darkened living room.

Blue bulbs in wall sconces provided some mood lighting and African masks threw ominous shadows against the wall. On another wall, Malcolm X raised his fist in a Black Power salute. A red lava lamp sat on a glass table in the corner.

But most of the light in the room came from the large screen of an Apple computer. A knight in full armor hopped around the screen, swinging his sword at an angry green dragon while dodging the dragon's fiery breath.

"One minute," said Darnell Livingstone without turning away from the battle. He sat in a new wheelchair, clutching a game controller and stabbing at it with his thumbs. The back of the chair sported a sharp white "C" and a pattern of white skulls on a black background. The wheels had three thick curved spokes of bright chrome, each spoke forming a shiny question mark.

Darnell lost the use of his legs back when he was with the Gangster Disciples, a top Chicago street gang with about thirty thousand members in maybe thirty states. Ten years ago, the Disciples successfully fought back an incursion by the Black P Stones, but during the war a bullet took out Darnell's spinal column, just above the waist. He was sixteen years old.

After three months in the hospital, Darnell quit the Disciples and went into business for himself. Because he'd given his legs to the cause, they let him. And they charged him a much lower street tax than they collected from the other independent operators in their territories.

I'd met Darnell when a criminal defense attorney hired me to dig up some reasonable doubt for a client charged with *unlawful use of a weapon*. Darnell was the defendant. He'd been busted for carrying a switchblade and he was guilty of it, but we got him an acquittal. Darnell told me to call him if I ever needed anything he could supply.

And a month ago, perhaps against my better judgment, I called.

The brave knight on the computer screen miscalculated, hopped in the wrong direction, and was consumed by the dragon's fire. Darnell flipped on a desk lamp and let out a baritone chuckle. He pivoted the chair around to face me. "That same motherfucker gets me every time. Level 4 is a bitch."

I offered my hand and he launched into a complicated soul-brother handshake. I followed along, gave up after the fifth maneuver, and said, "Jesus Christ, doesn't anybody just shake hands anymore?"

"Not on this block, Jimbo. Take a seat." I sat on a black leather chair and Darnell wheeled down a hallway and returned with a couple bottles of High Life and handed me one. He picked a half-smoked joint out of the ashtray and sparked it up. The flame threw light on his forearm, which bore an old tattoo. A heart with wings and horns and a tail, a six-pointed crown above, and a pitchfork on each side.

It made me think of Blake Sten's Hawk River tattoo. You expect members of a street gang to ink themselves with gang symbols, but how many IBM employees tattoo the corporate logo on their bodies? What does such a permanent and personal statement say about the corporate culture? Made me think that Hawk River had a lot in common with the Gangster Disciples.

I said, "Music's a little loud."

Darnell picked up a remote control and pressed a button and the music came down to a tolerable level. He said, "Saul Williams. You ever hear him?"

"No."

"Man's got something to say." He held the joint out to me.

"I'm good, thanks." I took a pull off the beer bottle and lit a cigarette, just to be smoking something. "Looks like Xzibit pimped your ride."

"No doubt. Got four-wheel independent suspension and all the motherfuckin' options. Called the Shockblade, cost me almost five grand. Worth it, too."

"Business must be good."

Darnell smiled. "Speaking of, how many you need?"

"Sixty should do me."

"That's what you said last time, but here you are again."

"I'll get another scrip from my doctor in a few weeks," I said.

"All right." He left the room again and I drank my beer and listened to Saul Williams. Darnell was right; the man had a great deal to say.

I thought about what I was doing here and how it would cost me my detective's license if I got caught. It was a risk I was willing to take. This was my second buy from Darnell, but it probably wouldn't be my last.

Darnell Livingstone came back with a pill bottle and traded it to me for $300. I swallowed the last of my beer, thanked him, and left.

"Be seein' you, Jimbo," he said as I closed the door behind me. The words landed on me like an accusation.

I drove home to my own apartment for a change. I'd been living at Joan Richmond's condo in recent days, returning home only to do laundry and exercise and pick up fresh clothes. I felt more at home in Joan's place than in my own apartment, but I had to admit that the proximity might have contributed to that loss of objectivity Terry warned me about.

It was time to spend a few nights at home, nightmares or not.

# CHAPTER SIXTEEN

**M**y Para-Ordnance was snug in its Kramer holster but the horsehide was not on my hip. I held it out in front of me, away from my body. Held it butt forward with the barrel facing my chest, placed it on the counter. I'd had another flashback episode at 4:00 A.M. and hadn't been able to get back to sleep after, so I was a bit fuzzy this morning and compensated with a pot of strong black coffee. As a result I was now both fuzzy and jittery and didn't want to take any chances. A quick reveal of your gun is never a winning plan when facing armed guards with shoot-to-kill authority.

The guards in the security hut seemed to appreciate my careful approach and managed not to shoot me. The younger one even smiled and the older one called me *sir*. I gave him my ID and told him that I had an appointment with Special Agent Holborn. He checked my name on a list and called up to the main building. I emptied all the metal from my pockets and took off my diving watch and sunglasses and put everything in a little plastic tray. Took off my jacket, shoes, and belt and put them on the X-ray conveyor and walked through the metal detector. The younger guard held an electronic wand at the ready but the metal detector didn't beep so all he got to do is stand there and smile at me some more. The older guard put my gun in a locker and gave me a claim check and returned my ID and asked me if I needed a shoehorn.

They seemed friendly enough.

A third armed guard arrived and escorted me from the security hut to the main building. Along the way, we passed an American flag and a City of Chicago flag and the FBI's own flag, just in case we became confused about our exact location. We passed through glass doors and entered the bright lobby of the new FBI Chicago Division Headquarters, where some more American flags and a big FBI seal left nothing to chance. A fourth armed security guard stood just inside the doors.

"How ya doin'?" I said.

"Please check in at reception, sir."

The guard who'd escorted me from the security hut took his position by the interior door and stood at parade rest. I approached the reception counter, where a young woman sat behind thick bulletproof glass. She had lots of curly hair and a full figure and a face that you'd expect to see in an ad for some beauty soap that boasts of its purity. I didn't know her name but I'd checked in with her a few times before and we nodded mutual recognition to each other. I put my driver's license on the counter, slid it under the glass.

"Two tickets for the 7:30 showing of *The Maltese Falcon*, please," I said.

She gave me a bigger smile than I'd earned. "Welcome back, Shamus."

I played along, "How's tricks, G-Girl?"

"That's 'G-Woman.'"

"I'll remember for next time."

She winked at me and said, "See that you do," then dropped the flirtation and checked my driver's license and nodded toward the seating area. "Special Agent Holborn will be down to see you." She slid my license back under the glass.

A couple minutes later the inner office doors opened and Special Agent Holborn walked my way. He wore black wingtips and a dark blue suit.

There are dark blue suits and then there are *dark blue suits,* and his was decidedly not off-the-rack. But Holborn wasn't on the take; he just spent a larger portion of his income on clothing than do most FBI agents. A lifelong bachelor with no kids, he could afford to look good.

I stood and held out my hand. Holborn took my hand and said, "Don't get up," and guided me back down on the couch and sat beside me. "What's up?"

"Maybe we should talk in your office," I said, "for privacy." Truth was, I felt slighted that he hadn't invited me in.

"I'm busy, Ray. You want my attention, tell me something."

I considered what would best get his attention. I said, "Is Jia Lun a spy for China's MSS?"

"I said *tell* me something. That was a question."

"Yeah, it was," I said. "Don't you want to know why I'm asking it?" I smiled at him and waited. When the silence became heavy, I added, "That was another question, by the way."

Holborn shot me a look. "I really don't have time for this." He glanced at his watch, sighed, stood up. "All right, come with me."

We passed through the inner doors and walked down a long hallway, past a granite display with photos honoring FBI agents who had fallen in the line of duty, and arrived at a bank of elevators. Holborn called the elevator and we got in and he punched a button and the doors closed and the elevator began to rise.

"Visitors are not normally allowed past the first floor," said Holborn. That was as close to an apology as I was going to get and I decided to acknowledge it.

"Well, thanks for seeing me," I said.

It seemed to me that Holborn still spent far too much of his energy keeping me in my place. But even if I didn't tremble at the sight of his badge, I'd always played ball when it counted and I'd even gift-wrapped the largest public corruption case of his career for him.

At least that's how I saw it—he might tell it differently. He'd probably say that I'd repeatedly held out information and broken more laws than there are commandments and shared evidence with the press that should've gone straight to the feds.

And we'd both be telling the truth.

I'd brought him another slam dunk just a couple of months ago when a woman tried to hire me to kill her abusive husband. That case had ended badly for me—and worse for the woman—but it was another gift-wrapped feather for Holborn's career cap. So I thought I'd done more than enough to merit a little respect.

We got off the elevator and walked down a narrow hallway. Framed photos of all the Chicago Division's honchos covered the wall, including the nation's first female special agent in charge. The current SAC was a handsome guy who looked like a movie star. Maybe George Clooney would play him on the big screen. Fifteen years ago, Treat Williams.

Holborn opened a door and led me into a long boardroom, closed the door behind us. We sat in two of the thousand leather chairs that surrounded an impressive table, its wood-inlay surface polished to a high shine. There was a six-foot flat-panel LCD screen on the end wall. Yet another American flag stood on one side of the screen. On the other side, a metal easel holding a giant pad of paper. The top sheet was blank.

I counted the chairs. There were twenty-two.

"Big room . . . we having company?" I said.

"My office, as you so generously called it, is a cubicle."

"Didn't mean anything by it," I said.

"Tell me what you heard about Jia Lun, and what you think it has to do with us."

So I told my story, including the scrubbing of Hawk River from the Joan Richmond murder file, but leaving out my conversation with Mike Angelo as I had with Terry. I also left out Tim Dellitt and Ernie

Banks, but I told him Blake Sten's story about Steven Zhang and Jia Lun and the FBI. Holborn took notes as I talked.

"And since you brought me up here," I concluded, "I assume that Jia Lun is in fact a Chinese agent."

"He is," said Holborn. "But that's an open secret, widely known throughout the intel community. So this Blake Sten of yours may or may not be selling you a line."

"Did he bring Zhang to you guys?"

"How would I know?" Holborn blew out a long breath. "You really don't have a clue how we work around here, do you?"

"You've never been the talkative one in our relationship, Agent Holborn."

"Watch it," he said with a glare that would make a lesser detective flinch.

"What?"

"Nothing."

Then I realized how he'd taken it. "Christ," I said, "do you hear a gay joke in everything I say?"

Holborn watched me closely for a second, nodded away the misunderstanding. "All right," he said. "You remember Hanssen?"

"Sure."

It was a famous story. The son of a Chicago cop, Robert Hanssen studied dentistry at Northwestern, but switched to an MBA. After graduation he went to work as an investigator in the CPD Internal Affairs Division, which probably didn't thrill his dad a whole lot. In 1976, Hanssen left CPD and joined the FBI. Within three years, he was assigned to Soviet counterintelligence. And unbeknownst to everyone, he became a spy for the Soviet Union.

Over the next two decades, Hanssen rose through the FBI ranks and did a lot of damage to the country. At one point, he was even tasked with finding the Soviet mole within the FBI. They actually put the mole in charge of the investigation that was supposed to catch the mole. He went straight for a few years after the breakup of the Soviet Union, then started selling secrets to the new Russian secret police, the FSB.

He wasn't found out until 2001. When they finally arrested him, he didn't howl or cry or protest his innocence.

He just said: "What took you so long?"

The Robert Hanssen story is right out of a John le Carré novel and it would take me an hour to scratch the surface. It is one of the most fascinating episodes in the history of the FBI.

Also the Bureau's biggest black eye, post-Hoover. At least, that we know about.

Holborn said, "In the wake of Hanssen, new operating procedures were implemented. The policy is called SCIFS, which stands for . . . Secret, Compartmentalized, Information . . ." He stopped and thought, smiled at himself. "Huh, can't remember the rest. Secret Compartmentalized Information . . . F . . . S." He shrugged. "Nope. It's not there. Anyway, what it means is, now we work on a need-to-know basis."

"That's gotta leave you guys pretty hamstrung."

"It's an imperfect world," said Holborn. "Anyway, we all work terrorism because that's the Bureau's main focus since 9/11, but otherwise it's strictly need to know. I don't work under the China desk, so I don't need to know."

"But I've just given you a need," I said. "If Hawk River engineered Joan Richmond's death to keep her from testifying to Congress . . . I'd think the FBI might take an interest in that. Or am I missing something."

"Sure we would," Holborn said, "but all you've offered is wild speculation. Looks to me like you're trying to get the Bureau to do your fishing for you."

He wasn't completely wrong. "How about this . . . I'll keep working it from my angle and see where it leads. And if it leads somewhere, I'll bring it to you. But in the meantime you could talk to your China guys, explain your need to know, find out if Sten was telling the truth." I reached inside my jacket and withdrew copies of the Steven Zhang and Blake Sten photos, put them on the shiny table.

Holborn picked up the photo of Blake Sten and his eyebrows danced. He didn't mention the burn scar or the weightlifter's neck. He didn't have to. "And if this Sten character was lying about bringing it to us, then what?"

"The photo of Zhang and Jia Lun could've been Photoshopped, but it didn't look like it. So let's assume for the moment that Zhang met with a Chinese MSS case officer. If Sten didn't bring it to the FBI, maybe he used it as leverage against Zhang . . ."

"Blackmailed him into killing the Richmond woman."

"That's what I'm thinking. Maybe. I don't know enough yet. Knowing if Sten brought it to you guys would be a big help."

Holborn gestured to the photos. "I can keep these?"

"Be my guest."

He put the photos between the pages of his notebook and stood up. We walked in silence to the elevators and rode down to the ground floor and walked out to the lobby.

"Okay," he said, "I'll ask. But I won't tell you what I learn."

"Agent Holborn . . ."

"Go do your private detecting, Ray. If you turn up something concrete, bring it back and perhaps we'll share information. Perhaps. But be warned—if you hold out on me, I'll put you out of business. I'm not getting played by you again."

"Hey, I had to stay alive," I reminded him. "And besides, you came out of it looking pretty good."

"Hardly the point," said Holborn.

"If I learn anything, you'll be the first to hear about it," I said. "You gotta know, I have no intention of taking on these guys alone."

And I meant it.

# CHAPTER SEVENTEEN

**I** **pulled out of the FBI visitor parking lot** and headed east on Roosevelt. A tan Crown Victoria turned in behind me, coming off Hoyne. Two white guys wearing suits and sunglasses. They settled into traffic three cars back. I could've circled the block to determine if they were following me, but I didn't want to overreact. My nerves were still raw from lack of sleep and caffeine overdose.

I continued east, turned north on Clark.

So did they.

I took Clark to Polk, turned east, and then north on Dearborn.

And so did they.

I picked up my cell phone and started to call Holborn just to thank him for the company, but the guys in the Crown Vic were now directly behind me, no longer trying to be coy about it. And the car didn't have government plates. I put the phone down and turned east on Jackson, crossed over to Lake Shore Drive, and headed north. Beyond North Avenue Beach the flow of traffic got faster and so did I.

To my left, luxury Lake Shore Drive condos towered over parks with trees showing the first blush of autumn on their leaves. To my right, joggers jogged and cyclists cycled up and down the path, and people frolicked with their dogs on the beach. Lake Michigan was particularly blue today, dotted with dozens of white pleasure boats. I've always wondered what the people on those boats do for a living, that they can spend the workday sailing. Nice work if you can get it.

When I slowed and exited onto Lawrence, the Crown Vic was still behind me.

So I went apartment hunting. I cruised the residential side streets of Uptown, stopping whenever I saw a decent building with a FOR RENT sign, and jotted down the address for later reference. But I didn't get out of the car. Just drove, stopped, wrote, and drove away again.

While I had the notebook handy I wrote down the license plate number of the Crown Vic. My escorts stayed with me the whole time and the guy in the passenger seat took a photo of each building where I stopped. They made no effort to hide their presence.

They seemed content to do this all day, but I soon grew tired of the game. I took Clark south and parked at a meter just north of Wilson and ducked into Max's Place, removed my sunglasses, and let my eyes adjust. Dim lighting fought to penetrate the haze and the dark wood surroundings soaked up what light made it through.

I bought three bottles of Old Style from Erica and took a stool, as Marvin Gaye called out from the jukebox for a witness. I pressed the Record button on my little digital voice recorder, dropped it in my handkerchief pocket. I took a swig of beer and lit a cigarette. I looked at my watch. It was just past noon.

My escorts entered the bar. They weren't big guys—the taller one was about five-ten, which put him an inch taller than me. The shorter one was maybe five-seven or -eight. They both sported receding hairlines and both were clean shaven. Their suits may not have been up to Special Agent Holborn's standards but they were above average and custom cut to help conceal their weapons.

They approached with a special swagger. Not the authoritarian FBI swagger, nor the militaristic strut that I'd seen on Blake Sten, and definitely not the aggressive bluster of the career criminal, but something entirely different. Something loose and dangerous. Something that said they were above all laws and they knew it for certain.

"Thank God you're here," I said. "I was beginning to think I'd have to drink all these myself." I gestured for them to take a beer but they didn't.

"Mr. Dudgeon," said the taller one, "we're with the Department of Homeland Security. We need you to answer a few questions."

"Sure. May I see some ID?"

"No, you may not." It wasn't the answer I expected.

"You serious?"

"Test me and find out."

"I guess I'll have to. You say you're government but for all I know you could be aliens from Neptune," I said. *And your car doesn't have government plates.*

"You had a meeting today with Special Agent Holborn at the FBI building," said the shorter one. "We need to know what you talked about."

"Then you should ask Special Agent Holborn," I said. "I'm sure you wouldn't mind showing him your tin."

"We want to hear it from you." On the jukebox, Marvin Gaye was done asking for a witness and was now wondering "What's Going On." That made two of us.

"Okay, I'll tell you," I said. "We were discussing an ongoing investigation into the recent wave of people posing as federal agents. Rumor is, some even claim to be with DHS."

"Listen, *fucktard,*" said the taller one, "you are going to talk to us. You do not want to be labeled as obstructing our agency's efforts to protect the homeland. Suppose we put you on the terrorism watch list. Could take *years* to clear your name. Suppose we contact the State of Illinois and tell them it is the opinion of the federal government that Ray Dudgeon is a security risk and should not be carrying a firearm or working with a PI license."

"I can't believe you guys operate like this," I said. "While we're supposing, suppose I divulged the content of my conversation with an FBI agent to a couple of guys who *said* they were with DHS. How much of a security risk would that make me?"

The shorter one said, "This is a very bad time for you to make enemies of us. America is at war."

"I couldn't help but notice." I stood up. "Look, I'm done with this conversation. If you show me some identification, I'll be happy to meet with you tomorrow at the Federal Center." *After I talk to Holborn and check you out with DHS.* "Failing that, you can call the Illinois Department of Professional Regulation and say nasty things about me." I pulled a business card from my wallet and placed it on the bartop. "Here, I'll make it easy for you—the number of my detective's license is on the card." I put my wallet away.

The shorter one picked up the card and stuck it in his pocket.

The taller one said, "I'm sure you've made a lot of bad decisions in your pathetic little life, Mr. Dudgeon. But this was the worst. You will be hearing from us again in the near future." They turned and left the bar.

I clicked Stop on my digital voice recorder. I put a cigarette between my lips and set it on fire. I reached for the second beer.

And thought some about my pathetic little life.

# CHAPTER EIGHTEEN

**Refused to show identification?"** Special Agent Holborn sounded dubious. "Are you serious?"

"That's what I said." I shifted the phone to my left ear and plugged the digital voice recorder into the USB socket on my office computer and downloaded the sound file to my hard drive. This was a conversation I wanted to save forever. Maybe play it back to myself on long winter nights.

"You're not exaggerating any of this?"

"I know, it ranks high on the weirdness scale," I said. "Hold on a sec." I unplugged the little Olympus from the computer, pressed Play, and held it to the mouthpiece. I waited until I heard the question about my meeting with Holborn, then pressed Stop.

"Who the hell do these guys think they are?" said Holborn.

"More important, who the hell are these guys?" I said. "After I realized they weren't FBI, my first thought was Hawk River but my intuition says no."

"Intuition is a fickle guide."

"True. But they could be legit DHS agents. Could be they're just assholes with egos, didn't want to lower themselves by showing ID to a gumshoe and thought they could tough it out of me. They suggested that their investigation has something to do with terrorism."

"They always say that. Even if it's true, they have no business asking you about our meeting. The Bureau has primary jurisdiction on terrorism."

"Where does DHS fit in?"

"DHS is a bullshit agency. But you didn't hear me say that." Holborn opened a desk drawer, closed it. Something clattered on his desk. "I'm recording. Play it again from the beginning and let it run through."

I did. When the recording ended, I gave Holborn the license plate number of the Crown Victoria.

"I'll be in touch," he said and broke the connection.

With no idea what to do next, I put a pot of coffee on and read the opening chapters of *The Book of Ralph*. It was good and it bothered me that it was good because I didn't want to admit that Jill's boyfriend had good taste in books.

But he did, damn him.

I wanted a cigarette. I denied myself, opted instead for another mug of coffee. It wasn't the same. The phone rang and I answered it and it was Terry Green calling to report that he had nothing to report.

"Everywhere I turn on this thing is a dead end," he said. "Someone's locked it down tight."

"Told you," I said.

"Yeah, you did. I've seen the CPD file on Richmond. You're right, it looks sanitized. And the cops just gave me the standard soundbite bullshit. And I can't get past Hawk River's media relations department."

"More sound-bite bullshit," I said.

"Natch. And Amy Zhang doesn't return my calls."

"But you'll stick with it," I said.

"Not much to stick with," said Terry.

"Bernstein . . ."

My meeting with Holborn had not gone as well as I'd planned, the tryst with the DHS guys (or whatever they were) had left me in a foul mood, and I hadn't had enough sleep. And now Terry was bailing on me. It was shaping up to be a hell of a day.

"My editor needs ink, you know how it is. Look, I didn't say I was closing the file but I've gotta focus on other stories. Leads that actually lead somewhere. I'll keep my ears open, but unless you bring me another avenue, I've got nowhere to go."

I decided not to mention the maybe-or-maybe-not DHS guys just yet. "For now, all I've got is confirmation that Jia Lun is an MSS agent."

"Yeah," said Terry, "I meant to tell you that. My people confirmed it as well. Apparently not that big a secret."

"So I heard."

"What's your next move?"

"Dunno. Think I'll take a closer look through Joan Richmond's place," I said, careful to use her last name. "If someone else cut the pages out of her diary, there won't be anything to find. But if she did it herself, maybe there's something I missed the first time around."

"Like what?"

"I don't know, Terry," I said a little peevishly. "Evidence. Maybe she wrote an opening statement that she planned to give in her testimony to Congress. Or something to back up her testimony."

"Safety deposit box?"

"No, I already checked. And there wasn't anything on her computer . . . but she had a box of CD-ROMs, looked like backups of her hard drive. I'll go through them again, look a little closer. And flip through all her books, see if any loose papers fall out. Hell, maybe I'll check for loose floorboards, disassemble lighting fixtures, tear open her mattress. Got nothing better to do."

"You could always call it quits, Woodward. Might be the smart play, under the circumstances."

"Not until I get justice for Ernie Banks," I said.

"You really sure you want to start tilting at windmills again? Almost killed you last time."

# PART II

We must guard against the acquisition of unwarranted influence,
whether sought or unsought, by the military-industrial complex. . . .
We must never let the weight of this combination endanger
our liberties or democratic processes. . . . Only an alert and
knowledgeable citizenry can compel the proper meshing of the huge
industrial and military machinery of defense with our peaceful
methods and goals, so that security and liberty may prosper together.

—President Dwight D. Eisenhower,
Farewell Address to the Nation—January 17, 1961

# CHAPTER NINETEEN

**I slept at home but had no nightmares.** Instead I had a memory-dream.

It was the day after I found my mother's body. My grandfather had flown up from Georgia to take charge of me and do all the things grown-ups do after someone dies. I was in my bedroom packing a suitcase. I could hear my grandfather talking on the phone in the living room, saying, "I've made arrangements for tomorrow; will your people pick up the casket at the airport, or is that . . . yes, thank you. Right, the family plot is at Westview. . . ."

I tuned him out and focused on packing. Jeans, T-shirts, underwear, socks. Chuck Taylors, bathrobe, Cubs jersey, baseball glove, jean jacket. I slipped my mother's diary into the suitcase, under the clothes, and zipped the case shut as my grandfather came into the room. He sat on my bed, patted the spot next to him, and I sat. He put his arm around my shoulders. I'd spent much of the day crying and his touch almost started me up again. If I looked into his eyes I'd bawl for sure, so I kept my eyes on the floor.

"Where's Mom now?" I said.

My grandfather cleared his throat. "Well, I imagine she's in heaven."

"I'm not a little kid," I said. "I know there's no heaven. I mean, where's her body?"

"At the hospital."

"What's a hospital gonna do? She's dead."

"The morgue is in the basement of the hospital."

"Oh."

"Don't worry, son, you'll get to see her again, at . . . in Atlanta."

"I don't want to see her again," I said, "and I'm not going to some stupid funeral."

My grandfather rubbed his rough fisherman's hands on his thighs and said, "You don't have to look in the casket if you don't want to. But you do have to go to your mother's funeral."

"But why?" It came out as a whine and I immediately hated myself, tried to sound tough, adding, "I mean, the bitch killed herself and . . . left me . . . to find her. Didn't even have the decency to do it somewhere else or even . . . put on some fucking . . . clothes."

The tears came again and there was nothing I could do to stop them. My grandfather put his sinewy arms around me and held me tight as I sobbed into his chest, where I was strangely calmed by the smell of Edgeworth pipe tobacco and Old Spice aftershave. After a couple of minutes I got myself under control. He went to the bathroom, came back with a box of Kleenex.

"I am so sorry that this had to happen to you, son," he said. "And you're right to be angry with her. It's okay." I blew my nose a couple of times while he pulled the pipe from his shirt pocket and lit it with a match.

"Human beings are odd creatures," he said. "Sometimes they take their own lives, and sometimes they want to leave the world as naked as they entered it. Your mother, Lord knows, she shouldn't have done what she did. But she wasn't thinking straight—people never are when they do that—and she wasn't thinking of you finding her, I promise you that."

I looked at him now and what I saw surprised me. There was the sadness, but also something else—failure? fear?—and I experienced one of those transcendent moments of objectivity, thinking *His daughter just killed herself and now he has to take in his grandson and he doesn't know what to say.*

But still I raged, not just at her, but at him and at the whole world.

"You don't know what the hell she was thinking," I said.

He didn't rise to that, just sat back down on the bed and puffed his pipe. "You're not a little kid," he said, "that is true, especially now. I said that humans are odd creatures, and they are. One thing they seem to need is the chance to say good-bye to their departed."

"Don't say departed," I said. "Dead." I wanted the word to hurt.

"Okay, their dead. You don't want to go to the funeral and you'll be angry with me for making you go. I understand that. But there's a good chance you'll suffer more in the long run if you miss it, so I'm afraid you'll have to go." He stood, maybe to make it final. "When we get to Atlanta, we'll buy you a suit at Rich's." He gestured with his pipe to the room. "I'm sorry we can't bring all your things home with us, but let's pick out some of your favorites. How about the covered wagon?"

"I don't want anything from this place," I said.

Vince was done serving subpoenas for his other employer and was once again following Dr. Boyfriend for me. To his credit, he stayed true to his word and didn't argue the assignment. When I told him we were almost finished with the gig, he gave me a sympathetic smile that hit harder than any argument would have.

I spent the afternoon alone in my office surfing the Internet and finding nothing of value. By five o'clock my eyes burned and I was incubating a headache. I decided to sleep at Joan's condo again, despite my previous resolution to stay at home. I was desperate for a night of uninterrupted sleep and told myself I could use the opportunity to conduct a more careful search of her place.

The decision successfully rationalized, I cracked open a beer and spent twenty minutes throwing darts, which gave my eyes a break from the computer screen and provided a workout for my shoulder. I didn't shoot particularly well, and wouldn't until after surgery and rehab. My problem was finding a consistent stroke. I'd shoot tight groupings for a few minutes, then I'd be all over the board again. I managed a couple of 140s but also missed the board occasionally and put a few new holes in the drywall.

Just as my shoulder was starting to complain in earnest, my cell phone rang. I left the darts in the board and answered before it went to voice mail.

"Ray Dudgeon."

"Um, yes . . . Mr. Dudgeon . . ." I recognized the tentative voice. It belonged to Amy Zhang.

"I'm glad you called," I said.

"Well, I just wanted . . . I want to apologize for my rudeness when you visited my home."

"Not at all. How are you doing?"

"Oh, I'm fine," she lied. "I'm sorry if I gave you the wrong impression before . . . I'm not in any trouble."

"That's good to hear," I said, "but my offer still stands, should you need any help."

"Actually, I could use your assistance with something. It's a silly thing, really, perhaps I shouldn't bother you with—"

"Go ahead," I said.

"Well, I'm at my mother's apartment. I just left to go home but my car won't start. It's an older car and I left the lights on and it appears I have a dead battery." There was a long pause on the line. "I would like to offer you a home-cooked meal, in exchange for a ride home, Mr. Dudgeon. That is, if you don't have other plans."

"No plans," I said, "but knock off the Mr. Dudgeon. It's Ray."

Amy Zhang promised to call me Ray and gave me the address on South Wentworth and I promised I'd be there within the hour.

# CHAPTER TWENTY

**I didn't know what triggered Amy Zhang's call** for help, but it sure as hell wasn't a dead car battery. On the drive to Chinatown, I stretched the tension out of my neck and tried to clear my mind.

My phone rang and I looked at the little screen. The call was coming from Isaac Richmond's house. I didn't have anything to say to Richmond yet, so I let the voice mail get it.

The sun had slipped below the horizon and the sky was on fire as I turned south onto Wentworth and passed through the Chinatown Gate. To my right stood the majestic On Leong Merchant Association Building, its pagoda roofline silhouetted by the sunset, its elaborate terra-cotta masonry still beautiful but quietly petitioning for repair.

Grandma's apartment was two blocks down on the same side of the street, above a beauty salon. A quick visual scan of the area revealed nothing and no one unusual.

Just a typical evening in Chinatown.

The street was a mass of movement as people ducked in and out of gift shops and restaurants and medicinal herb shops. A group of young Chinese tough guys stood around a tricked-out Subaru, smoking cigarettes and combing their hair and trying to look like James Dean. Something traditional and melodic spilled from a second-floor window but couldn't compete with the Chinese punk music that blared from within the Subaru. Old people, hunched and shuffling, ignored the James Deans as best they could. Scattered among the locals were some white and a few black faces—couples on dates, tourists clutching maps and cameras and exotic culture.

The exterior door was unlocked. I entered and climbed a narrow stairwell to the second floor, found apartment 2A and knocked "shave and a haircut" on the hollow door.

Amy Zhang opened the door and let me into a modest living room that could've been in Beijing, except only the rich in Beijing could afford an apartment that size. She wore a simple white dress and her hair was tied back in a ponytail. I was struck again by her beauty, but the circles of exhaustion under her eyes were even darker now.

A skinny girl around ten years of age sat cross-legged on the floor watching a SpongeBob SquarePants cartoon on television. I've never seen a kid who could watch SpongeBob without laughing, but the girl just sat there staring. Didn't even crack a smile. Amy spoke in Chinese to the girl, who stood and came over to us.

"Theresa, this is Mr. Dudgeon," said Amy Zhang. Theresa didn't look up at me. She looked at my right hand and stuck hers forward.

"How do you do, Mr. Dudgeon."

I shook her limp hand and said, "Hello, Theresa," and she returned to the television. I felt a presence behind me.

Grandma stood hovering in the kitchen doorway, partially obscured by a small fish tank on a pedestal. She wore a shapeless dress that looked like it was made from white sackcloth, and a furious scowl.

I said, "Pleased to meet you, ma'am." Grandma grunted at me, then spoke to Amy in rapid-fire Cantonese. She sounded angry.

"Excuse us for a minute." Amy led Grandma into the kitchen. I couldn't understand them, of course, but Grandma raised her voice and used the phrase *gweilo* repeatedly, so I knew they were arguing about me. *Gweilo* is a derogatory term for Caucasian. It means "ghost man" or something similar.

I sat on a chair near Theresa. If she was listening to the argument from the other room, she didn't show it. If she was listening to Sponge-Bob, she didn't show that, either. I'm not very good with kids and I didn't know what to say.

I said, "In my day it was Rocky and Bullwinkle."

"They're still on," said Theresa without looking away from the screen. "They're good, but SpongeBob is better."

I said, "You like staying with your grandma?"

"It's okay. Mom says I can't come home yet. Our house is for sale. My dad is dead." She said it like she was telling me that her shoelace was untied. Just a statement of fact.

"Yeah, I'm sorry about that," I said.

Theresa reached forward and turned up the volume. "This part is funny," she said.

On the screen, SpongeBob was prancing around with a butterfly net, catching purple jellyfish and exulting. Theresa still didn't react, even though *this part was funny*. She'd cut off our conversation and I wanted to respect that. I turned in my chair and looked out the front window onto the street below and the hair on the back of my neck stood up.

Directly across the street was a Bubble Tea shop. At street level, the reflection of the western sky had prevented me from seeing through the window, but the sky was dark now and from this angle I could see everything.

At the counter behind the window, a man in a long black leather coat stood not drinking his tea and not reading his newspaper. He was a *gweilo*, he was big, and he was a tough guy. Looked like a boxer.

Or a soldier.

He stood at the counter and kept his eyes on the door where I'd entered the building. He periodically flipped a page of his newspaper or raised the plastic tumbler and put the straw in his mouth, but he never more than glanced away from the door.

Here was Amy Zhang's *dead battery*.

He should've worn a baseball cap. Then I wouldn't have been able to tell where he was looking, from this high angle. I watched him until the argument between Amy and Grandma sputtered out and Amy came back into the living room, purse in hand. She put her arms around Theresa and kissed her cheek and they said their good-byes in Chinese. From the tone and body language, I imagined Amy was saying something like *Be a good girl for Grandma . . . I'll see you tomorrow . . . I love you.*

But she could've been saying anything.

As we descended the staircase to the exterior door, I said, "You know, I've got jumper cables in my car, we can try to get yours started and—"

"Please," Amy's hand touched my forearm and she stopped on the stairs. She rallied with, "I really don't feel like driving tonight, let's just take your car."

"Sure," I said. We resumed our descent. She probably knew that I knew she was lying, but now was not the time for that conversation.

Amy slowed until I was a couple of steps ahead and fell in behind me. I got the car keys in my left hand and shook the tension out of my right and took a slow breath and visualized sweeping my jacket back and drawing my gun. Then visualized the ten brisk steps from the door to my car, unlocking the door with my left hand, putting Amy in the passenger side . . .

I pushed the door open and focused on the car and started walking. I forced myself not to look directly at our man but instructed my peripheral vision to pick him up.

It did.

He'd abandoned his newspaper and bubble tea and stepped out of the shop and onto the opposite sidewalk as I opened the passenger door.

"Don't look at him," I said, "just get in." Amy got in and I closed the door and walked around to the driver's side.

The man across the street was now getting into a silver Chevy Malibu.

I cranked the ignition over and pulled away from the curb, heading south on Wentworth. The man in the Malibu didn't pull a U-turn, but drove north. That meant losing us wasn't as important to him as not being made. Which was good news, but didn't mean he wouldn't loop around the block and try to pick us up again. I continued south and turned a sharp right on Twenty-sixth Street.

"Don't look at who?" said Amy from the passenger seat.

"Please," I said, "let's not pretend you called me about a dead battery."

"I don't know what you're talking about. I didn't see anyone."

"You're a lousy liar, Amy."

"And I don't appreciate being called a liar."

"Then take 'lousy' as a compliment," I said. "Best I can do."

Amy folded her arms across her chest. I focused on my driving. We passed under the train tracks and I took Canal Street north and kept an eye on the rearview mirror, but no silver Malibu appeared. I took note of each car in the rearview, and a couple blocks later I got in the left lane and slowed and engaged my left turn signal. A red Toyota got behind us and also signaled a left turn.

At the intersection I clicked off my turn signal and went straight through.

The Toyota turned left. After a few more blocks, I did the same thing in the right lane and a similarly innocent blue Land Rover turned right.

Still no silver Malibu. We continued north to the Canal Street Bridge and over the Chicago River.

I swung a left on Eighteenth Street and we passed under the Dan Ryan and into the University Village neighborhood where Amy lived. I circled one block, then another.

There was no one following us. I took us a few blocks north, then west again.

Could I have been letting paranoia get the best of me? I didn't think so. I went the long way to approach Amy's town house from the west. If we went straight there, we'd be approaching from the east, so if someone set up surveillance, he'd do so on a cross street to the west.

And there it was. The silver Chevy Malibu, parked just back of the corner a block west of Amy's town house. Our man sat in the car, looking east. I dictated his license plate number into my little recorder as we passed.

Amy never even glanced at the car.

# CHAPTER TWENTY-ONE

There's a television in the living room. I'll get dinner started." Amy hung up her coat and drifted into the kitchen. Just like that. Like there wasn't a man sitting in a car at the end of the block. But I watched her through the kitchen doorway and she checked to make sure the back door was locked before washing her hands and starting on dinner.

I sat on the couch and took the phone from my pocket and listened to my voice mail. Isaac Richmond wanted me to come in and give him a progress report. Good for him. I deleted the message and put the phone away.

I turned on the television, kept the volume low, tuned it to CNN. It was the same old same old. Political prostitutes on the left and right talking past each other, spinning the facts and shilling their talking points to America. When Wolf Blitzer reminded me, for the sixth time, that he was *part of the best political team on television,* I reached my limit. Blitzer had been a reporter once upon a time. Now he worked for the marketing department.

I switched to WGN and found the Cubs playing a meaningless game against the Brewers. Neither team was going to the playoffs, but these are the games where you get to scout the September call-ups. The Cubs had some talented kids in the pipeline and next year looked promising.

Next year. The official mantra of Cubs fans everywhere.

Amy came into the room with a bottle of red wine and two glasses. She stopped short and froze, staring at the television with a lost expression on her face.

I turned it off. "What's wrong?" She didn't answer, just turned from the dead television screen and faced me with the same lost look, eyes focused about ten feet behind me. "Amy, what is it?"

She found her way back to reality. "I'm sorry. For a second I . . ." She put the glasses on the small dining table and poured the wine. "Steven loved baseball," she said without looking up. "Anyway. Dinner's ready, please sit."

I sat in the chair with its back to the wall and scoped the room. I stood and moved Amy's chair and placemat to the right, took the centerpiece off the table and put it on the floor. If Malibu Man tried to breach the front door, I'd have a direct shot at him without Amy or a bowl of plastic fruit getting in the way. If he came in the back, I'd have to get up anyway.

I sipped some wine and Amy returned with a brighter expression on her face and a plate in each hand. She paused for half a second, taking in the changes I'd made to the table, but didn't say anything.

"So," I said, "what do we call this dish?"

"Spaghetti Bolognese. And garlic bread." She put the plate in front of me, and it was. She took her seat and picked up a fork. "You were expecting chicken chow mein and egg rolls?"

"Well . . . yeah, I suppose I was." I felt like an idiot. "So I guess this means no fortune cookie for dessert, huh?"

The tension broke and Amy smiled.

"Spumoni," she said.

The pasta was perfectly al dente and the sauce was homemade using fresh tomatoes and oregano. A little diced pancetta rounded out the ground beef. It was excellent and I told her so.

We drank wine and ate, and she told me about her love for Italian cooking: its methods, ingredients, and textures.

I refilled our wineglasses. "You speak the language of an aficionado," I said.

"It's true. All my life, cooking was what you did so that you could eat well. When I switched to Italian, it became a joy, and I guess a hobby."

"What triggered the switch?"

Amy sipped some wine. "Turning thirty, actually. My mother is an excellent Chinese cook. I could never equal her skill in the kitchen." *And earn her approval* went unspoken. "So I found cooking frustrating. Eventually I accepted that it was not an area of my life where I would excel, and it became just another household duty. But five years ago we moved to this neighborhood and Little Italy is right next door. I fell in love with the food and the way they talk about food, and it was all new to me."

"And you turned thirty."

"I did. Four years ago. And I decided to challenge myself and see if I could excel at Italian cooking."

"I'd say you won that challenge."

"Thank you." She sipped her wine again and her face grew serious. "I'm not turning my back on my culture."

"I didn't suggest that you were."

"I still cook Chinese a couple of times a week to keep in practice and take a break from Italian."

"America's a melting pot," I said.

"Exactly. Why not take the positive that you find from every culture, including the one you grew up with, and create your own personal culture?"

"No reason not to," I said.

"I mean, isn't that true freedom?" Amy finished the wine in her glass. That made two. "I don't drink much," she said. "I mean, I don't drink often. I have a low tolerance." She twirled a little spaghetti on her fork and ate it, then returned to her subject. "But most people

think you're betraying your culture if you do that. That you're a traitor somehow."

I drank some wine, said, "Tribalism is both the most unenlightened
and most pervasive of human instincts."

Amy nodded, "Yes. Who said that?"

"I did."

"Well, you're right," she said. "It's always Us and Them." She
caught herself and let out an embarrassed smile. "How did we get
onto this heavy topic?"

"You turned thirty," I said and smiled back at her.

"Sorry. I guess I got carried away." She sat straight and smoothed
imaginary wrinkles out of her dress. "But I do love to cook Italian. My
latest project is wild mushroom risotto."

"I'd love to try it sometime."

The smile ran away from her face. "This is not a date," she said.
"We're not on a date." She stood and collected the plates, avoided eye
contact.

"I never thought this was a date, Amy." She still didn't look at me.
"Amy?"

"I think you should go now," she said to the empty plates.

"Okay." I pushed my chair back and walked to the front door,
slipped into my shoes. "But what do we do about the man in the car at
the end of the block? You know, the one you insist on pretending isn't
there."

Amy flew into the kitchen and I heard dishes and cutlery clatter
into the sink, followed by a couple of sharp sobs. I stood and waited
and a minute later she returned.

"I'm sorry. Please stay. I-I just want to be clear . . . I'm not looking
for a lover. What I need right now is a friend."

What she needed right now was a bodyguard. I nodded. "But you've
got to stop pretending you're not in trouble." I fished my car keys from
the pocket of my coat. "I'll just be a minute. Lock the door behind me.
We'll talk when I get back."

\*   \*   \*

Malibu Man was still sitting at the end of the block. If he thought there was any chance that I'd made him on our approach, he'd have moved to another spot, so I took his location as a positive. I walked down the steps to my car, opened the trunk, and reached in for my overnight bag.

The contents had shifted when I'd taken corners at speed and the stuff I kept at the back of the trunk was all over the place. The first aid kit, yellow jumper cables, and heavy police flashlight were familiar enough, but the black electrical cord gave me a start. It had been riding around in my trunk for months and I'd forgotten it was there.

It was just a four-foot length of heavy cord, folded in half, ends bound together with duct tape to make a handle. But unlike fire or public speaking, it was the worst weapon I could imagine.

I'd once been tied to a chair and flogged with a similar cord. Flogged close to death. I'd had a hard time getting over the experience. I figured familiarity would help rob the implement of its power, so I'd made one of my own and kept it on the passenger seat for a while. When the sight of it finally stopped triggering flashbacks, I'd tossed it in the trunk, behind the first aid kit.

I picked the cord up now, felt its heft. It didn't inspire the same paralyzing sense of dread that it once had. What I felt now was maybe worse. A desire to use it on someone.

I tossed the cord into the trunk. A few deep breaths brought my heart rate back down. I grabbed my overnight bag and headed back up the walkway to Amy Zhang's front door.

# CHAPTER TWENTY-TWO

**A**my retreated to the kitchen to make a pot of tea and I sat in the living room considering the relative merits of calling the police.

Contrary to what you see on television, private eyes don't just set up surveillance in a residential neighborhood whenever the urge strikes. First you check in at the nearest police station. You show your ID to the desk sergeant, explain that you'll be conducting a surveillance on such and such a block and give him the plate number and description of your car. And if you decide that the desk sergeant is that kind of cop, you grease his palm. It's a tricky dance.

If you do the dance successfully, then when a worried civilian calls the cops about some guy sitting in a car all night, the cops will assure the civilian that they know about the guy in the car and everything is fine.

Malibu Man didn't strike me as the kind of guy who follows such etiquette. And anyway, he hadn't had time to check in. So I could call and act like a worried civilian and the cops would dispatch a prowl car to check him out. And that would motivate him to terminate surveillance for the night. But if I did that, he would know he'd been made.

And they'd be more careful next time.

I decided not to act. Amy returned and poured fragrant Lapsang souchong into cups. We drank the smoky tea in silence for a minute. She put her cup down and brushed a stray hair out of her eyes.

She said, "Was he still there?" *Progress.*

"Still there. Who is he?"

"I really don't know. I've never seen him before. He was hanging around in front of my mother's building when I arrived. The way he avoided looking at me, it caught my attention. I watched him from the window for a while. He didn't leave. So I called you."

"Do you always arrive at the same time?"

"Between four and four-thirty."

"Every day?"

"Every weekday. Weekends I go in the morning." So they knew her routine.

"You said you've never seen him before, but you've seen men like him," I said.

Amy thought a while before answering. "Not . . . I don't know," she sighed. "After Steven . . . did what he did . . . I thought that I was being watched. There was often a man in a car outside—not that car and not that man, but someone similar—and sometimes I thought I was being followed. But then it stopped, and for the last month I didn't see anyone. Until today."

The timing made sense, if my theory was correct. Someone at Hawk River had convinced Amy to go along with a cover-up, and they'd kept an eye on her for a while. Probably dropped by a couple of times to test her, as she'd implied during our first meeting. They couldn't waste manpower forever, so once they were reasonably sure she was sticking to the deal, they'd eased off. But my visit to Joseph Grant put them on edge, and then Terry's call pushed them over the edge.

So they put a man on her again. If my theory was correct.

I picked up the teapot and refilled our cups. "You're still not telling me everything."

"I still don't know if I can trust you." She looked at me steadily.

"Not much choice. You don't have anyone else."

Her eyes moved away, down to her teacup. "Trusting the wrong person is worse than having no one to trust." *One step forward, two steps back.*

I wanted to say something harsh, forced myself to tone it down. A bit. "Knock it off. I know you're in a difficult position but I'm getting tired of it. You want me to stay, you have to talk to me. Bottom line. I can't help you without information."

Amy didn't speak or meet my eyes but offered an almost imperceptible nod of her head. I said, "Good. Steven's mental illness was an act, wasn't it?"

Slender feet rose to the couch and she hugged her knees to her chest. A silent tear ran down her left cheek. When she spoke, it was so quiet I had to strain to hear her. "I spend a lot of my time hating Steven these days. Really hating him. I don't hate him for what he did to Joan Richmond—and that probably makes me a bad person, but I don't. I hate him for what he did to me and what he did to Theresa." A new tear followed the path of the first, and then another on the other side. "And I hate him for what he did to my husband."

"Meaning?"

"Meaning I watched as Steven killed the man he was, the man I knew, and became someone else. Could he have been pretending? I can't allow myself to believe that. But if he wasn't, then he drove himself insane by conscious effort. Right in front of me. He annihilated himself. He took my husband and Theresa's father away from us . . . *before* he shot himself. Do you understand?"

"I think I do."

Her arm moved in a gesture of futility. "And how do I come to terms with that? Joan Richmond's father is having a hard time coming to terms with her death? How do *I* come to terms with *that*?"

Amy's tears flowed freely now and she didn't wipe them away. They rolled down her face and fell onto her dress, making little dark spots on the fabric.

I didn't know what to say. I crossed to the couch and sat beside her and put my arm across her shoulders. It felt awkward and I started to think I should retreat. Then she curled her body toward me and buried her head in my chest. I put my other arm around her back and held her as she sobbed for a very long time. I stroked her silken hair and rocked her gently until the convulsive gasps subsided.

I kissed the top of her head and immediately wished I hadn't. But she didn't take it the wrong way. She sat up and sniffed and wiped her face with her sleeve and put her right hand on my chest.

"I shouldn't have had any wine. I'm sorry."

I brushed tear-soaked hair out of her eyes, "It's okay."

Her eyes met mine and didn't run away. "Maybe I can trust you," she said. She wiped her eyes, blew her nose loudly into a Kleenex.

"Charming," she said and grabbed another tissue from the box.

"We still need to talk a little more. Can you do that now?"

"I guess. I'm just so tired. I'm tired of looking over my shoulder, tired of not knowing what's going to happen next. Tired of trying to think of what I can do about it, when I really can't do anything." Amy curled into the fetal position on the couch, facing the room, and rested her head on my right thigh. "Do you mind?" she said.

"No."

"Can you— can you pat my head again?"

"Sure." I put my hand gently on her head.

After a minute of silence she said, "When I was a little girl and had nightmares, my mother would come into my room and sit on my bed and pat my head like that." She wiped her nose with the tissue. "I just wish this nightmare could be patted away."

"You and me both." I stroked her hair.

"All right," said Amy, "ask your questions."

I said, "You knew that Steven worked for Hawk River."

"Yes."

"And that he was fired."

"Yes."

"What reason did he give you?"

"He said that a man named Sten was framing him. Sten had manufactured evidence that made it look like he was stealing from the company." Amy's exhaustion was taking over and her voice sounded sleepy, far away.

"Stealing what?"

"I don't know. Information to sell. Steven wouldn't tell me anything more. He said that Sten had built a strong case and he couldn't fight it. He just had to take it. I knew Steven for sixteen years . . . he had the strongest character of any man I've ever met. I'd seen him handle stress that would kill most people. But I'd never seen him so scared . . . so helpless, as the day he was fired from Hawk River. "

It's harder to lie convincingly in that grogginess before sleep and I figured this was probably my best chance for getting Amy to tell the truth, uncensored by fear. Fear is a mighty censor and although Amy was opening up, she was still measuring her words carefully.

I said, "Sten told me that Steven was stealing employee records and trying to sell them to the Chinese government."

"That's absurd. Steven would never do—would never have done that. That's one thing I am absolutely certain of."

"He said that Steven was in debt over his head. Gambling."

She sat up and there was fury in her tired eyes. "Oh sure, he's Chinese so he must have a gambling problem. Bullshit."

"I'm not making the accusation. I'm just telling you what Sten said."

"Steven did *not* gamble. We lived within our means. And he hated the Chinese government . . . even more than I do. I can't believe you're—"

I held up my hand. "Stop. I'm on your side here. I'm just trying to figure out what Sten was up to." I reached out and put my hand on Amy's shoulder, guided her back down to the couch. She didn't resist and settled with her head on my thigh again. I said, "Why would Sten set him up?"

"I don't know. Steven wouldn't tell me. He said it was for my own good, that it was better for me not to know. I pushed him, but he wouldn't say."

"Any guesses?" I put my hand back on her head.

"I think he learned something about Hawk River when he was working on their computers. Something he wasn't supposed to know. Something bad. So they framed him and fired him and threatened to go to the police and press charges if he complained. That's what I think. But I'm guessing."

"And maybe he shared what he learned with Joan Richmond. She quit less than a month later."

"Perhaps. They spoke on the phone a few times after he was fired."

"Did they continue to have contact after she quit?"

"They spoke on the phone occasionally. And we had Joan over to dinner once, just after she started her new job. She felt badly about what they'd done to Steven, even though it wasn't her fault. She promised that she'd hire him for any IT work she needed at the department store. And she did."

"Did you see Joan again, other than that dinner?"

"No."

"Did Steven?"

"Not that I know of, until he got the contract at HM Nichols. They spoke on the phone every month or so."

"Back to the dinner. What was the conversation like?"

"They didn't talk about Hawk River, if that's what you mean. As I said, Joan told us how sorry she was about the way things turned out there, and Steven assured her that it wasn't her fault, but that was it. We tried to have a pleasant evening. We talked about the dinner. I made veal marsala. We talked about the neighborhood. And music. I should say, *they* talked about music. Steven loved American pop music and Joan recommended a lot of bands he should listen to. I didn't really pay much attention. Music is not my thing, so I focused on Theresa and got her to bed." Amy was drifting off as I stroked her head and her words were slurring.

"Anything else?"

"Um, not that I can, uh, remember. It was a long time ago and it was . . . none of it seemed important at the time . . . just, you know, a social dinner, like . . . any other . . ." Then she said, "Am . . . so . . . tired . . ."

There were more questions but they could wait until morning. I took my pistol from the holster on my hip and put it on the coffee table in front of me and settled against the back of the couch. I patted Amy's head some more and listened to her breathe.

Once she was asleep, I slid her head off my thigh and onto a sofa cushion, turned off the lamp at her end of the sofa, moved to a recliner facing the front door. Took the gun with me, put it within reach on a side table.

She was a beautiful woman. Not the kind of beautiful that you see in the movies or magazines. Beautiful and smart and not yet defeated by all that she'd been through. Not yet defeated, but tired and running out of energy. Running out of fight.

And this new round of fighting was my fault. They'd stopped following her before I got involved. I'd walked right up to the mouth of the cave and poked at the sleeping monster with a stick. I'd even brought Terry into it, handed him a stick, too.

And now the monster was awake.

You learn to watch out for red flags when working on a case, and if there are enough of them, you get out. I couldn't even *see* this case for all the red flags. But to get out would be to abandon Amy. There was no way around it.

My grandfather often said, "In for a penny, in for a pound." It was an expression he picked up from the Brits, back when he was in the navy. Back when the British pound was worth three bucks.

I watched Amy sleep and thought, *In for a penny, in for a pound.*

# CHAPTER TWENTY-THREE

**F**or Amy Zhang, morning came laden with regret. She was reluctant to answer more questions—didn't even want to talk about the previous night except to say that she shouldn't have had any wine and had said too much. And I pressed her aggressively, which just made things worse.

I'd been outside four times since sunrise. No Malibu. No occupied cars nearby of any make or model. Amy and I now stood in her bright kitchen. At an impasse. I tried various angles but she still wouldn't talk about it. I grew frustrated and said something unpleasant. Now we stood bathed in morning sun, facing each other, saying nothing. I thought she might bolt from the room. She didn't. She approached me tentatively. Then leaned against me, her ear to my chest. Despite my frustration, I put my arms around her.

She said, "Thank you for last night. I needed to cry on someone. And God knows, I needed the sleep. But I find this hard to accept. Without the wine clouding my head . . . it just seems too absurd. I'm supposed to believe that you were working for Joan Richmond's father and you suddenly decided, for no reason at all, to risk your life on my behalf . . ."

"And it's easier to believe that Hawk River sent me to test you again," I said. "I thought we were past that." I touched her chin but she wouldn't look up.

She said, "If you are working for them—"

"Hey—"

"No. If you are working for them, then you'll go back and report that I can't be trusted." She said it without emotion, like she was working on a math problem. "And that's that. They'll kill me. Or you'll kill me."

"Amy, stop it."

"I just want you to know, Theresa knows nothing about it. Do you understand? I told her nothing."

"That's enough," I snapped. "Cut it out. I'm not working for them."

"Then why are you doing this for me?"

I considered mentioning justice for Ernie Banks, but that was far too glib. She deserved the truth. I owed her that.

"They left you alone a month ago, right? Why the hell do you think they're back? I'm the one who started asking questions about Joan's murder. I'm responsible for this."

Amy looked up at me. I couldn't read her expression. She said, "You didn't start this."

"Neither did you," I said.

"No, but I'm in it. You don't have to be."

I brushed a hair out of her eyes. "I do have to be."

She broke contact, moved to the other side of the kitchen, folded her arms across her chest. "Please, no questions this morning. I need some time to think."

That was my limit.

"Okay, I'm done," I said. "The back-and-forth game gets old real fast. You need some time to think? Fine." I snatched my car keys off the kitchen counter and stalked to the front door. Amy ran after me.

I slipped into my shoes and coat and unlocked the door. I said, "Don't do anything stupid while I'm gone. Do not visit Theresa today.

Call and make an excuse. You've got the flu, you don't want her to catch it. Lock the door behind me and don't leave the house. If anything happens, call my cell. I'll be back tonight."

"Ray, I'm sorry. Please try to understand, it's hard for me to—"

I didn't stick around to hear the excuses and apologies. I left her babbling at the front door and walked away.

I stopped at my office and called a contact at DMV, gave her the Malibu's license plate, hung up the phone, and wrote a check for a hundred bucks and put her home address on the envelope. I dropped the envelope down the mail chute in the hallway.

Then I tossed darts at the board until my fax machine buzzed and spat out the answer.

The car was a rental. Rental cars move around the country, sometimes on one-way hires. But I got lucky. This car's "home base" was a rental agency in Chicago, at the north end of the Magnificent Mile. I left the office and called Vince from my car. He didn't answer so I left him a voice mail. Called Terry, left him one, too.

I drove the rest of the way to North Michigan Avenue on autopilot, regretting my blowup with Amy. *She has every right to be wary . . . she'd be crazy not to be. In her shoes, you'd be just as guarded . . . maybe more so. Hell, no maybes about it. Some guy just shows up at your door and generously offers to save your life? You'd never believe him.*

Still, her reluctance bothered me and I had to remind myself not to take it personally. Truth is, the previous night had been the most intimate I'd had with a woman in a very long time. And I hated to see it lost this morning.

By 11:30 I was standing in the little white office of a car rental chain, talking to a skinny kid in his late twenties. The kid had a tangle of blond curls perched on his head, a shark's tooth on a hemp string around his neck, and the demeanor of a surfer who got stoned in California and woke up in Chicago.

"Dude, I'd love to help you, really," said the kid, "but I'm not allowed to give out that kind of info, ya know? I mean, like, I could get fired."

I shifted my hand on the counter so he could see the fifty-dollar bill peeking out from under my fingers. Not so long ago, a twenty would've made an impression on a kid like him. Now it took a fifty.

He wiped his mouth with his hand, said, "I'd like to, but my manager can see if I call up customer info on the 'puter . . ."

"Forget the computer," I said. "Tell me what you remember about the customer."

"Well, he was, like, big? You know, tall? A mean-looking dude, kinda like a cop, but different. Hair real short. Had a long black coat, he put it right there on the counter. And the dude was built." It was the same guy.

"Remember his name?"

"Naw, man, it was yesterday. We get, like, a lot of customers." No one had come in since I'd been there. I looked around the empty little office.

"Yeah, I can see that."

"Well, most of 'em come in at the end of the day. There's a lunch rush, too."

"When did he come in?"

"Oh, he came in early. Like, nine, ten in the a-m. Wait!" The kid's eyes rolled to the top of his head as he brought a memory into focus. "His name was John. John, something." He thought some more. "Dude, I'm drawing a blank on the dude's last name."

"All right, what about mannerisms or anything unusual he said, or—"

"Wait! I got it! Smith. His name was John Smith. I'm sure of it." He seemed proud to have remembered.

"Tell me you're kidding."

"No, I swear. That was the dude's name, on his driver's license. Credit card, too. John Smith. I remember now, for sure."

He didn't seem to think there was anything wrong with the name

John Smith and it's true enough that there are plenty of John Smiths in the world. But I'd bet a week's worth of City Hall graft that this particular dude was not really named John Smith. I was striking out.

"Anything else? Scars, tattoos, anything?"

The kid broke into a wide smile. "Yeah, man, good thinking. Right on. Dude had a tattoo on his forearm. Kinda like a bird or something."

I grabbed a pen from the counter and sketched the Hawk River logo on a scrap of paper. "Like this?"

"Shit! Yeah, dude. Right on! That's it exactly."

I left the kid with the fifty and headed back to the parking garage. I'd learned exactly what I'd expected to learn and learning it didn't make me happy.

Amy had speculated that if I were working for Hawk River, I'd report that she couldn't be trusted. Right now Malibu Man was reporting that I'd spent the night with Amy. Which meant they might send someone to lean on her and make her tell them what she told me. I didn't think she'd handle that meeting very well.

But if they killed her, I'd still be around to alert the cops, so they'd probably want to take care of me first. That probably gave me a little time to work.

Probably.

I started for the garage of the 900 North Michigan building and then remembered that I hadn't eaten today. I cut through Bloomingdale's and into the building's expansive atrium, which stretches six stories high and boasts a lot of sand-colored marble and chrome accents and long-hanging ferns. A bright and luxurious shopping mall, for bright and luxurious shoppers.

I bought a ham and cheese panini and a bag of plantain chips from King Café, sat near the green marble fountain and watched people buy things they didn't need at Gucci and Christofle as I ate.

My phone rang. The call display told me it was Vince.

"Vince, I need you on something."

"Okay, but I gotta tell you what's going on here."

"Where are you?"

"Wabash, just south of the office. In the diamond district."

"Look, doesn't matter. I need—"

"Ray, you're gonna want to hear this first."

"Go."

"I'm shadowing Dr. Glassman. He's shopping for an engagement ring."

*Shit.* I opened my mouth to speak, but nothing came out.

Vince said, "Sorry. But I figured you'd want to know."

"Yeah, thanks." *Maybe I can get over there and talk to her . . . is she on days or nights?* I couldn't remember.

I snapped out of it, said, "Write down this address . . ."

"Hold on." There was a pause on the line. "Okay, hit me."

I gave him the address. "A woman lives there. Amy Zhang. Chinese. Five-one, one hundred pounds, midthirties. Pretty. Don't approach her. Just park out front and watch the place. If any bad guys show up, don't let them get to her."

"We expecting bad guys?"

"Maybe."

"I'm on it."

"Vince?"

"Yeah?"

"Take your gun."

I broke the connection and dialed Amy Zhang. She answered on the second ring.

"It's Ray. Just listen. I'm sending someone over. He'll be driving a blue Ford Escort. His name is Vince Cosimo. Black hair, about six-four, big guy. He works for me. He's going to watch out for you until I can get back."

"Okay." Her voice was very small and I knew what she was thinking. If I was working for Hawk River, Vince was the guy sent to kill her.

"I told him not to approach you. He'll just sit in his car outside. You don't have to invite him in."

"Okay."

"Okay." I hung up and started for the garage. It occurred to me that I might be spending a few nights sitting in Amy Zhang's recliner. I needed a new book. I turned around and headed up the escalators to the Waldenbooks on the sixth level.

I browsed through the Current Events section, focused on books covering the wars in Iraq and Afghanistan. I flipped through the indexes, looking for Hawk River and the names of the other private military corporations. Found a few. I took one of the more promising titles to the cash register and paid for it, then crossed to the other side of the atrium and took the escalators back down to the ground floor.

I stopped again at King Café and bought a large black coffee to go. In the little parking garage lobby I stuck a credit card into one of those machines that most garages now have so they don't have to pay a cashier. The machine charged my card $18. I'd been there just over an hour.

About ten yards into the garage, I remembered that I'd left my credit card in the machine, went back to get it. *You have got to get some sleep, you're not twenty anymore.* I'd gotten maybe three hours on Amy's recliner, and I was feeling it in a big way. The coffee would help.

I headed back to my car, thinking about the miracle that is coffee. I was practically nose to nose with the guy when he spoke.

"Ray Dudgeon."

I stopped dead. There was a fighting knife in his right hand. The tanto blade was anodized black but the sharpened edge glinted in the fluorescent light of the garage.

He said, "You're coming with me."

It took some effort to tear my eyes away from the blade. I looked up to a face I'd never seen before, tried to smile, and said, "Sure, I'll come along, just don't cut me."

My right thumb flicked the plastic lid off the Styrofoam cup and I threw twenty ounces of steaming coffee at his face and ran like hell. His scream echoed through the garage as I flew down the ramp and jerked open the door to the lobby. I cut back into the mall, where there were civilians. Witnesses. Security guards.

It wasn't until I was into the mall that I realized I'd been cut. No pain, I just felt the blood trickling down my left arm.

*Fuck it, worry about it later, keep running . . .*

Faces of startled shoppers blurred past as I tore through the mall but no security guards came into view. I heard his footfalls echoing off the marble floor as he ran into the mall behind me and I realized I wouldn't make it out onto Michigan Avenue. My lead wasn't big enough. I'd have to stop and heave the door open and he'd catch up and sink the blade between my ribs.

I turned and ran up the escalator, took the metal steps two at a time. *Clang-clang-clang.* I didn't dare slow to turn and look back.

At the top I pivoted and ran for the next up-escalator, chanced a look down. He was coming up the escalator, fast. *Clang-clang-clang-clang-clang.* His face was bright red from the burning coffee but he was still faster than me. My lead was shrinking.

I yelled, "He's got a knife! Call the police!" into the open atrium. My voice reverberated through the place, bouncing off flat slabs of polished marble. A woman down below screamed. Another woman's voice echoed, "Call the police!"

I hit the next escalator and continued my frantic climb. When I got to Level 3, I took another quick look back. My call for help hadn't made him give up the chase and he was gaining. He ran into a man on the escalator, knocked him facedown on the metal steps, and scrambled right over him.

The place was filling up as people came out of shops to see what the commotion was about. I crashed into a woman and sent her and a half-dozen bags flying in all directions. I didn't stop to help her.

I just kept running, climbing, frantic, out of my mind, no destination, running, climbing, thinking *Too crowded to draw your gun . . . why are the cops taking so long? . . . he's gaining ground . . . don't look back, keep going, faster. . . .* My lungs were fire and my thighs were rubber and I could feel myself slowing but I pressed on.

I reached Level 6 and collapsed against a pillar to the right of the escalator, my chest heaving. I realized I was still clutching my book.

*Clang-clang-clang-clang-clang.* . . . He was coming fast up the final escalator. I couldn't run anymore. I got into a crouch, held the book like a shield, and turned so my left shoulder was facing the escalator.

*From the legs, Dudgeon. From the legs.* . . .

He hit the metal landing at the top of the escalator and I tossed the book at his face and he raised his hands to protect his face. His hands were empty. I sprung upright, using all the remaining strength in my legs. My left shoulder slammed into his chest in an upward trajectory, knocked him off-balance. His arms flailed at the air and he started to fall backward down the escalator. But as he twisted his torso to try and right himself, he fell against the handrail and flipped over.

I lurched toward the railing and grabbed handfuls of air.

He fell six stories with nothing along the way to break his fall. There was a terrible popping sound as his head hit the marble floor and burst open like a watermelon.

# CHAPTER TWENTY-FOUR

**O**kay, tell me again. What exactly did the man say to you in the parking garage?"

"He said, 'Ray Dudgeon. You're coming with me.' He had a knife in his hand."

I'd already told it twice. My story was: I'd stopped at the mall to grab a sandwich and maybe do a little shopping. I'd decided to buy a book, picked up a coffee for the road, and then I'd been confronted on the way back to my car. I saw no reason to say anything about my visit to the car rental agency, so I'd left that out.

Now we were going over it a third time.

"He menaced you with the knife?"

"Yes, he *menaced* me with the knife."

"But you had your gun . . ." The detective gestured to my gun, in an evidence bag on the table.

The interview was being conducted in a Thai restaurant on Level 6 of the shopping mall. The mall had been shut down and sealed off and witnesses were being interviewed in another restaurant on another level.

The restaurant was empty of customers and staff. There were a bunch of cops milling around. A Latino EMS guy was examining the cut on my left arm. My shirt was off.

"Yes, I had a gun. But I didn't notice the guy until he was right in front of me. I had a book in one hand and a cup of coffee in the other. And knives scare the shit out of me."

"Uh-huh," he said. Unimpressed.

"I'm telling you, the guy had a knife."

"Relax. We know. The knife was in a sheath on his belt."

I nodded at the horizontal cut on the outside of my arm, a few inches above the elbow. "You'll find my blood on it."

A uniform came into the restaurant, signaled to the detective. The detective looked at me without expression. "Be right back," he said. He picked up the bag with my gun in it and left.

The EMS guy had flushed the cut with hydrogen peroxide and was dabbing at it with sterile gauze. He said, "You'll need stitches for this. Better go to the hospital when you're done here. I'll put some butterflies on it for now." A trip to the hospital would mean a three-hour wait in the emergency room. I didn't have time for that.

"Can't you stitch it?"

"They'll do a neater job of it at the hospital. Less scar."

"Look, these guys may need to take me in, it could be a long time. Don't worry about making it neat, just stitch it good so it won't open up." I leaned in close, added, "Fifty bucks."

The EMS guy stiffened. "I'm a professional, have some respect."

"Hey, no offense. I'm just trying to get it done. Please?"

He sighed and rustled around in his tackle box. "I don't want to hear complaints if it leaves a ridge."

"Thanks."

I lit a cigarette and smoked while the EMS guy stitched my arm. Smoking wasn't allowed in the mall. Under the circumstances, I figured the chances of getting busted for it were slim. The cops had given me coffee and I used the ceramic mug as an ashtray.

The detective returned along with another cop in a brown suit. The detective said, "This is Captain Samberch."

*Captain.* CPD captains don't normally hang out at crime scenes. Crime scenes are populated by officers and detectives and sergeants, and an occasional lieutenant if the stiff is someone really important or if the case looks like a heater. But a captain?

Samberch said, "The famous Ray Dudgeon. Chicago's own Goo-Goo private eye." Goo-Goo comes from *good government*. It's a dismissive term for a government reformer, or any foolish idealist who thinks he can clean up public corruption. But Samberch said it without any real edge.

I dragged on my cigarette, said, "Yeah, I was thinking of adding it to my business cards. That a good idea?"

Samberch chuckled, pulled up a chair. "And you can put it in red neon in your window, above a big flashing eye." Still no edge. Just friendly teasing. Just a couple of guys, shooting the shit. He signaled to a cop near the bar and the cop brought a couple fresh mugs of coffee. Samberch reached into his breast pocket, pulled out a flask, and unscrewed the top. It was brushed stainless steel like Mike Angelo's flask, but Mike's was a lot bigger. Then again, Mike was a lot bigger than Samberch, rank notwithstanding.

Samberch held the flask over my coffee mug. "A little Irish?"

I nodded. "Much obliged, Captain."

He poured a good double shot into my coffee, screwed the top back on the flask, and returned it to his pocket. I drank some, nodded my thanks to him. I was still feeling shaky and sick from the postadrenaline hangover, and it felt good going down.

He looked wistfully at his own mug, shrugged. "On duty," he said by way of explanation.

The EMS guy was done stitching my arm. He put a strip of gauze over his handiwork and taped it in place, packed up his tackle box.

"That'll hold."

"Thanks, man," I said. He left and I buttoned my shirt. Now it was just Captain Samberch and the detective whose name I'd forgotten. And me. I drank some more boozy coffee. Lit a new cigarette.

Samberch spoke first. "Detective Oliva brought me up to speed on your statement. We're downloading video from the building's security system. You have any idea how many security cameras there are in a place like this?"

"Lots?"

"Good guess. So it's taking a while. But I think we'll find that you're telling it straight." He offered a reassuring smile. "We've interviewed most of the witnesses and they tell it like you told it. I mean with all the contradictions and inconsistencies that you get from eyewitnesses. So far, they all say he was the aggressor, you ran, you called for police. Some say he had a knife, some say no. Some say he had a gun. One guy swears he had a hammer. You know how it is."

I did know how it was. What I didn't know was why Captain Samberch was being so collegial. "Will I get my gun back?"

"It's being tested now. Doesn't smell like it's been fired and nobody was shot. You may get it back when we're done, if it tests clean." He sipped some coffee. "But I'm curious why you didn't use it, if your life was in imminent danger. I would've shot the guy."

"I was just asking him about that, Captain," said Detective Oliva.

I said, "The thing is, we were too close at first and my hands were occupied. In retrospect, after I threw the coffee on him and put some distance between us, I should've turned and drawn my gun. But I thought I could get away. Thought I could get out to Michigan. I didn't think he'd chase me through a crowded mall. He did." Samberch watched my eyes intently as I spoke and I didn't look away. "And then there were just too many civilians in the way so I couldn't draw on him, couldn't risk it. Not only was my gun not fired, it never even cleared leather."

Samberch nodded. "Makes sense," he said. "But you should've taken him out in the garage."

"Yeah, I said that. It was a mistake."

"Would you say that you panicked?" Trick question. For lethal force to be justified, you must be in reasonable fear for your life. But if you admit to panic, you can't claim that you were reasonable.

"No, I didn't panic. I just tried to find a way out where nobody gets hurt. Unfortunately, he pressed me into a corner by giving chase, until I had no options."

*Truth is, I panicked.*

He nodded again. "Very good. A lot of people in this town would love to see you busted," he said.

"So I've gathered."

"I'm not one of them. And neither is Detective Oliva."

"Thank you," I said, "I appreciate that."

"Okay. Tell me what you know about the dead guy."

"I don't know anything about the dead guy."

"Come on, Dudgeon. We're helping you out here. Now you have to help us out."

"Believe me, I'd love to know who he was. But I have no idea."

"Really?"

"Really."

Samberch sighed, "Then you are in some serious shit, my Goo-Goo friend." I shrugged my lack of understanding to him. He said, "Because the guy with his brains splattered all over the floor out there isn't just some thug."

"You know who he is?"

"I don't know who he is. I know *what* he is." He snapped his fingers and got the attention of a uniform who brought a couple of evidence bags to the table. In one bag was the knife in a leather belt sheath. In the other bag was a diving watch.

Samberch said, "See, we have a problem with your dead guy. First, he had no wallet on him, no ID, nothing. Now that's not so unusual. If he came here to ice you, he'd leave his ID at home in case something went wrong, right?"

"Sure," I said.

"But then we look at his clothes. No manufacturer's labels. None. Not even laundry marks."

"So he cut the tags off."

"Wrong. They never had tags to begin with. Custom made, no tags, no manufacturer's mark. Same with his shoes. Even his belt." Samberch opened a bag and brought out the dead man's diving watch, handed it to me. "Look at that."

It was a high-quality watch with substantial weight, precision fit and finish. Unidirectional ratcheted bezel and automatic movement. I examined the face, the crown, turned the watch over and inspected the back. A very high-quality watch, but not a mark on it to identify the manufacturer. Sterile.

I'd never seen a sterile watch but I'd read about them in books. My blood ran cold and the room began to close in on me.

"Uh-oh," I said.

"You got it. And it's the same thing with the knife." Samberch took the watch and put it back in the bag, drank some coffee. "Only time I've seen a watch like that was Vietnam. Standard issue to black-ops CIA guys. Right?"

"Yeah, but not just CIA. From what I've read, all sorts of covert intelligence guys get them. And not just American."

"Guy have a foreign accent?"

"No. Sounded like a TV anchorman. Had that nondescript, nonregional American accent."

"So not a Chicago guy, either."

"Not unless he purposely got rid of the accent."

"You can understand how little pleased I am about this," said Samberch, tapping the evidence bag with his index finger.

I met his eyes. "Doesn't please me a great deal, either."

"I'm sure."

"Did he have any identifying scars or tattoos?"

"From the neck up there's not a lot we can say, for obvious reasons. His body is clean. We'll run his prints, see if we get a hit. We'll get his face from the security video. In the meantime, I suggest you give some thought to motive. You may not know who he is but you can make a list—members of your fan club who might send a guy like this."

I considered asking him if he wanted me to include city employees—both current and those serving time—on my list, but I decided to keep my trap shut. We'd just met, but so far I liked Samberch and I figured him for a right guy. There was no percentage in acting like a wiseass.

Someone behind me caught the captain's attention. He stood and walked over to the bar area, where a laptop computer had been set up. I started to follow but he held his hand up.

"Stay seated, Dudgeon. You don't get to see this."

So I waited while Samberch and Oliva and a bunch of other cops watched various streams of security video on the laptop computer. I drank the rest of my coffee and someone refilled my mug and I drank that, too, and smoked another cigarette, and thought about how I'd screwed up.

The car rental kid didn't know where I'd parked my car, so he couldn't have dropped a dime on me. And no one had followed me from Amy's house to my office. So the dead guy had picked me up when I left my office. When I was busy worrying about Amy's suspicions, busy feeling rejected. Put simply, I'd allowed myself to become distracted and I'd made myself an easy target. Same thing in the garage.

*Damn, that was bush league, Dudgeon. A major malfunction. And after lecturing Jill about paying attention to her surroundings? Way to go, man. Way to set an example. You better smarten up, get your head in the game . . .*

I cut the self-flagellation and focused on the facts. The guy who came after me was not some run-of-the-mill hit man. A hit man would've just come from behind and popped a couple of small-caliber bullets into the back of my head. This was different. So I doubted that this guy had anything to do with my past sins. It seemed obvious that his attack was related to the Joan Richmond case, but assuming that the obvious is true can get you in a lot of trouble.

And then there was the nagging feeling that he just wasn't a Hawk River kind of guy. Holborn had warned me that intuition is a fickle guide, which is true. But it's not something to ignore, either. And mine told me that this guy had a lot more in common with those two maybe-DHS guys than he did with Joseph Grant and Blake Sten.

Samberch and Oliva returned to the table.

Samberch said, "Good thing for you this happened where it did. The whole place was covered. You were never off-camera."

"So I'm in the clear?"

"Looks that way."

"Thanks."

"One thing. What was that at the end, as he was falling . . . you try to catch him?"

I didn't have an answer.

I said what would make sense to him. "I wanted to question the guy, find out who he was working for."

He nodded. "Hang tight awhile, we'll see about your gun."

"Thanks."

"Oh, and Goo-Goo?"

"Yeah?"

"You plan to get chased by guys like that, you ought to give up smoking." Samberch turned and walked out into the mall.

Oliva handed me my book, said, "Yours?"

"Thanks."

"It'll keep you occupied while we finish our work." But he didn't leave, just stood there looking down at me. He gestured toward the book. "My brother's over there."

"Iraq?"

"Fourth tour. It's a bad war."

"It's a war," I said. "Wars are bad."

He shook his head. "Afghanistan is a right war. Iraq is a wrong war. Makes a difference."

"I'm not much into politics," I said.

"Yeah. You think it's about oil?"

"Maybe."

"I think it's about oil." Detective Oliva was a man carrying a heavy load. He said, "The guy who came after you . . ."

"Yeah?"

"Whatever you're working on . . . got anything to do with this?" He gestured to the book again.

"No."

Oliva looked disappointed. "All right. I'll see you later." He turned to go.

"Detective."

"Yeah?"

"Hope your brother gets home safe."

"Me, too."

# CHAPTER TWENTY-FIVE

**I**t was past 8:00 when I pulled out of the garage and onto Walton. My gun was back on my hip and the police had released me without charge. That was the good news.

The bad news was everything else.

I turned my phone on and called Vince on speed-dial.

He answered with "Shit, you okay?"

"Yeah, why?"

"You're all over the fuckin' radio, is why. I left you four messages. They say you tossed some guy off a sixth-floor balcony."

"Call you back." I pulled to the curb and turned on the radio.

" . . . *identity of the assailant is still unknown. More details after the break.*" I lowered the volume as some guy started barking about how much better my life would be if I covered my house with vinyl siding from Amazing Siding. Even if I had a house, I didn't see how vinyl siding could help me right now.

My phone rang. It was Terry.

I said hello and Terry said, "Hey, you okay?"

"Yeah, I'm all right, thanks. Call you back in five." I hung up.

The phone rang again.

"Yeah."

"Ray Dudgeon?"

"Yes."

"Hi Ray, it's Judy Bobalik, Channel 2 News . . ."

"Oh Christ."

"Sorry. I know it's been a long day but you're the lead at ten."

"Lucky me."

"Hey, I'm just doing my job. We're shooting a stand-up in front of 900 North. Can you drop by and give us an on-camera?" The radio finished selling me stuff and the news came back on.

"Judy, I'm sorry, I gotta go." I hung up.

*"Our top story at this hour—Death on the Mag Mile. Nine Hundred North Michigan Avenue was the scene of a dramatic foot chase this afternoon, ending in the death of a man the police are still trying to identify."* A disinterested cop voice came on, reading a statement. *"Just before one o'clock this afternoon, local private detective Ray Dudgeon was assaulted by a man with a knife in the parking garage of 900 North Michigan Avenue. He fled into the shopping mall and the assailant followed, chasing Mr. Dudgeon up the escalators and causing minor injuries to two bystanders. The assailant caught Mr. Dudgeon on Level 6 of the atrium. Mr. Dudgeon knocked him over the guardrail and he was killed on impact with the floor. For now, the deceased is a John Doe. We are working to establish his identity. Thank you, that's all I have at this time."*

A reporter barked a question about the extent of my injury. *"Mr. Dudgeon sustained a cut to his left arm requiring stitches. He was treated at the scene and released."* Another question, about the motive for the attack. *"Still under investigation. That's all I have at this time. Now if you'll excuse me. . . ."*

My phone rang again and I flicked the radio off. The call display said it was coming from Isaac Richmond. The guy who got me into this mess. I let it go to voice mail.

After a minute, I checked my voice mail. Eighteen messages. The four from Vince, plus three from Terry. One from Sasha Klukoff, reporting that he'd found a potential buyer for my Shelby. And Special Agent Holborn left a message saying that he couldn't be reached after six, but to call him tomorrow before noon. The next eight messages were from reporters, all looking for a quote about the day's top local story. WGN was leading its nine o'clock broadcast with it and it was the lead for all the ten o'clocks, too. The local papers and radio stations also wanted in on the act.

Throw a guy off a balcony, and the whole world wants to talk to you.

The last message was from Isaac Richmond, who implored me to call back ASAP. Yeah, right. I'd call him tomorrow if I felt like it.

I deleted the messages, thinking *There's no way Jill won't learn of this.*

After Vince told me about the engagement ring, I'd had the crazy idea to show up at her door with protestations of love and proposals of marriage. My ring wouldn't be any match for Dr. Glassman's, but the tears in Jill's eyes when I last saw her told me that her love for me wasn't dead. On life support perhaps, but not dead.

And now this. *Maybe I should call her now, before she hears about it on the news . . .*

I called Vince instead.

"You hear it?" said Vince.

"I heard it. How's it going there?"

"Fine. The Chinese babe peeks out at me through her curtains every hour or so. Nobody else around. Just regular activity. I've patrolled the surrounding blocks a few times, at random intervals like you showed me. I'm the only one out here. No bad guys yet."

"All right. How long are you good for?"

"I can go 'til morning, easy," said Vince.

"You sure?"

"No problem. I stocked up for an all-nighter just in case."

"Okay, if anything happens or if you start falling asleep, call my cell. Otherwise, I'll be there to relieve you in the morning."

I hung up and called Terry and he asked me again if I was all right. I reassured him that I was fine.

"I take it this was related to the Joan Richmond thing," said Terry.

Only a fool ever tells a reporter anything off the record but when that reporter is your best friend, the term actually means what it says. Between Terry and me, it is a blood oath.

"Think so," I said. "But I have no actual knowledge. And I suspect he was working for someone other than Hawk River, but that's also speculation."

"Based on?"

"I don't know, call it a hunch. You know anything about a CPD captain named Samberch?"

"Samberch . . . One of the good guys, from what I hear."

"That was my impression, too. How about a Detective Oliva?"

"Never heard the name," said Terry. "Want me to ask around?"

"That's okay, I was just asking." I cranked open the window and lit a cigarette. "Got any news for me?"

"Actually, yeah. An update on the committee hearings. You remember Bill Combes, worked city council when you were at the *Chronicle*?"

"I remember Bill. Nice guy. Parrothead. Scuba diver."

"That's him. He covers the Hill for Reuters now. Anyway he's got a source. An aide to some congressman on the OGR committee. Says the hearings are in free fall. Everybody's playing it cool but it's starting to look like Joan Richmond was the star witness. They don't have much else, and they're beginning to look a little foolish."

"I assume Hawk River's lawyers are now yelling *partisan witch hunt*."

"We're still at *fishing expedition*. But if the committee doesn't produce something resembling a smoking gun pretty soon . . ."

"I've got diddly," I said. There was no reason to bring up Malibu Man. All he told us was that Hawk River was nervous. And we already knew that.

Terry cleared his throat and said, "Listen . . . you know I gotta ask you for a quote about today . . ."

"Sure." I tried to think of something. Whatever I said next would run in the next morning's *Chronicle,* and would no doubt be read by the dead guy's employers. It was an opportunity to send a message. I auditioned various statements in my head but none seemed right. And the more I thought about it, the angrier I became.

"Ray?"

"Hold on, I'm thinking."

What do you say to the men who just sent an assassin into your life? *I'll be a good boy, please don't send another*? How about, *Eat shit and die, motherfuckers*? Somehow neither seemed appropriate.

"Got your pen?"

"Shoot."

"I have some advice for the people responsible for today's attempt on my life. Next time, send someone who can fly."

After a few seconds of silence, Terry said, "Have you completely lost your mind?"

"Well, not completely," I said.

"I can't print that."

"Why not?"

"Because I don't feel like being responsible for your untimely demise, you idiot."

I stubbed my half-smoked cigarette out in the car's little ashtray. "I got lucky today, Terry. Only reason I'm still breathing. If I hadn't had a steaming coffee in my hand . . . the guy was way better than me—I never would've gotten to my gun in time."

"And how does rubbing their noses in it improve your chances next time?"

"It probably doesn't. But it tells them that I'm more angry than afraid." I could picture the meeting: the decision maker who sent the assassin being grilled by his superiors. If they started questioning previous assumptions . . . if they paused to rethink strategy . . . it just might help me.

Or maybe I was rationalizing.

"Are you more angry than afraid?" said Terry.

"Not by a long shot," I said.

# CHAPTER TWENTY-SIX

**M**ausoleums and gravestones appeared and disappeared as the beam of my headlights swept the grounds of Mount Pleasant Cemetery. I parked next to the small stone building that served as the head groundskeeper's residence and rang the doorbell.

Gravedigger Peace opened the door and shook my hand. He greeted me with his familiar crooked smile, but the smile looked a little forced and his face looked gaunt. He wore a baggy T-shirt with CHICAGO GREEN—a fast-rising local band—silk-screened on the chest.

Gravedigger led me inside and I sat on the couch in the living area while he went to the fridge and pulled out a couple of beer bottles. There was an open bottle of bourbon on the coffee table in front of me and a half-filled rocks glass next to the bottle.

He got another glass from a cupboard, sat across from me, put the glass on the table, and handed me one of the beers. I poured some bourbon into the empty glass but didn't pick it up. Drank some beer instead.

I looked him over. We'd gotten together a few times during the summer but I hadn't seen him since July. I guessed he'd lost maybe ten pounds. He had never carried extra weight, was always muscular and compact, and had always seemed taller than he was. But with the added weight loss, he looked small. Still strong, but underfed. And he looked older.

He still hadn't said anything, and small talk would be an insult. I said, "You're looking thin, Gravedigger. No dishes in the drying rack, no cooking smells." I nodded at the bourbon bottle. "So I'm guessing that you've been drinking your dinner recently." Nothing in my tone but the concern of an old friend.

"You don't miss much," said Gravedigger. "If I ever need a detective, you got the job."

Gravedigger's eyes glistened and they were red around the rims. He wasn't slurring drunk but just drunk enough, and staying that way for a while, the way a drinker sometimes does. *Maintenance drinking* is what I call it when I do it, which isn't as often as it once was but probably still more often than it should be.

"What's going on?" I said.

"Shit. Heavy shit."

Gravedigger and I had known each other since we were in diapers. As children, we lived on the same block, went to the same schools, got into trouble together and usually got out of it together. I watched as Gravedigger's father became increasingly abusive until he finally broke Gravedigger's arm and left the family for good. And Gravedigger watched as my young and overwhelmed single mother spiraled into depression until she finally killed herself. So we'd each seen behind the other's mask more times than we could count. The closest thing I'd ever had to psychotherapy was the occasional drunken all-nighter with Gravedigger, talking about our *heavy shit*. And I had no doubt that he would say the same.

So I wouldn't be searching Joan Richmond's place tonight.

I said, "You've got me 'til morning."

"Thing is, I'm not sure I want to talk about it," said Gravedigger. He winced, corrected himself, "Scratch that. I'm not sure I *can* talk about it. Not while you're so damn sober."

I understood. I drank the bourbon in my glass and chased it with a swig of beer, then refilled the glass.

"So talk. I'll drink with you." I watched Gravedigger's eyes retreat to somewhere far away. We drank in silence for a minute.

"Had a visit," said Gravedigger. "Had a visit from Mark Tindall."

Mark Tindall was Gravedigger's original name. It was his name back in the sandbox and it was his name when he dropped out of high school. It was his name when he became a mercenary and went to Africa, when he served time in a Nigerian prison, and when he returned to Chicago badly broken and struggled to put himself back together. But then he found the job at the cemetery and in that job he found a place where he could live with himself. He quickly rose to the rank of head grounds-keeper and, in a surprising move, legally changed his name to Gravedigger Peace. He would never again answer to the name Mark Tindall.

Gravedigger got two fresh bottles of beer from the fridge, sat back down, and said, "You know, I thought I'd killed that guy. Thought I'd gotten rid of him for good." His voice carried a strong note of futility. "Then you look in the mirror one day, and there the motherfucker is, staring back at you."

This was bad. This was worse than bad.

"What exactly did you do, Gravedigger?"

Normally Gravedigger only smiled with the left side of his mouth. This smile was even, and it looked cruel. "Look at you," he said, "Mr. Detective."

"Jesus, you know enough of my skeletons to know I'm not judging you, I'm worried. Tell me what happened."

He went to the closet and put on a jean jacket lined with fake sheepskin, grabbed a battery-powered lantern. "Come with me," he said. "Bring the bottle."

We left the house and walked to a grave about ten yards from Gravedigger's front door. We sat on the grass. He put the lantern on the ground, near the new headstone. Not much information on it. The name Walter Jackson and the years of his birth and death. Walter Jackson died at forty-seven.

I knew the name. Gravedigger told me about him during some of our drunken all-nighters after he came back from Nigeria. Walter Jackson had been Mark Tindall's commanding officer in the mercenary outfit in Africa. He was a black man from Georgia, had been with Special Forces, left the military and became a soldier for hire. He'd saved Gravedigger's life.

"He was killed in Ramadi," said Gravedigger. "It was on the news."

I remembered the story now. Five civilian contractors slaughtered and their bodies burned in the street. I remembered the video of young Iraqi men dancing around the fire, chanting their fury and waving machine guns around.

I said, "I saw it. The name didn't hit me at the time. I didn't make the connection. I would've called."

"I know you would." He reached out for the bottle and I gave it to him. He poured a little bourbon on the grave and made a toasting gesture at the headstone, then took a swig from the bottle and handed it to me and I drank some, too. He said, "Sarge put it in his will, to be buried here, by me. And that's an honor. But it fucked with my head something fierce. And Mark Tindall showed up."

I knew I didn't want to hear the answer but I had to ask again. "What did Mark Tindall do?"

His eyes welled up. "Something bad. Something really fuckin' bad."

"I'm sorry."

"Yeah. I am sorry, too." His hand shook slightly as he held it out for the bottle.

"Did the other guy deserve it?"

"Other guys. There were two of them. No, they didn't deserve it . . . not really."

"But maybe a little bit," I said. Grasping at straws.

"Shit, nobody deserves what happened to those guys. They deserved a good beating. I overreacted. I mean, *they* attacked *me* . . ."

"So it was self-defense," I said.

"Yeah. No. Hell, I could've incapacitated these guys with *both* hands tied behind my back and a cast on one leg. But Mark Tindall wanted blood. And he got it."

"Still, they *initiated* the violence, right?"

"Yeah."

"Well, you can't start a fight and then expect it to end on your terms. We're a long way from the schoolyard where you can start shit and then call *Uncle* when it doesn't go your way." I reached for the bottle, took another swig. "From where I sit, he who initiates violence waives the right to his life, because he didn't respect his intended victim's right to live."

"That's very nice in a philosophy classroom," snapped Gravedigger, "but I'm not talking about their fuckin' *rights*, man."

"Okay, you're right. I'm sorry, I was just looking for a way to make it better."

"This isn't something you can *make better*." Gravedigger blew out a long breath and went far away again, to a place he wished he'd never been. We were quiet for a while.

*Time to reevaluate. Gravedigger's a mess—there's no way he can help with Amy Zhang's protection. And the last thing he needs is to toss ideas around about how to deal with your little mercenary problem . . .*

"You smoking these days?" Gravedigger's voice brought me back.

I pulled the pack from my pocket and shook out a cigarette for myself and tossed him the pack. Lit mine, tossed him the Zippo. He took a deep drag, held the smoke in his chest for a few seconds, and blew it at the night sky.

After a minute he said, "Remember when you said that sometimes a good man does bad things?"

I remembered. It was just after Gravedigger returned from Africa and I was trying to help him find a way to forgive himself.

"It was ten years ago," I said. "I was younger then."

"Thing is, a good man can do one bad thing. Anybody can fuck up. Once. But just once."

"People have been known to make more than one mistake in a life-time," I said.

"This ain't stealing pencils from the office supply cabinet or put-ting a dent in someone's car and not leaving a note. And you don't take the moral temperature of a man by his intentions. Intentions are bullshit. You are what you do, not what you intend." He dragged on the cigarette. "Mark Tindall was not a good man, you know? He'd done far too much. He was not redeemable. There was no way to live with that. All I could do was kill the guy."

Amy told me that Steven Zhang had killed the man he was—annihilated himself, she said—and become someone else. And then he'd really killed someone. Gravedigger had done the same thing, but then he'd stopped killing. He said, "I just had to start over as someone new."

"Some people believe that we start over every day," I said, "and our actions determine who we are on that day only. That we don't carry our accomplishments forward. Or our failures. Every new day brings the same opportunity and imposes the same responsibility. You dig?"

"Yeah, I've read all those books. But we both know it's more com-plicated than that." He stubbed his cigarette out in the grass. "I'm working on it."

"Let's head in," I said, "it's getting a little cold out here." I stood and grabbed the lantern. It was time to get some distance from Walter Jackson's grave.

# CHAPTER TWENTY-SEVEN

**I made a pot of coffee** and a box of macaroni and cheese. There was a package of Vienna hot dogs in the fridge and I cut a couple into the macaroni. I didn't make a point of the food or the switch to coffee and Gravedigger didn't say anything, either. But he ate. And he screwed the cap back on the bourbon.

We talked about the last couple of months. The relapse into Mark Tindall was a onetime thing, sparked by Walter Jackson's death and two young knuckleheads who thought they could take on a guy in his late thirties who stood five-six. Of course, they didn't know about Gravedigger's past. Or about the rage. He didn't want to talk specifics and I wasn't sure I wanted to hear them, so we didn't go into the details of what had happened. I knew enough to understand how it was affecting him, and that's all I wanted to know.

We focused instead on the aftermath. The relapse had shaken his belief in the existence of Gravedigger Peace, but it had not broken that belief. Gravedigger was still Gravedigger, but he'd had to kill Mark Tindall a second time and it was painful work. He was self-medicating with booze, but he insisted that he never drank before his work was done for the day and I believed him.

He'd get through this. He might not ever be quite the same, but he'd get through.

We put our dishes in the sink and I refilled our mugs and we moved back into the living area.

Gravedigger smiled—a real smile—and said, "I think we've talked this thing to death." He sipped some coffee. "And it helped. Thanks for being a nosy bastard."

"It's what I do best."

"Now let's talk about your problems."

"Who said I had any?"

"When everything's fine, you call and say 'let's get together for a drink next week.' When you call and say 'can I come over now?' I know there's trouble."

"Fair enough," I said. "But I think we'd better leave it for another time."

"That's a negative," said Gravedigger.

"I think it might be bad for you."

"You come here with trouble, and we *don't* talk about it because you decide I can't handle it, and then you get killed. Now *that* would be bad for me. I appreciate the concern but I'm okay. You can stop treating me like a mental patient."

"It has to do with your previous occupation. You're sure you want to hear it?"

Gravedigger let out a big laugh. "Perfect! Just perfect. You gotta love the absurdity. I mean, the timing! It's like the universe is poking us both in the eye with a stick." He unscrewed the cap from the bourbon and poured a little into our coffee, still chuckling. "Ah, what the hell? Why not? What do you want to know about the mercenary business?"

So I told Gravedigger about Steven Zhang and Joan Richmond and their history at Hawk River. I told him about closed-door congressional hearings and scrubbed police files and the malignant threats coming my way, about DHS bullies and Amy Zhang's fear and the guy in the Malibu. He listened intently as I talked, elbows on his knees, leaning forward.

Then I told him about the attack in the parking garage.

"Jesus, Ray. You could've mentioned that a little sooner. Isn't that what you reporter types call *burying the lead*?" I hadn't been a reporter in over nine years, but I let that slide.

"I'm trying to keep it in context of the overall problem."

"The overall problem? They tried to kill you today." Gravedigger lit a new cigarette. "You ignore that problem, you won't be around to worry about the overall problem."

"If I let myself obsess about that," I said, "it'll paralyze me. Compartmentalize to survive, that's my motto." But there was a sick feeling in my gut and compartmentalizing was a struggle and I wished he hadn't focused on that particular part of the story. "Anyway, I have a reluctant ally at the FBI. After what happened today I think I can convince him to get involved."

Gravedigger rolled his eyes. "The FBI doesn't stand a chance."

"Let's not go overboard here," I said. "I know these guys are powerful, but—"

"Powerful? You ever see Eisenhower's *military industrial complex* speech? Ike wasn't messing around. He tried to warn us but we were too stupid to pay attention. And now it's too late. There's just too much money at stake. How'd you like Hawk River's head office?"

"It was very nice," I said.

"Bet it was. Check out the board of directors at any of the defense companies, and their lobbyists, too. What do you see? Retired pentagon brass, senators, congressmen. It's a revolving door between the federal government and the gravy train. Powerful? They run the fucking country."

"I don't buy into those shadow government conspiracies," I said. "Too paranoid."

"I'm not talking about that," said Gravedigger. "There's nothing shadow about it, it's right there in front of us, just like Eisenhower said. All you gotta do is follow the money. The defense establishment, the oil companies. They run the joint. I know. I used to work for them."

"Okay, if they run the joint and the politicians are just hired hands, then why is Congress investigating? Just putting on a good show for the voters? I don't buy that. Nothing personal, but you're not the *least* paranoid guy I've ever met."

Gravedigger sipped his coffee and his voice was a bit calmer. "Look, I'm not saying they own *every* politician. I'm saying they own enough of them. And if a handful of do-gooder congressmen start investigating, look what happens. Some crazy-acting guy kills this Richmond woman, then conveniently offs himself. Hell, if she'd been famous, the papers would've called him a lone nut assassin. Since she was a nobody, they just called him crazy. Mark my words, the congressional hearings will amount to nothing. And you can take that—"

"Okay, whatever." The sharpness of my tone surprised me. "They run the world, they don't run the world . . . that's a distraction I really don't need right now." I felt a little queasy. *Keep a lid on the fear.* I took a deep breath, reached for the pack and lit a cigarette.

Gravedigger nodded an apology my way. "The guy who came after you today, you said you didn't think he was a Hawk River guy."

"He didn't seem *military* enough to me, for what that's worth. Not much more than a hunch really."

"But I think you could be right. That detail about the sterile watch—"

"And knife. And clothing. Not a label on the guy."

"Right. See, most of the mercs I've known are label obsessed. Rolex, Strider, Larry Vickers, SureFire . . . these guys are constantly showing off their brand names."

"Still not much to go on," I said.

"Yeah, but let's just play that out. If he wasn't working for Hawk River, then logic says he's with the DHS guys who fucked with you in the bar."

"If they are DHS, which I doubt."

"Right. But they gotta be government. Like you said, the G is the only other party who stands to benefit." He finished his coffee, put the mug down hard, went to the fridge, and brought back a couple bottles of beer. He looked across the room at nothing for a minute before speaking again.

"Once upon a time, I had a gig in Somalia. The outfit I worked for was a British company. But our client on this gig was CIA. They couldn't send their own paramilitary guys—it was too politically sensitive and they needed to maintain *total* deniability, not just *plausible* deniability. We were supposed to take out some asshole warlord posing as a man-of-the-people politician." Gravedigger shrugged, "We took him out, all right. And his family."

"And what does this tell us?"

Gravedigger shook off the memory. "My point is, these operations happen all the time. CIA, DIA, DEA, you name it; if it's got three letters, it probably hires contractors to do shit it needs to be able to deny. I'm telling you, there are a *lot* of black ops that get contracted out whenever and wherever the government needs deniability. You can bet Hawk River gets its share of these gigs, no matter what bullshit Joseph Grant fed you. And let's say your Joan Richmond was gonna talk about it. It's Hawk River's mess, so it's their job to clean it up. But the government guys get nervous, maybe they think your Blake Sten is fucking up. So they send a guy to take you out."

It actually made sense, despite Gravedigger's paranoia. But I still didn't want to believe it. "I don't know . . ."

"Then paint me a more logical scenario."

I couldn't.

"Fine," I said, "let's run with that, see where it leads: Amy said that she thought Steven Zhang learned something bad while working on Hawk River's computers. Blake Sten fires Zhang, ostensibly for trying to sell company records to China. Joan Richmond quits less than a month later. Zhang and Joan maintain regular contact for over six months before she has a job to offer him. Congress starts holding hearings to investigate billing practices of various defense contractors, including Hawk River. And Joan is scheduled to testify. If Zhang shared what he learned with Joan, it may have been the motivation for her to quit, for them to stay in contact, and for her to testify. With me?"

"Sure."

"But. They're both dead. So what would make Joseph Grant's government friends nervous enough to take me out? Amy could talk, but she doesn't really know anything of substance. She can't even admit to herself that Steven was faking his mental illness. And Blake Sten showed me a photograph of Steven Zhang meeting with a Chinese MSS agent. Even if it was a frame-up, Sten has the photo to back up his version. So if Amy did kick up a fuss, they could just spin it as a delusional grieving widow. Killing me does nothing but invite unwanted attention. Unless . . ."

"Unless Joan Richmond or Steven Zhang had some physical evidence that Sten was unable to recover," said Gravedigger, "and everybody's afraid you'll find it."

So I would be searching Joan Richmond's place tonight, after all.

# CHAPTER TWENTY-EIGHT

**I** **sat on the floor of Joan Richmond's living room,** surrounded by books. A pot of coffee in my gut and angry music on the stereo to keep me awake. I'd started searching at 2:30. It was now coming up on 5:00 A.M. I was exhausted.

The soundtrack for my search included The Stranglers, The Who, The Stooges, and now The Clash. All bands starting with *The*, and all rebelling against authority. It wasn't a conscious choice—I'd just reached for the next disc at hand, so long as the music was energetic enough to keep me from drifting.

It had been twelve hours since I'd taken any Percocet and my shoulder was screaming but I couldn't risk falling asleep. There were plenty more rebellious bands in Joan's collection that started with *The*, but I was running out of places to search.

And running out of time.

The CD-ROM backups of her computer system were exactly what they seemed and held no secrets. I'd unzipped the cushions on her couch, kneaded all her throw pillows, examined the seams of her mattress and box spring, detached the headboard from the wall, felt through the lining of her clothes, pulled all the pictures off the walls and looked behind the frames, peeled back her rugs, looked under lamps and shelves and drawers and anything else that could be looked under. And now I'd flipped through all her books.

Nothing.

The prospect that I would never find what I was looking for loomed large. Whatever Steven Zhang may have found on Hawk River's computers was nothing more than data—he could've saved that data onto a USB flash drive smaller than my thumb. Hell, he could've saved it on a Micro SD card smaller than my thumb*nail*.

I reshelved the books while Joe Strummer sang about police and thieves fighting in the street. I poured another cup of coffee and sat at Joan's kitchen table with my notepad and reviewed the notes I'd made at Gravedigger's house.

Gravedigger and I had talked through various other scenarios, but the only one that made sense was that Joan Richmond had been in possession of some evidence and Blake Sten had been unable to recover it. If that scenario was right and if I could find Joan's evidence and get it to Special Agent Holborn, it would be Game Over. At that point killing either Amy Zhang or me would be suicide for Hawk River and would serve no purpose for their government friends.

The only problem was, I couldn't find it, either.

*But that doesn't mean you can't make them believe you've found it.*

The idea hit with blunt force. It seemed so obvious. I could run a bluff. Risky as hell, and normally I wouldn't even consider it. But after what happened the previous day, nothing was more risky than inaction and I was out of options. I had to do *something* to shake things up.

So I would run a bluff. First step: plant a story in Delwood Crawley's "Chicago After Dark" column at the *Chronicle*. Crawley was the top gossipmonger in town, a man with many contacts and few scruples. I didn't like him and he didn't like me, either, but we'd developed a kind of barter system. Occasionally he'd call on me to do some investigative legwork—following up on some scandalous rumor or another. And in return, I could plant items in his rancid column when I needed to.

I flipped to a blank page in my notebook and tried to emulate Crawley's hack prose style. My third attempt yielded this:

*Developing story . . . Whispers in Washington: A little bird— or more accurately, a big hawk—tells me that we can expect shocking developments in the congressional Oversight and Government Reform committee hearings, as early as next week. New information is winging its way to DC and a rushing river of scandal will soon flow all the way back to Illinois. Break out the life vests, Aurora! . . . more to come.*

It was terrible stuff but it sounded just like Crawley.

The second step was to feed Crawley the story. If I could get it to him today, it would run in tomorrow's paper.

Step three: I'd courier a clipping to Joseph Grant, just to be sure, and he'd have it by the end of the day.

I knew it wouldn't save me, but it might buy a little time until I could think of something better.


When I stopped at my apartment for a change of clothes, the light on my answering machine was flashing "1." The message was a hang-up. I dialed *69. I recognized the number recited back to me by the phone company Fembot. The call had come from Jill's apartment. So it was a reasonable assumption that she'd learned about my latest demonstration of why she shouldn't worry about my chosen profession.

Still, she'd called. Even if she hadn't left a message, she'd called.

I thought back to January, a few weeks after she'd ended our relationship. The Outfit scandal had exploded all over the news and my name was everywhere, along with the names of some dead guys and a bunch of public servants under arrest.

She'd left a message that time. I was on my way down to convalesce at my grandfather's house in Georgia and I checked messages from a pay phone in Kentucky. Jill's message said she just wanted me to know that she was glad I was okay. That was all she said. But that should've been enough. I should have called her back. I didn't.

There were plenty of reasons. I was badly injured and my mind was a mess and I didn't know what to say to her. I thought I should wait. Thought I should take some time to get my head together and figure out what I was going to do next. Figure out what I had to offer her. A change of career? A normal life? Kids? I didn't know.

So I waited. And the longer I waited, the harder it was to pick up the phone. By the time I did call, months had passed and she had moved on. She was dating the man who would eventually go shopping for an engagement ring while Vince watched from the shadows.

And now she'd called again. Didn't leave a message this time, but she'd called. I thought about calling her back. *Hey, honey, I'd love to get together right now but I'm a little busy with people trying to kill me. I'll call you later if I'm still alive. In the meantime, please don't marry the other guy . . .*

Maybe not.

On the way to University Village, I drove around in circles to be sure I hadn't grown a tail. It was not yet 7:00 A.M. and I knew Delwood Crawley wouldn't be in but I called and left a message on his voice mail, asking if we could meet later. Then I left a message for Special Agent Holborn, told him that I was available on my cell.

Again I thought about calling Jill. Again, I didn't. I drove a circuit of the blocks surrounding Amy's town house and found no bad guys parked nearby. I pulled to a stop behind Vince's blue Escort.

Vince's *empty* blue Escort.

*Shit.*

# CHAPTER TWENTY-NINE

**I** **drew my gun, flew up Amy's front steps** and hammered on her door and jabbed at the doorbell. Looked up and down the block. The street was empty. And quiet. I hammered on the door again.

A few more seconds passed and the door opened.

Vince said, "Keep your pants on. I had to check, make sure it was you."

"Jesus, Vince. I thought you'd be in the car." I holstered my gun and stepped inside and Vince locked the door behind me.

"Amy invited me in after she saw the news on TV." He offered up a sly man-to-man smile. "I think she likes you. She was really worried about you."

"Where is she?"

"Upstairs, sleeping." Vince stretched. "And speaking of sleeping, I'm beat. Can I go now?"

"You see anything?"

"Niente. No bad guys, no nuthin'. Just a regular night on a quiet street."

"Okay, thanks. Get as much sleep as you can and be back at four."

"Will do."

"Also, pack a bag. I want you to stay on Amy's couch awhile."

Vince nodded. "Listen, uh, if I'm gonna be here 24/7, working . . ."

"Yes?"

"Well, I'm not gonna be able to take any process-serving gigs for Argos."

"Right. You're working for me full-time for the next while."

"But, see the thing is, I don't have a daily rate. We never talked about that. What's the job pay?"

"Oh yeah, sorry. Four hundred bucks."

"For how many days?"

"Per day. Four hundred per day."

Vince broke into a wide smile. "Excellent. Cool, thanks." He turned to leave.

"Vince."

"Yeah?"

"Is Jill on days or nights right now?"

Vince thought for a second. "She had yesterday off, goes back on days this morning. Shift starts at eight."

"Thanks." He headed down the front steps. "Get some sleep," I called after him. I needed some myself, badly, but that would have to wait until Amy was awake and could stand watch. In the meantime, breakfast would keep me going.

I fried a couple eggs and some bacon, read the morning paper while I ate. The police still didn't know the identity of the man who attacked me. Not at press time, anyway. The story told me nothing new but Terry had indeed quoted me, against his better judgment.

*When reached by the* Chronicle *for comment, an angry Ray Dudgeon said, "I have some advice for the people responsible for today's attempt on my life. Next time, send someone who can fly."*

Perhaps not my finest moment. But Terry had helped sell the quote by describing me as *an angry Ray Dudgeon,* and it didn't read like false bravado. Rather, like a guy come slightly unhinged. Maybe a little more than slightly.

And despite the obvious attempt at humor, I didn't think Jill would love the quote a whole lot. Of course, I hadn't been thinking of how it would read to her when I said it.

"Good morning."

I looked up from the paper. Amy stood in the kitchen doorway. She wore blue jeans and a red UIC sweatshirt. Her hair was in a ponytail, her hands jammed into the back pockets of her jeans. Bare feet, toenails painted red.

I closed the paper, tried to control my anger, failed. "I don't suppose you've had a chance to read the paper."

"I saw it on television." Amy looked at her delicate feet. "I'm sorry. I wanted to believe you but . . . I was scared, I didn't know what to think. When I saw the news, I knew for sure you weren't with them."

"You sure? Because I can go back out there and get myself killed if you need more convincing." *You're being childish, Dudgeon. She was trying to protect her daughter. Let it go.* I took my plate to the sink. "It's all right, forget it. Just tell me what you know and don't leave anything out this time."


We sat in the front room and Amy told her story again. It was the same story, right up to the point when Steven Zhang went nuts.

She said, "You asked before if Steven was faking his illness. I still find it hard to believe . . ."

"But he was, wasn't he?"

"Yes. God . . . yes I think he was. I mean, he put on a good act but I didn't really . . . you know, like when you see an actor in a movie and you can't point to anything specific that he's doing wrong but you just don't believe him? I asked him—I said, 'Why are you doing this?' and he responded with all sorts of delusional raving, but . . ." Amy shrugged. "And there was something in his eyes. Like he knew what he was doing was hurting me and he felt terrible about it." She let out a long sigh. "If he really had been as disconnected from reality as he was acting, he wouldn't have looked at me like that."

I'd already concluded that Steven Zhang's illness was phony. The fact that Amy thought so too was fine, but ultimately useless to me. I needed something concrete, something I could work with.

"You thought Steven had learned something bad on Hawk River's computers."

"Yes."

"And whatever he found, he had to save. On a CD-ROM, a flash drive, SD card, portable hard drive, whatever."

"Yes." Amy's eyes grew wide. "Yes, that's right! A week after Steven started acting crazy, Joan called me. She asked about his sudden illness and I told her I didn't understand it, either. Then she said that Steven was supposed to give her something; he had some important computer files and she needed them very badly. She was extremely agitated about it. Most of all, she sounded frightened and I remembered when Steven was fired from Hawk River, he said that it was for my own good not to know any details, that he was trying to protect me. In my mind, the two things fit together."

"Good thinking," I said.

"Joan asked me to ask Steven about it. She wasn't able to get through to him and she thought maybe I could. I asked him a number of times, whenever he seemed lucid, but he immediately started ranting about how everybody was in on some giant brainwashing conspiracy against him. Like my asking triggered him to amplify the craziness."

"Do you know if Joan ever got what she was looking for?"

"I know she didn't. She called a few times to see if I'd found out from Steven. The last call was the day before . . ." Amy kneaded her hands in her lap.

So I'd spent a night tearing through Joan's apartment for nothing. She never even had the damn thing to hide.

*Which means it could still be right here . . .*

"I need to search Steven's office upstairs."

"You won't find anything." Amy reached forward and touched my arm to stop me from standing. "I'm sorry, I should have told you all this before—"

"Don't worry about that now," I said. "Just tell me, why won't I find anything?"

"Well, this goes back a long time," said Amy. "All the way back to China." Her voice echoed reluctance. This was not an easy topic, but then none of our conversations were easy.

"That's okay," I said, "go ahead."

She took a deep breath, let it out. "All right. You need some background. In 1989, Steven and I were both student organizers in the June Fourth Movement."

"Tiananmen Square?"

"Yes, Tiananmen was what the world saw on television and that was the largest of them, by design. But there were protests all across the country . . . it was massive. And it was carefully coordinated, timed to coincide with Gorbachev's visit, when there would be news media from all over the world. Planned for many months on university campuses, in dorm rooms and study halls and cafeterias. The universities in Beijing were the main planning centers.

"Steven was a leader in the prodemocracy student movement. He had written influential dissident essays that were secretly distributed among the campuses. Those essays inspired many students to join. To me they were like the writings of Thomas Paine, forbidden in China but widely read in secret. I was eighteen years old, an undergraduate studying languages. The prodemocracy movement soon became my passion. And I became an organizer on campus." As Amy told her story, she stopped looking at me and seemed to retreat into herself. Like she was alone in the room, telling herself the story.

She was silent for a minute. Then she said, "We believed that the Americans would stand up. The UN. The whole Western world would stand up for us when they heard our cries, and the Party would be forced to enact some democratic reforms. We weren't expecting utopia, just a few reforms. A little less corruption. A small step toward democracy. We really believed it was within reach. Of course we were wrong. No one stood up for us. And the government crushed us."

Television images of Tiananmen Square flashed through my mind.

A sea of people standing together under the glare of Mao Zedong. Student leaders making speeches through bullhorns. Thousands of people, the young and the old, sitting cross-legged on the ground, staging a mass hunger strike. The statue of the *Goddess of Democracy,* hastily carved in Styrofoam, facing Mao's portrait, staring him down. Tanks and trucks full of soldiers with rifles, surrounding the square, waiting for the order to move in.

And as they made their approach, the solitary young man who stood defiant before the tanks, daring them to run him over.

And then chaos. Truncheons cracking heads and rifles firing into the crowd and clouds of tear gas choking protesters. Limp and bloody bodies being carried away, buses burning in the streets, the *Goddess of Democracy* felled by a tank and quickly reduced to Styrofoam rubble by the People's Liberation Army.

*People's Liberation Army.* What a name.

"I was rounded up with the rest of the organizers and sent to prison," said Amy. "I was given a ten-year sentence. It was very bad in prison. We were not treated well. After a year, I was given medical parole."

"What was wrong?"

Amy looked at me again and smiled without any humor. "A medical parole is just an excuse to send a political prisoner into exile. You see, because I was well known to the movement I became one of the *June Fourth martyrs,* as we were called. And martyrs inspire. So the government offered us medical parole, on condition that we leave the country—for medical treatment, is what they say in public—and never return. It's a common practice—a convenient way to get rid of troublemakers without creating more martyrs. I was put on a plane to America and told that if I ever returned, I would disappear into a prison labor camp and never be seen again."

"Did Steven come with you?"

She shook her head. "Steven was offered medical parole," she said, "but he refused it."

"Why?"

"If you leave the country, you have turned your back on the struggle. You have taken the easy way out. Exile is not honorable for someone considered a martyr."

"That's pretty harsh."

"In China, life is harsh. You couldn't understand." She was right; I couldn't even imagine. "For three years Steven refused medical parole. Finally he gave in. He came to Chicago and we were married."

My cell phone rang. The call display said it was coming from the FBI. I held my finger up in a "one minute" gesture and answered as Amy went into the kitchen.

Special Agent Holborn said, "I've got to admit, you're harder to kill than I ever would've guessed."

"Thank you," I said. "Got anything for me?"

"Two things. First, the plate number you gave me."

"The DHS guys."

"Are you sure they were Illinois plates?"

"Absolutely. *Land of Lincoln* and everything."

"Then either they're counterfeit or you wrote the number down wrong."

"I gave you the right number," I said.

"Then it's counterfeit. No such plates exist. Not in Illinois."

"That's interesting."

"I thought you'd think so."

"You guys ever use counterfeit plates? Like when you're undercover and you want to dress your car as a civilian?"

"Ray, we're the government. We can get genuine civilian plates whenever we want. Genuine civilian cars, too, if we need them."

"Yeah, I'm just looking for a reason why a couple of DHS agents would ride around with counterfeit plates on their car."

"If you think of one, I'd love to hear it."

"You said two things. What's the second?"

"I spoke to the China desk. Your Blake Sten never brought them anything about Jia Lun meeting with any Steven Zhang. They've never heard of Steven Zhang. Or Blake Sten, for that matter."

"Thought you weren't going to tell me what the China desk said."

"I figure you earned it yesterday."

"Thanks."

"My pleasure," said Holborn. "Stay alive, and call me when you learn something."

# CHAPTER THIRTY

Amy and Steven Zhang built a new life together in the United States, became citizens, had a daughter, saved their money, and brought Amy's mother to Chicago. They embraced their adopted country with the intense gratitude felt by immigrants from oppression.

But they could not forget the way things were back home and those who continued the struggle, and they felt some measure of guilt for the blessings of their new life. So they decided to exercise their new freedom to help.

Steven used his computer skills to set up special Web sites. One site gave tips on building a backyard koi pond and keeping your fish healthy. Another was a guide to Chicago's Chinatown for the casual tourist. A couple of years ago, he added a site devoted to Italian recipes and cooking techniques. Completely innocent Web sites, but behind them he built *blind pages*. You could surf around the sites all day, click every available link, and you'd never stumble upon the blind pages. On those blind pages, he posted news articles about China that appeared in the Western media but were censored back home. He posted the articles as large image files, making them invisible to word-search applications.

Amy wrote the copy for the main sites. And she used her job as an English tutor at UIC to recruit Chinese students. The students sent e-mails back home, to kids on university campuses in Hong Kong and Beijing, and those kids forwarded the messages to kids on campuses in other cities throughout China. The e-mails looked trivial enough— a lot of prattle about the life of a college kid. *Oh, and by the way, I found this really cool site about Chicago's Chinatown, or koi ponds, or Italian cooking.* And certain words within the prattle told the reader what extensions to type, in order to get to the blind pages.

It was a clever system and they were able to funnel a lot of news past the censors. Their big mistake was not doing enough to disguise ownership of the sites. Steven opted for private registration of the domain names, but that's easy enough to get around if you really want to find out who owns a site and are willing to spend a few bucks. If you did, you'd find that the sites were registered to Zhang IT Consulting. And the ownership of Zhang IT Consulting was a matter of public record.

As Amy told me all this, I realized how I'd underestimated her when we first met. Living in a city like Chicago, you meet cabdrivers who were doctors in their home country, waiters who were engineers, and so on. My own mechanic, Sasha Klukoff, was a professor in Russia back when it was the Soviet Union. You meet these people, but it never occurs to you that some of these cabdrivers and waiters and mechanics were also political dissidents in their native countries. Even political prisoners. Now I saw Amy Zhang through new eyes. She was a fighter, and a survivor.

And then she told me how it all came crashing down.

"The night that Steven died, after the police had gone, I was packing a suitcase. Theresa was at my mother's and I was going to join her there. I couldn't stay here. The place . . . it was a mess." I'd seen the police photos and I knew what she was saying. "I had to get out of here. I was packing a bag and a man came to the door. He was a huge man, with a terrible burn scar on his face."

"Blake Sten," I said.

Amy nodded. "He didn't say his name but Steven had described him to me. He showed me a photograph of Steven in a coffee shop with Jia Lun."

"Did you know that Jia Lun worked for the MSS?"

"Before I saw the photo? I knew that he was an important journalist and his reporting always supported Party policy, so he was connected to the Party. That's what I knew. Sten explained that Jia Lun was a professional contact of his. Then he showed me printouts of our Web sites, including the blind pages. He had the paperwork proving that Steven owned the sites. The last thing he showed me was another photo." Amy closed her eyes, opened them slowly. "It was taken on the tarmac of an airport in Shanghai. You could read the signs on the building in the background. In the foreground there were six PLA soldiers. They had a man in handcuffs. Yan Benli. He had been one of the June Fourth martyrs, sent to New York on medical parole. He gave lectures here, trying to persuade the American government to take a harder line on human rights in China. He disappeared a year ago. He was supposed to give a lecture at the New School. He never showed up. His body was never found and he's still listed by the New York police as a missing person. In the photograph, he stood between Jia Lun and Blake Sten."

"Sten was in China?"

"Yes. And he told me that the same thing would happen to me if I raised questions about Steven's death, or his illness. And I would never see Theresa again."

It all made sense. The photo of Steven Zhang and Jia Lun wasn't proof that they'd had a meeting; it was proof that Blake Sten could *engineer* such a meeting. Sten hadn't shown me any other evidence and he hadn't brought it to the FBI, so the content of their conversation could've been completely innocent. All he had to do was send Jia Lun into the coffee shop and snap some photos. Jia Lun could have approached Steve Zhang and struck up a conversation about the weather and Blake Sten would've gotten the photo he needed.

Sten might've used the same coercion on Steven: *I have influence with the Chinese government. Look at this photo of you and Jia Lun—I made that happen. Now this other photo—Jia and me, delivering one of your fellow dissidents to the PLA. I could do the same thing to you and Amy. Look here, I even have the records of your Web sites. You'll both disappear into labor camps, and you'll never see Theresa again. There's no way out for you. But you can save your wife and daughter . . .*

Maybe. But why would Blake Sten have that level of influence with the Chinese government? I had no answer for that one.

Amy said, "Sten went to the door and two other men came in. They searched the house for hours, took everything apart. They spent a lot of time in Steven's office. They even took the hard drive from his computer."

If three guys from Hawk River hadn't found it, I wouldn't. Amy was right—it wasn't there. *Damn.*

"When the police came back, I described Steven's recent behavior but did not mention my suspicions, or Blake Sten. And as I told you, I was being watched after that. A week later, someone else came to the door—not Blake Sten—and asked me to tell him what I knew about Steven killing Joan. He made no pretense. He said that he worked for Sten and he wanted to hear it the way I told it to the police. There was another visit a week after that. Sten again. It was the same thing, he wanted me to tell it over again. I think really he just wanted to scare me again. Remind me of what would happen if I didn't go along. A week after that, they stopped following me. Until you arrived." Amy was silent for a minute. Then she said, "And that's everything. Now I've told you all that I know. Can you do anything with it?"

"I'm not sure," I said. "If I had the computer files . . . I think I could get you and Theresa into Witness Protection. But you'd have to tell everything you know to an FBI man I know. And you'd have to testify, if it comes to that."

"If I testify, would they be able to keep us safe?"

"They'd try. They're pretty good at it, but there's no way to know for certain."

"Because I don't think Blake Sten will let me live. Once he finds whatever Steven had . . . or once enough time has passed not to raise suspicions . . . I think I'll have some kind of accident. Or I'll just disappear and Sten will earn some credits with his contacts in China."

She was probably right.

My grandfather's voice echoed in my head, dispensing advice both simple and profound: *Never make promises you can't keep, son.*

I said, "We're not gonna let that happen, Amy. I promise."

I was fading fast, desperate for sleep. Clear thought now required conscious effort. If I didn't close my eyes soon, I'd be totally useless. I went out to my car, did a quick circuit of the surrounding blocks, saw nothing, and parked in front of the town house again. I'd brought a couple of portable door jammers from home and I showed Amy how they worked. Then set one up on the back door, the other on the front. I made sure all the blinds were fully closed and gave her instructions to stay away from the windows.

It was 9:20. I swallowed a couple of Percs, set the alarm in my cell phone for 3:30 and placed it on the coffee table. Placed my gun next to it. Pulled the coffee table close to the couch and stretched out.

By the time Amy put a blanket over me, I was asleep.


The phone woke me at 2:05. Delwood Crawley said he would be at Riccardo's at 5:30. I said that I would be there and we hung up on each other. I'd been hoping for a full six hours of sleep, hadn't quite gotten five. It would have to do. I rose from the couch suffering from a bad case of bed head, managed to calm it down with a soak under the bathroom faucet. Brushed my teeth. Slapped on some deodorant. Felt almost like a new man.

I found Amy reading the newspaper in the kitchen. She wanted to visit Theresa. She hadn't gone yesterday and this was the longest they'd been apart since Steven's death. We had time to get to Grandma's for a quick visit and be back before Vince arrived. There was still no one watching Amy's house and I couldn't think of a reason to say no.

So we went. And there was no surveillance set up at Grandma's place in Chinatown, either.

As we entered Grandma's apartment, Theresa flew into the living room and into Amy's arms. There followed hugs and kisses and Amy smoothed Theresa's hair down the way a mother does. Theresa led Amy by the hand and we all went into the kitchen, where a chubby Chinese girl in her early twenties sat at Grandma's kitchen table. Schoolbooks were spread across the table. Amy introduced the girl as Samantha and told me that she was Theresa's tutor, until the time was right for Theresa to return to school.

Samantha had long hair, dyed very black. Black eyeliner generously applied, and black fingernails. Black cargo pants and pink Chuck Taylors. A matching pink Hello Kitty T-shirt. About a thousand string bracelets, some with pukka shells, others with little skull beads. I might've guessed Goth, but the pink shoes and the Hello Kitty T-shirt said something else. I think she may have been what kids of her age call Emo. Whatever that means.

Although her English was better than most American kids, it was not her native tongue and I wondered if she might've been one of Amy's UIC students who, until recently, had helped smuggle news to university students in China.

Samantha told us that Grandma was out grocery shopping, and Amy put the kettle on the stove. I left them in the kitchen and sat out in the living room, by the front window.

There was still no one watching the place.

I thought it through: Sten gave me a story to feed my client. *I sincerely hope that, once you pass all this to Mr. Richmond, he can move on, too,* he said. And just in case that was too subtle for me, he'd followed up with the assault on Ernie Banks. A clear message: *Put this case to bed. Now.* I hadn't allowed Tim Dellitt to buy me off the case, so an unambiguous threat would be the natural next step for a guy like Sten. But then Terry called Hawk River with questions about Steven Zhang and Joan Richmond. Sten couldn't know if Terry had been put into motion before my visit, so Terry's call didn't tell him if his threat had achieved its goal.

Sten needed to know if I was still on the case. I'm usually a pretty hard guy to tail (despite my screwup the previous day) so it would require a team. Waste of manpower. Easier to simply put Malibu Man on Amy. If I were pursuing the investigation, I'd turn up in Amy's life. If I didn't turn up, then either I'd dropped the case or I was such a lousy detective that I wouldn't get anywhere anyway.

But once I'd spent the night in Amy's house, Sten knew. She'd let me stay overnight—Sten would assume she'd told me everything. So there was no need to keep a man on Amy. Whatever damage Amy could do by talking to me had been done. I was the threat now. They could take care of Amy later. And killing her before me would be a serious tactical error.

It was too soon after the attempt on my life for Sten to move on me. I was too hot. If I'd convinced the police that there would be another attempt, there might even be a CPD team shadowing me for a few days, ready to swoop in and grab anyone tailing me. Better to wait. Regroup. Restrategize, in the light of recent events.

And if I was correct about the identity of my attacker, Blake Sten was as surprised by the attempt on my life as I was. Maybe, like me, he was right now wondering what the hell just happened.

Amy broke the silence of the drive back to her house with, "I still haven't told her. How Steven died. But I will have to, before she returns to school."

"Or before she gets on the Internet," I said.

"Oh my God. I hadn't even thought of that."

"Amy, you've got to tell her."

She ran her fingers through her hair. "She's so young and she's already been through so much. I don't know how. I don't know what words to use . . ."

"It doesn't matter how, just tell her." It came out a little harder than intended. "For Christ's sake, the longer you wait, the worse it's gonna be. If she finds out somewhere else, it'll be a double betrayal—her father kills himself, and then her mother lies to her about it."

Amy looked out the side window as we crossed over the Chicago River. She said, "But how do you explain suicide to a child?"

*My mother's cold body naked on top of the sheets, an empty pill
bottle beside her, a half-empty bottle of Sambuca on the nightstand. My
grandfather's inadequate words: "Human beings are odd creatures. . . .
She wasn't thinking straight—people never are when they do that."*

"I have no fucking idea," I said.

"Am I making you angry?"

"I'm not angry."

"You sound angry."

I took a deep breath. *Just tell her, Dudgeon.* I spoke with a forced
calm. "Look, I'm not angry, it's just . . . okay, here's the thing . . . my
mother killed herself when I was thirteen."

"Ray, I'm so sorry."

"Me, too. Anyway, it was a long time ago. Point is, you need to tell
Theresa the truth and go through this thing together. Probably the
only thing that saved me when my mother killed herself was that her
parents took me in and we all went through it together."

Amy thought about that. "She'll never get over it."

"Not completely, no. But you're making it worse by keeping it from
her."

I wanted to shut up and say nothing more. But I heard myself say,
"When this trouble is over . . . when your life returns to whatever new
version of normal you can make of it . . . after you've told her . . . you
know, I could visit with her. Tell her about my mother. Maybe it would
help her to talk with someone who's been there."

I didn't look at Amy. I couldn't. What if I looked and saw pity on
her face? What if she said *No, thank you* in that too-polite tone of
hers? I just kept driving, kept my eyes on the road.

Amy's warm hand covered mine on the stick shift.

"Thank you. You're a nice man."

Was I? Did I really want to talk with Theresa so I could help her?
Or so I could help myself? I couldn't honestly say.

"You don't know me, Amy."

We rode the rest of the way in silence.

# CHAPTER THIRTY-ONE

**R**ic Riccardo was a WPA artist and popular bon vivant who styled his eponymous restaurant after a Parisian café and commissioned six of his fellow WPA artists to paint large murals in the bar area, depicting the Seven Lively Arts. Riccardo's own painting depicted Dance. The place doubled as an art gallery and drew a lot of local artists and jazz musicians. In the late '40s and for some years after, it was the only downtown restaurant in Chicago that extended a genuine welcome to black people.

Because it was hip and because the martinis were huge, Riccardo's also attracted a loyal clientele from the nearby newspapers and ad agencies. It became the official hangout of the local scribblers when they felt like going upscale.

The news scribblers stuck around through new ownership, despite a slow decline in the food and decor, until they were the only customers left. After a few failed attempts to revitalize the place, Riccardo's finally closed down in 1995.

Another part of the Real Chicago gone, while publicly traded national chain *theme park* food factory restaurants opened all over the neighborhood and even the news business became just another part of your mutual fund's investment portfolio.

It reopened in 2000 as 437 Rush. Part of a chain, but at least it was a local chain. Phil Stefani promised to re-create the original vibe of Riccardo's, and he did a pretty decent job of it. The place had a lot of mahogany, black-and-white tile floors, wavy glass dividers, and framed photos of many of Chicago's prominent editors and columnists through the years. Stefani even commissioned Gregory Gove to paint a new mural over the bar, celebrating jazz. Soon the reporters and ad guys returned and everyone still called it Ric's, holding on to the past like nothing had changed.

Sometimes that's the best you can do.

I entered through the revolving door and was greeted warmly by Paulo, who told me that Delwood Crawley was waiting for me at a table in the back room. I glanced at the bar and spotted Scott Jacobs and a couple of young *Sun-Time*s reporters whose names I couldn't recall. Went over and said hello, then headed to the back for my date with Crawley.

Crawley's trim three-piece suit was a pale shade of gray that matched both his waxy skin and his thinning hair. He wore a blue shirt with white collar and French cuffs, and a paisley bow tie. He saw me coming, took a long sip of his drink, and reached for a monogrammed silver cigarette case on the table. Long bony fingers extracted a cigarette and lit it with a silver Dunhill lighter that matched the case.

"I cannot fathom how you manage to stay in business if you can't even make it to a meeting at the appointed time." His English accent was crafted to portray a social status higher than that which he'd enjoyed as a young man.

"Come again?"

"I said, 'you're late.' "

I glanced at my watch. I was seven minutes late.

"I had to stop at the bar and say hello to some real reporters." I sat down across from him.

Crawley blew a stream of smoke just over my head. "Thank good-

ness I don't fancy myself a reporter. You might've hurt my feelings."
He smiled, "That is, if I had any." The accent was particularly strong
today. Probably practiced it at home.

The waiter arrived and Crawley ordered a Kansas City skirt steak,
*well done,* and the waiter winced. He was gonna catch hell from the
chef. I didn't really want to break bread with Crawley but I'd been for-
getting too many meals lately. Might as well kill two birds.

"I'll have the filet," I said.

"And how would you like that cooked?" the waiter pleaded.

"Blue," I said. The waiter smiled.

"Disgusting," said Delwood Crawley.

He ordered another double Johnnie Black on the rocks and I ordered a glass of the house red to go with my steak.

I opened my notebook and ripped out the page where I'd written
the 'graph I wanted to insert in Crawley's column. I slid the page across
to him. He reached into his breast pocket and pulled out a leather case
and put on his reading glasses. He read the item.

"Oh my dear boy. Is *this* your attempt to approximate my style?"

"If it's not purple enough, I apologize," I said.

Crawley looked at me over the top of his glasses. "It's purple
enough. It is not *clever* enough."

"Just run it as I wrote it."

"Please," he scoffed. "*Whispers in Washington: A little bird—or
more accurately, a big hawk—tells me . . . ?* That is beyond dreadful.
I simply cannot allow it to run under my name. Not in its present
form." He hit me with a condescending smile. "I'll fix it up."

"You'll run it as I wrote it. Verbatim."

"I see. Sending a coded message, are we? Why not use the personal
ads like everybody else?"

I almost said *It has to be seen as news,* but I didn't want to offer him
the legitimacy. I said, "It can't be seen as coming from me."

The waiter brought our drinks.

Crawley slid the paper aside and folded his glasses and put them on
top of the paper. He stubbed out his half-smoked cigarette and imme-

diately lit a fresh one. He'd once told me that the toxins in a cigarette become more concentrated as you smoke it down—that by smoking only the first half of each cigarette, he could smoke three packs a day and keep the health risks negligible.

That was Delwood Crawley all over. The guy thought he could outsmart cancer.

He said, "Tell me, what sort of trouble are you in this time?"

"I don't think so."

"Now my feelings *are* hurt," he mocked. Another serpent smile. "Don't you trust me?"

"Not as far as I can throw a piano."

"All right then. If you refuse to share anything juicy and you insist that I run that tripe you penned, it's only fair that you pay for my dinner."

"Deal. Let's move on."

I lit a cigarette of my own, fully planning to smoke it all the way to the filter. But the steaks arrived and I stubbed it out after a couple of drags.

Crawley made a face when I cut into the meat and blood leaked onto the plate. He gestured with his fork, "Well, it fits you, anyway." He took a bite of his gray, overcooked steak, chewed for a long time. "This latest murder of yours was particularly gruesome."

I knew he'd bring it up and now he had. But I hadn't expected him to call it murder.

"Self-defense," I said.

"I'm sure the barbarians on the police force were content with that explanation but it didn't appear that way to me." He said it with a smile, of course.

He was goading me. There was no way it could've looked any other way. I cut off another piece of meat, ate it.

"Didn't know you were there," I said.

"I saw the security video from the mall."

"Who showed it to you?"

"Come now, you don't actually believe that I would reveal a source.

In any event, something as titillating as that is always bound to find its way out of police evidence."

Titillating. Strange word choice. Probably said a lot about Crawley.

"Anyhow, the footage is being leaked to television outlets." He dabbed at his mouth with a white linen napkin. "I should think it'll be all over the telly by tomorrow. Perhaps even later this evening."

In my mind I saw Jill watching television. Watching me kill a man. *Goddamn.* I drank some wine. *Take it easy, Dudgeon. Just get up to Jill's place before the nine o'clock news . . .*

"It's been edited down to thirty seconds," he said, "and only long shots, but it's clear enough. It appeared to me that you acted quite deliberately indeed. I suppose how it will appear to the average television viewer is dependent upon which parts they show and how the newscasters spin it . . ."

I ate some more steak as he talked. The steak was excellent a minute ago. Now I couldn't taste it at all.

"I don't suppose," said Crawley, "that they'll show the part where the man's head hits the floor and everything spills out. As I said, bloody gruesome . . . too grisly for the evening news, I'd wager." He cut off a piece of meat and chewed it happily. He was enjoying the hell out of this.

My phone vibrated. I left the table and stepped into the hallway. The phone's little screen read: FBI HQ.

I answered and Special Agent Holborn said, "I have an urgent message for you: go visit your client."

I glanced at my watch: 6:12. "Now?"

"He's expecting you at seven."

"I don't understand. Who—"

"I don't understand, either. And I'm not particularly happy about serving as your secretary. That was the message that I've been told to deliver. I've delivered it."

"*Who* told you?"

"I'm not at liberty to say."

"Oh, come on, Holborn . . ."

"The call came from National Headquarters. I wasn't invited to ask questions. Gotta go." The phone went dead in my ear.

Back at the table I said, "Something's come up. Your deadline's eight?"

"Eight o'clock, never changes," said Crawley.

"Hold the piece until you hear from me. I'll call you before eight. If I don't call, trash it."

Crawley drained the last of his scotch. "Very well. But must you really play it for such high drama?"

# CHAPTER THIRTY-TWO

**A**t 6:47 Isaac Richmond opened the door and I stepped inside. He didn't say anything, just closed the door and led me into his study. This time he didn't sit at the coffee table. He took the power position—the tall leather chair behind his desk. He didn't offer me a seat. It wasn't to my advantage to stand before him like a soldier under his command, so I sat anyway.

"Why have you been avoiding me?" His tension was palpable. And contagious.

"Our agreement was that I report to you biweekly," I said. "It hasn't been two weeks since my last visit."

His face flushed. "I made it very clear that I was buying sixty days of your life." And his voice was getting louder. "If I call, you answer. And if I tell you to report, *goddamn it,* you report."

"I've been a little busy," I said. "Perhaps you've seen the news."

Richmond shot to his feet and stabbed the air between us with his index finger. "You're fucking right I've seen the goddamn news! And I want a full explanation."

This was a very different Isaac Richmond than I'd seen previously and I didn't intend to give him anything until I learned why.

"Full explanation," I said. "Man tried to kill me. I killed him instead."

"Is that supposed to be funny?" Stabbing the air again.

"I didn't find it funny at all," I said. "Why don't you stop pointing at me, sit down, and tell me what's got you so riled."

Richmond sat. His mouth tightened, twitched. "The man was not trying to kill you." Quiet anger now. "I sent him to pick you up and bring you here."

The words came back on me like a distant echo: *Ray Dudgeon . . . You're coming with me.* I knew in an instant that it was true. I didn't want to believe it.

"He cut me," I said.

"After you scalded him."

"He chased me with a knife," I said.

"No, he did not. I've seen the police report. He sheathed his knife. His hands were empty when you threw him to his death." Richmond fixed me with a hard look, waiting for an answer.

I said, "Okay. But. He approached me with a knife in his hand. I simply defended myself. What the hell would you do if a man pulled a knife on you in a parking garage?"

Richmond looked away, let out a long breath. "Much the same, probably." When he looked at me again, the anger had receded into the background. "What a goddamn mess."

I said, "The knife was unnecessary. Why not just ask me to come see you?"

"I told him you'd been avoiding me, that you wouldn't even take my calls. Told him not to give you the option of refusal."

"Poor judgment on both your parts." I wasn't about to give him even an inch on this.

"I didn't tell him to use a knife. I thought he'd bully you, verbally."

"I don't bully well."

Richmond's mouth twitched once. "So I've heard." He picked up the telephone receiver, pressed a button, said, "Gentlemen, come in here a minute." He held up a hand to cut off my question and cradled the phone.

The door opened and two men entered.

The DHS agents. I felt dizzy, like the earth's axis had just shifted.

The taller one gave me a curt nod and I managed a nod back at him. The shorter one didn't even look at me.

Richmond said, "You're surprised," and I turned to face him.

"Little bit, yeah."

"I'll explain. Wouldn't have been necessary, but things have gotten out of hand and standard operating procedure no longer applies." He had all of his composure back now. He was Colonel Isaac Richmond, leader of men. "In short, this is the lay of the land: What I told you before was true. My daughter was murdered and I was uneasy about the speed with which the police cleared the case so I made a few calls to friends in Washington."

"These guys?"

"Their superiors."

"What agency? 'Cause it sure as hell ain't DHS."

He didn't answer me.

"What agency?" I repeated.

"Not relevant. My contacts were former clients in the intelligence community. They didn't know if Joan's murder was engineered by Hawk River but they had an interest in finding out. So they contracted me to coordinate the operation. These two gentlemen, and the man you killed, were sent to assist under my direction."

I felt like a rube. "Jesus," I said, "I can't believe I fell for your grieving father routine and I've been working for the *fucking* government the entire time."

The taller guy behind me said, "Your patriotism is noted."

Without turning I said, "You power monkeys use the Constitution for toilet paper, so skip it. You couldn't *spell* patriotism."

"Enough," said Isaac Richmond. "I've spent my entire life protecting this country from enemies foreign and domestic—I will not be lectured. From a legal standpoint, you've been working for me, not the government."

"A fine distinction at best," I said.

"Get over it," said Richmond.

*He's right, Dudgeon. Focus on what's in front of you . . .*

Still I burned with anger. I pressed it down and focused on what Richmond was saying . . .

". . . hiring you was not my first choice, believe me. But it was the best choice we had, given the circumstances."

"Circumstances being the government wanted to know if Hawk River was behind Joan's murder, but they couldn't be seen investigating. When you called your friends, they had the perfect cover. Getting me to do your legwork solidified the cover story and preserves deniability for your client. A father hiring a private eye to look into the death of his daughter? Who would question that? No reason to suspect a government connection."

"Very good. I'm impressed." He didn't sound impressed.

"But this isn't a true investigation," I said. "If they need deniability, then this is a containment operation."

"Potentially. Depending on what we learn."

"Let's say it does become a containment op. The final task of which is my death, if they really want to be sure of containment. Wouldn't that be the logical endgame?"

"Don't be stupid. Of course not. If the operation had gone as planned, you never would've known anything about it."

"But you're telling me now."

The taller man at the back of the room spoke again. This time I turned to face him. "Whatever you want to believe, Mr. Dudgeon, we are not in the business of murdering innocent Americans. Our operation has national security implications and we will do whatever is necessary to protect its secrecy. But as long as you aren't planning to expose the operation's existence, then you have no reason to fear for your personal safety." His tone was radically different from when they'd braced me in the bar. They'd sent their genuine tough guy—

their action man—to bring me in, and I'd killed him. I'd gotten lucky as hell and I knew it, but they didn't.

So the tough guy talk was out, but the intimidation was now in even greater force than before.

I turned in my chair and said to Richmond, "I have no intention of exposing your operation. I'll send you a check for the balance of what you've paid me." Pushed my chair back and stood up. "Been nice knowing you."

I turned to leave. Stopped. The government guys were aiming their handguns at my chest.

Behind me Richmond said, "Sit down, Mr. Dudgeon. We're not through with you yet."

What choice did I have? I sat.

"Let there be no misunderstanding," he said, "you are working on this case until I tell you that you are no longer working on this case. And I don't give a rat's ass if you don't like working for the government. You will share with me everything you've learned, and then you will go out and learn some more. Once this operation comes to a conclusion, you will go on with your life. And you will not reveal the existence of this operation to the press, the Chicago police, the FBI, or your neighbor's cat. Understood?"

I understood. I understood that I'd been played by professionals. I understood that I held no cards in this game, had no leverage, was way out of my league. I understood that simply walking away from the table was not an option. I understood just fine.

I said, "I'm told that the video from the shopping mall is being leaked to the press. It didn't come from me, but it'll keep this story going for another news cycle or two."

"That doesn't concern us. The police will not learn anything about the man you killed. His prints will not match anything in a database. He had no identity and we have no need to correct the record of how it went down. You just stick to your story—you don't know who he was or why he was trying to kill you."

"I can do that." *It beats saying I killed a man for asking me to come to a meeting.*

"And I think you'll find that your friend Terry Green has suddenly lost interest in the story." He didn't elaborate and I figured I'd get the details from Terry later. "Now that we're clear on the ground rules, we'll put the past behind us and move forward. Let's hear your report."

So I told him what I'd learned so far. Most of it, anyway. Did my best to minimize Amy's part in it. Left out the Web sites that she and Steven had made and Blake Sten's visit to her home following the murder. Told him that both she and I *suspected* Steven was faking his illness and *suspected* that he'd gotten something off Hawk River's computers that Joan had intended to share with the congressional committee.

Maybe guys in the intelligence community operate on hunches more often than they claim, but for whatever reason, Richmond didn't ask me to provide rationale for my suppositions.

He just said, "I expect you to follow up on these suspicions and bring me what you learn—without delay."

Then I told him about Tim Dellitt's visit to my office and Blake Sten's threats and the assault on Ernie Banks. I explained my visit to the FBI in sketchy terms—a few half-truths and a couple of lies. Told him that I'd tried to get Holborn invested so I could call on the FBI for help if Sten's threats escalated. And I told him that Holborn wasn't much interested in what I had to say.

Richmond was a smart man and I don't think he fully believed me. But he was fully committed to his own objective and he sifted through my verbal report for the nuggets that would lead him to that objective.

"Your suspicions are supported by Hawk River's attempts at intimidation," he said, "so we will proceed on the assumption that there is some evidence—computer file or whatever—still floating around out there. Until now your task has been to learn the truth about Joan's murder. That remains a goal. But moving forward, your *primary* task is now to locate that evidence before Blake Sten does. And bring it to us."

Some grieving father. I nodded, "Got it. Justice for your daughter runs a distant second to covering the government's ass, right, *Colonel*?"

"You're dismissed."

I stood up. "No wonder Joan was so unhappy."

His face flushed again. He said to the government spooks, "Step outside, gentlemen."

Richmond looked at the desk blotter for a while after they left, then his mouth twitched three times. He straightened his spine and looked up at me and there was a deep pain in his eyes that couldn't be faked.

"You little prick," he said. "I have given my entire adult life to my country. Sacrificed the normal family life that most men enjoy. Sacrificed any real chance of happiness . . . for me or for my daughter. But because of what I do, people like you have the luxury to piss and moan about the Constitution. And when my government calls, I answer, regardless of personal feelings." He took in a deep breath, let it out. "If you don't see a grieving father, Mr. Dudgeon, you're not looking close enough. Now get the hell out of my house."


I hit the road and was surprised to learn that it was only 8:05. It felt hours later. I quickly looped a few blocks to be sure no one was following me, then hit Lake Shore Drive and stepped on the gas. I could still make it to Jill's place before the nine o'clock news, with time to spare.

I pulled out my cell phone and called Delwood Crawley at the *Chronicle* and got his voice mail. I'd just missed his deadline for tomorrow's paper but now I wanted to be sure he didn't run it the next day, either. Or any other day. So I told his voice mail that the piece was dead and should stay that way.

I exited at Belmont, cruised slowly past Jill's building. The lights in her apartment were on. I turned left on Broadway, cut across Oakdale and pulled into Binny's, bought a bottle of red wine and a pack of minty gum. Got back in my car, but didn't put it in gear.

My mind raced and zigzagged around like a ferret on speed. Understandable after the meeting I'd just had, but I needed a very different headspace to approach Jill. And I needed it fast. My watch said 8:43.

I dug around in the CD case, pulled out Keith Jarrett's *The Köln Concert*. It had been a long time since I'd allowed myself to play it. It was the soundtrack of happier times with Jill. I inserted the disc, rolled down my window, and lit a cigarette.

I closed my eyes, listened to the music, stretched my neck, and felt some of the tension dissipate. Remembered lying with Jill on her couch, bodies intertwined, drinking wine and making out, Keith Jarrett on the stereo. I let the image linger for a while.

My watch said: 8:50.

*Now or never.*

I stubbed out my cigarette, grabbed the small bottle of mouthwash from the glove box, took a swig, and spat it out the window. Tossed a few pieces of gum into my mouth and chewed. Took the gun off my hip and locked it in the glove box. Pulled out of Binny's parking lot and drove the few blocks to Jill's place.

Fate was kind and offered me a parking spot directly in front of the yellow brick courtyard apartment building where Jill lived. Two stone lions sat on pedestals at the courtyard entrance. Sam and Florence. Jill and I had named them in honor of Sam Spade and Florence Nightingale—archetypal figures of our chosen professions. It was the silly kind of thing that couples falling in love do after a romantic dinner and a bottle of wine.

We named them on our third date, and after that we often greeted them by name as we passed.

Sam and Florence. They were us.

I looked at them now, thinking *They're cast in stone and rooted to their respective pedestals, ten feet of empty space between them. Might as well be ten miles. They couldn't close that gap if they wanted to.*

Were they us?

Time to find out.

# CHAPTER THIRTY-THREE

**I** **pressed the doorbell and the exterior door** buzzed open without my having to identify myself, like Jill was expecting company. I walked down the hallway, my heart pounding against the inside of my rib cage. Knocked on the apartment door. Took a breath. The door opened.

A woman I'd never seen before said, "You're not pizza."

"No, I'm not pizza. I'm Ray Dudgeon. I'm looking for—"

"Oh, *you're* Ray." Big smile. "I'm Sandra. Come on in, Jill's just in the bathroom."

Sandra seemed a bit tipsy. An empty wine bottle stood next to a full ashtray on the coffee table. Two wineglasses, mostly empty. A suitcase on the floor and a blanket on the couch.

The television was off.

"Jill's been letting me crash here while I look for a place, and helping me drown my sorrows." She touched my arm, leaned forward, and spoke in a conspiratorial tone. "And I've been helping her drown hers. Just so you know, I'm on *your* side. No use both of us making the same mistake."

"Thanks," I said.

"Don't mention it, I'm always on the side of true love." She suppressed a giggle as the bathroom door opened and Jill stepped into the room.

No engagement ring on her finger.

"He's not the pizza," said Sandra.

Jill stared at me with her mouth open for a few seconds. "No, he's not."

"You just gonna stand there?" said Sandra.

Jill walked forward like there might be land mines hidden in the floorboards, stopped a few feet from me. Just out of reach.

I said, "I didn't know you had a houseguest. I just, I know that you called earlier and I need to talk to you . . ." Awkward as hell, with Sandra staring at us. Would've been awkward anyway, but this was ridiculous.

"I see. Um, perhaps you can ring me tomorrow . . ."

*Sure, that'll be great. I'll just give you a call after you've watched me kill someone on television . . .*

I said, "No. I really need to speak with you right now." I stepped forward and took her hand in mine. "Just come with me. Don't ask why." I held eye contact and waited for an answer.

Sandra broke in with, "Oh, for God's sake, just go with him! This is the most romantic thing I've ever seen."

"Will you shut up?" Jill shot a glare at her friend.

I took a chance and walked toward the door and didn't let go of Jill's hand, silently praying that she would walk with me.

She did, and we left without another word to Sandra or each other.

We were in the car, a few blocks south on Halsted when Jill broke the silence.

"I've had half a bottle of wine on an empty stomach. Otherwise I might've said no. Your timing was perfect."

She didn't know the half of it.

I said, "Sandra seems nice."

"She is. Going through a rough time, though."

"Just left her husband."

"Yes."

"Decent enough guy, but it wasn't true love," I said.

"She told you all that in two minutes?"

I nodded, "Not in so many words but, yeah, she told me that. Sounds like a cautionary tale, if you ask me."

Jill reached over and touched my face. "Not now. We can talk later. Right now I really just want to pretend for a little while." She reached forward and turned the music up a bit. Then reclined her seat slightly, pulled her knees up, and put her feet on the dash.

"Okay," I said. "What are we pretending?"

She closed her eyes. "I want to pretend that everything is fine between us. I want to pretend that I'm not involved with another man. That nobody tried to kill you yesterday . . . that you aren't followed by the shadow of death everywhere you go . . . that you're going to live to be an old man. I just want to pretend that we have a future."

It felt like a punch in the gut. I pulled the car over to the curb, stopped, turned in my seat to face her.

"Spend the night with me and I'll pretend whatever you want."

And then we were on each other, grasping and stroking and kissing, her tongue like fire on mine, her hand pulling the back of my head, pulling me into her.

When we came up for air, Jill fixed me with a wild look and said, "You better get me to a bed before I come to my senses."

I put the car in gear and hit the gas. My apartment was a good twenty minutes away through traffic.

Joan Richmond's place was only ten blocks.


I dug the HM Nichols keychain from my pocket and got the door open and we practically tumbled into the place, tearing at each other's clothes like a couple of teenagers. I kicked the door shut, reached out an arm, felt for the dead bolt and locked it as Jill kissed me again. We knocked a few things over on the way to the bedroom and left a trail of clothes in our wake.

What happened next was beyond intense. It rose from yearning to reckless to frenzied, infused with a manic passion that bordered on frightening.

As we approached the apex, Jill said it. Said it twice. Then again, and again until it became like a rhythmic pleading mantra:

*I love you. I love you. I love you, I love you, I love you . . .*

Jill cried for a minute after she climaxed, the way some women do, triggered by the sudden release of built-up tension. I held her as she cried, stroked her hair and told her she was beautiful.

Then we lay together without speaking, me on my back, Jill nestled in beside me, the full length of her body against mine. I'd spent some time propped up on my elbows and now my shoulder was killing me but I didn't want to get up for drugs so I tried to tune out the pain and focus my attention on other senses. The pungent smell of our love-making mingling with her perfume, the sweet and sour taste of her still on my lips, the soft texture of her hair between my fingers.

A perfect moment. I wanted to live in it forever.

Jill snuggled in a little tighter. Her index finger traced meaningless patterns across my chest. But something subtle changed in the room. We lay the same way, breathed at the same pace, but the mood was different. Jill was no longer in the moment. She was *thinking about things.*

"Think a little louder," I said. "I can almost hear you."

She tugged gently on my chest hair. "It's gone a lot more gray this year."

"Time marches on."

"I think it may be marching a little faster for you than most," she said. "How long has it been?"

I thought back to the last time Jill had seen me without a shirt. The night I'd shown up at her door bruised and bleeding. Not the most romantic of evenings, but that was the last time.

"Nine months, two weeks," I said.

"It was almost all brown, now it's mostly gray. That's pretty fast."

I looked down at my chest. The hair on my head had gone a little more gray this year, but not enough that you'd call it salt-and-pepper. Not yet. But my chest hair was now decidedly more salt than pepper.

She was right—it had happened fast. And I hadn't even noticed it.

"Lack of sex," I said. "Stick with me, kid, we may even be able to reverse the process."

Jill smiled sweetly, kissed me on the lips. She propped up on one elbow, ran her finger along the line of stitches on my left arm, her face now serious. "Six inches higher, he'd have filleted your fish." Her finger ran up my arm to the old tattoo of a mean-looking fish that had been a present to myself on my eighteenth birthday, then back down to the stitches. "Does it hurt?"

"Not much."

She looked at me like she was trying to decide something, but her piercing blue eyes offered no clue what it was, just that it was major.

"I almost hung up before the beep when I called," she said. "But I couldn't. Part of me wanted you to hear the hang-up on your machine, wanted you to know that I'd called." She sat back against the headboard, pulled the sheet up, covering her breasts. "God, I'm so confused . . ."

I didn't know what to say and didn't want to say the wrong thing. I sat up, took her face in my hands, and kissed her softly. "What we just did . . . that wasn't pretend. That was real. And that could be our life together."

"Sure, until some guy cuts your throat instead of your arm."

*Shit, here we go again . . .*

"Yes, Jill, until then. And that could happen a week from now or a year, or ten years, or never. In the meantime, you'll be spending your life with the man you love, instead of hiding in something safe. Right?" I could hear my voice rising and anger seeping into my tone. "And excuse me for pointing out the obvious, but if the safe choice were making you so fucking happy, you wouldn't be naked in a bed with me right now."

"Please don't get that way. I can't handle it."

*Easy, Dudgeon . . . don't do the same old thing again . . . don't blow it now . . .*

"Sorry, I'm just frustrated by the argument." I took a breath and tried a new tack. "Look, you once told me that you might be able to accept it if you understood why I do what I do. And I brushed you off. That was wrong. I don't want to do that again. So give me a chance to tell you."

Jill sighed, "Do me a favor, get my cigarettes? They're in my purse."

I left the room, searched the wreckage in the living room, found her purse on the floor, next to an overturned lamp. I picked up the purse, pulled out a thin paperback—the same book of poetry she'd bought when I saw her last—grabbed her cigarettes and lighter, returned the book to the purse and the purse to the floor.

I hadn't smoked in Joan's apartment before. It didn't smell like a smoker's place and I hadn't seen any ashtrays and, even though Joan was dead I hadn't wanted to smoke there. I got a bread plate from the kitchen to use as an ashtray and filled a glass with wine.

*Make it a conversation, not an argument,* I reminded myself on the way back to the bedroom.

"I don't mean to change the subject," said Jill, "but I can't concentrate until I know where I am. It's been bugging me." She gestured at the floral-print sheets and smiled. "I'm guessing a woman lives here, unless you've really gotten in touch with your feminine side."

"I'm looking after it for a client."

"A PI house sitter?" She held up a hand in apology. "Wait, it's none of my business. I'm certainly in no position to be getting jealous."

"I've never met the woman who lives here," I said. "Really. She's away, and her father's a client. I'm doing a gig for him and the place is just kind of a fringe benefit, a free place to stay. My apartment's in boxes, I'm moving next month."

"Where to?"

"Don't know yet. Maybe Uptown." With a light tone I added, "In a perfect world, I'd be moving into your place." It fell flat and Jill just looked away and dragged on her cigarette. "Right, one step at a time," I said.

"Tell me why I should be okay with you working in a job where people try to kill you, Ray."

"First, people don't usually try to kill me, so—"

"I've barely known you a year and it's happened on two separate cases."

"Fair enough. Bad year. But if nothing else, it proves that I'm pretty good at staying alive." Another smile went unreciprocated.

*Not the time for banter, you idiot . . .*

"All right. I'm not going to lie to you and say it'll never happen again. I can't make that promise." I lit a cigarette for myself. "I've done a lot of thinking, and I've come to accept that this is part of who I am. I can't change that. But I can change in other ways. I can get better at the whole communication thing." I dragged on my cigarette, held out my hand for the wineglass and drank some, handed it back. "Truth is, I'm still trying to figure out why the job has become so central . . . part of it is . . . for instance, I'm on a case right now—"

"The one where a guy just tried to kill you."

"Yes. And there's a woman who's in a lot of trouble—"

"The woman who lives here," said Jill.

"Different woman. And this woman has a little girl. Both innocent people, caught between some very bad people. Truth is, without my help she won't survive the mess she's in."

"And for some reason you need to save innocent people from bad people?"

"Well, not exactly. Sort of. It's an extreme example. But sometimes this job gives me a chance to stand up for a few underdogs." *And stand up to a few bullies.* But I didn't say that out loud. "And that's something I need to do."

"There are other ways to stand up for underdogs."

"Yeah, but I work better on the edges of the system. I pretty much have to be on my own, I don't really fit in . . . I'm not good with the politics and compromises and corruption. A lot of people can dismiss that stuff but it eats at me. Killed my career as a reporter. I'd make a lousy lawyer, and you wouldn't feel any better if I were a cop, which I'd also be lousy at . . . You could say I have a problem with authority . . ."

The explanation had started lame and was falling apart, going in circles. *Just tell her the truth . . .* "And there's more to it than that," I said.

"What?"

I stubbed out my cigarette.

She put her hand on my knee. "I need to know."

*You've got nothing to lose . . .* "I have a lot of anger inside."

"News flash," said Jill with a wry smile.

"Okay, obviously. Right. But the job purges it, I don't know why. It eases the pressure. And I need that, too."

"And if you couldn't ease the pressure, what would happen?"

"I don't know. Look, I'm still trying to figure it out. I'm telling you what I know so far." *But not everything . . .* "And I'll get better at it, I promise, but you can't expect it all at once. Okay?"

I moved beside her with my back against the headboard, reached out, and drew her close. She rested her head on my shoulder and her hand on my chest.

After a minute I said, "The man who attacked me yesterday, you know what happened, right?"

"I know what they said on the radio. And, God help me, I read Terry's article in the *Chronicle* this morning. I didn't want to read it, but I had to. That's when I called."

"Okay, so you know the details. Thing is, some asshole in the police evidence room has leaked the mall security video to the press. So it'll be on television, probably for a couple of days."

"And?"

"I don't know," I said. "You know what happened, but seeing it is different. I guess I'm afraid it'll change the way you feel about me."

She didn't respond to that. She said, "When you killed that man . . . how did you feel?"

"Scared."

"No, I mean after you killed him. How did you feel about it?"

"I didn't feel anything," I said. "No wait, that's not true . . ." I refilled the wineglass, drank some, and passed it to Jill. "I felt a lot of things, some of them contradictory. I felt repulsed, sickened by . . . well, the guy fell a long distance and, you know, it wasn't nice to look at. So there was that. And I felt angry as hell that the bastard attacked me, put me in that position. Kind of righteously indignant, if that makes any sense. And worried, you know, that the cops would find a way to hang a charge on me for it. Eventually I just felt empty."

We sat in silence and I thought about the one feeling I'd left out.

*I felt powerful.*

Jill passed the wine and I drank some. I said, "And then I thought of you and how this might kill any chance for us, and I felt . . . despair."

Jill said, "I'm not going to watch the news. I don't need to see it."

And then she kissed me.


Sometimes when you dream, you know things that aren't apparent onscreen. In my dream, Jill and I were married, for example. And we had a ten-year-old daughter. The girl wasn't in the dream; I just knew that she existed and knew her age. Maybe she was in her room sleeping, I don't know.

Jill and I were in a bed. The bed had the same floral-print sheets as Joan Richmond's bed, but it wasn't Joan's bed or Joan's apartment. It was our bed, in our own place.

It was a sex dream. We were in the sixty-nine position, Jill on top.

My excitement woke me and for a few seconds I didn't know what was happening, thought I was caught somewhere between the dream and reality. Then I realized that I was awake and Jill had my penis in her mouth.

Greatest wake-up call ever invented.

I shifted my position and made it mutual.

After it was over, we didn't say anything. Just kissed and hugged and purred at each other for a while and fell asleep embracing.

The sky outside the bedroom window was still dark, but the light in my heart was that of a thousand suns.

# CHAPTER THIRTY-FOUR

**W**hen I woke up in the morning, Jill was not beside me. I slipped into my boxers, trudged out to the living room. Her clothes and purse were gone. I looked at my watch: 8:15. She'd be at work by now.

A note lay on the kitchen counter.

> Ray,
>
> I watched the news this morning in the living room while you slept. I know that I told you I didn't need to see it, but it turns out I did need to.
>
> It was horrible.
>
> I'm not saying that you were wrong and I understand that you had to protect yourself, but the way you pushed that man over the railing was just so vicious. On television, you looked like a completely different man than the one I know. A stranger.
>
> The man I saw on the television scares me, and I'm not sure I want to be near him.

And yet I realize that he is you.

I do love you. But I don't know if I can handle the violent life you've chosen. I don't think I can.

Thank you for pretending with me. That part was beautiful.

Jill

Under the note was another piece of paper. It was a page torn out of the book of poetry Jill had been reading. On the page, a short poem titled "Onions," by someone named Bryan Owen.

It read:

> *She said I'm like an onion –*
> *I had so many hidden layers.*
> *I told her that*
> *if she stopped peeling*
> *she wouldn't cry so much.*

*Fuck.*

There was an e-mail on my office computer from Delwood Crawley. The subject line was: *Couldn't resist.*

The message said:

> Made a call to check what congressional hearings are underway. Your item said "hawk" and "river" and "Aurora" so it was easy enough to decipher. And far too delicious to resist. I made it the lead item in this morning's column. Sorry, old boy. Nothing personal.
>
> —Delwood

This day was getting better by the minute.

I picked up the phone and called Vince on his cell. All was quiet on the Amy Zhang front. They were getting along fine and Amy was kicking his ass at Scrabble for the fourth straight game. I told him I'd check back in a few hours.

Then I dialed Special Agent Holborn at the FBI.

An hour later Holborn entered my office, sat in one of my client chairs, and gestured at the full bottle of beer on the desk in front of me. Or maybe he was gesturing at the empty one beside it. Then he took a long look at his watch, although I'm quite certain he already knew the time.

"Oh look," he said, "it's ten-thirty." Another glance at the beer bottle. "In the morning."

I decided not to tell him that breakfast had been a slug of cold vodka from Joan Richmond's freezer. I lifted my beer in a toast. "Top o' the mornin' to ya."

"Having a bad day?"

"With skills like that, you ought to be a detective," I said.

"You don't seem drunk," he said.

"I'm not." Which was true. "I'm just trying to keep my head from exploding." I took a swig of beer. "How's your head these days, Agent Holborn?"

"I don't usually make house calls, Ray. What's on your mind?"

"Influence, corruption, interagency clout. How far your head office would go to do favors for their friends in the intelligence community. Things like that."

"In English, please."

"Let's say I brought you evidence that Hawk River had Joan Richmond killed to keep her from testifying to Congress. Circumstantial, but strongly suggestive evidence."

"Let's say."

"And let's say I brought you a witness who is being extorted into silence by Blake Sten."

"Yes . . ."

"Number one—could you get said witness and a child into the Federal Witness Protection Program? Number two—would you actually follow through with the investigation, or would you get a call from National Headquarters telling you to spike it?"

Holborn made a face that suggested resentment of my implication. "I can't answer number one. I'd have to meet with your witness and hear her story."

"Her?"

"I'm not an idiot. Steven Zhang's widow. That's who we're talking about, is it not?"

"Okay."

"Okay, I'd have to meet with her, hear her story. But if I thought she was credible and if it was clear that Sten's actions were on behalf of Hawk River, then yes, we could probably get her into the program."

"And number two? Would you be allowed to follow through?"

"What makes you think I wouldn't?"

"Recent history."

"Meaning?"

"Meaning, when your superiors in Washington instructed you to pass that message to me, they were doing the bidding of our DHS thugs with the phony license plates. Only they're not DHS."

"What are they?"

"I was hoping you could tell me," I said. "Here's what I know: They work for a federal agency that's part of the intel community—"

"Hardly narrows it down."

"An agency," I continued, "that sometimes makes use of mercenaries, on a classified basis. An agency that has occasionally contracted out work to a retired military intelligence colonel, Isaac Richmond."

"That's all you've got?"

"Pretty much. They pointed their guns at me yesterday. I surfed around the Net this morning looking at guns and my best guess, they were Sig Sauer 228s. That narrow it down?"

"Current flavor of the month for CIA," said Holborn. "But also popular with DIA, and a million other intel guys. So, not really."

"Which agency would have the most influence at the Bureau?" I said.

"Wait, you're barking up the wrong tree. The intelligence community is far bigger than you think. Beyond CIA and DIA, each branch of the military has its own intel division, as does the Department of Energy. And Treasury. There's the NSA, NRO, NGA, DEA, INR . . ."

"I get it."

"Oh, I don't think you do. I'm not even close to done—there's ODNI, within which you'll find the ISE, NCTC, NIC, NCIX, SSC. Of course, the Coast Guard, which is now part of DHS, has their own division. And we've got ours at FBI. And then—"

"Stop please, you're giving me a headache."

"You already have a headache."

"Well, you're making it worse."

"I'm making a point," said Holborn. "You're not going to know who these guys are, and even if they tell you who they are, you're still not going to know. Hell, you could see their paychecks and still not know. The intel community is not just huge, it's interconnected. A multiheaded beast. Like Typhon."

"Or King Ghidorah," I said.

"Not enough heads," said Holborn. "And unlike Ghidorah, Typhon would eat Godzilla's lunch."

"Okay," I said, "*Typhon the Multiheaded Beast*. Tell me about Typhon."

"When I first started with the Bureau, one of my trainers—old guy, had over twenty years in the intel division—told me a story. Back in the late '60s, early '70s, he was sent to work at HUD."

"Housing and Urban Development?"

"The very same. See, the Bureau was tracking domestic terrorism in a big way. Remember, this was the time of the Weather Underground, Symbionese Liberation Army, and God knows how many other wing nuts blowing up mailboxes and robbing banks and shooting cops. He was assigned to the Black Panther Party, and the Panthers did a lot of recruiting and organizing in the housing projects. So this FBI agent became a caseworker at HUD, visiting poor folks in the projects, making sure they were getting their benefits and sending their kids to school, that kind of thing. He worked at HUD for six years and only his direct superior knew he was FBI. His paychecks came from HUD, his income tax forms said HUD, his coworkers thought he was just another one of them. But the whole time, his *real* job was to be the FBI's eyes and ears in the projects."

"Why so cloak-and-dagger?"

"Paranoia, mostly. Comes with the job. One of the reasons I don't work intel. But in his case, it wasn't unreasonable. If word leaked to the Panthers, he'd have been a dead man. Anyway, that's just one example. When I was stationed at the Miami Division, I worked with a new guy. Junior field agent, right out of Quantico. Good guy. We worked together for three years, then he was reassigned to the intel division, sent overseas. Couple years later, he was killed in the line of duty somewhere in Eastern Europe. Only then did I learn that he was CIA, had been the whole time. Guy worked with me every day for three years, got the same paychecks I did. But he was never *really* FBI."

"Christ." I took a swig of beer.

"I'm telling you, in the world of intel, it's Alphabet Soup. CIA, FBI, DEA, whatever. You never really know who you're dealing with."

"Well, whoever these guys are, they work for my client. Actually, my client works for their superiors. Basically I've been sucked into some kind of officially nonexistent containment op."

"You ought to keep better company," said Holborn.

"Thanks for the hindsight. They suspect Joseph Grant and Blake Sten are behind the murder, and they're concerned that any airing of Hawk River's dirty laundry might lead back to some classified paramilitary operation that they'd just as soon not have known to the public. And more importantly, they do not want the existence of their operation exposed. Not to the press, not to Congress, and not to the FBI. They were not ambiguous on the subject."

"Uh-huh."

"Agent Holborn, I'm risking my life by telling you this. I need you to understand that."

Holborn sent me a smile that I think was supposed to be reassuring and said, "Go on."

"They knew I'd been to see you and they don't seem to mind if Sten gets nailed for the murder, but they would mind very much if the involvement of the government in a cover-up comes out. If you reveal what I've told you about that . . ."

"My focus is Hawk River," said Holborn. "Period. I don't give a crap about their containment operation."

"Good. But if I bring you a case and then their boss swings some clout with your boss, and the case gets shut down . . . I'll have Hawk River after me and no backup. Isaac Richmond and his Alphabet Soup guys won't risk the secrecy of their mission to step in and pull my ass out of the fire. See my problem?"

"Ray, I'm a cop. A damn good cop, if I do say so myself. If Hawk River is interfering with the oversight work of Congress, that is a crime of the highest order. If you bring me evidence, I will pursue it. Doesn't matter which agency these guys represent. They may have influence enough to pass messages through my superiors, but they don't have the clout to scuttle an investigation of something that serious. Nobody does."

"I'm sure you believe that, Agent Holborn. I'm just not sure you're right."

Holborn glanced at his watch and stood up. "You know you can't handle this alone or you wouldn't have called me here. Bring me the woman. Let me hear her story. We'll take it from there."

I nodded. "I'll talk to her, call you later."

Holborn nodded back. For two guys who didn't agree on much, we were nodding at each other an awful lot these days. He stopped with his hand on the office door, turned and said, "By the way, a couple of tough guys are casing the lobby downstairs."

"Shit. Alphabet Soup."

He shook his head. "They don't match the description you gave me."

"Oh?"

"These guys are both well over six feet. Look like they lift heavy weights for fun. Very short haircuts. And they have dead eyes."

"Soldier types?"

"Everything but the uniforms."

"You could've told me this when you arrived," I said.

Special Agent Holborn wrinkled his nose at me.

"I like to make a dramatic exit," he said.

# CHAPTER THIRTY-FIVE

**I called Terry and got his voice mail** and left a message suggesting we meet later for a drink. I wanted to hear his version of how he "lost interest" in the story, as Isaac Richmond had promised.

With a fresh pot of coffee for fuel, I took stock of the situation.

No doubt, I'd oversold my position to Holborn. I had the witness, but I didn't have the evidence and didn't know how to get it. But I needed the FBI invested in this mess, fast. And it was a mess.

On one hand I was under pressure from the Alphabet Soup guys to find the evidence against Hawk River. Not so they could prosecute Grant and Sten, but so they could bury the evidence and cover their asses. And if I were able to find the evidence for them, that would leave Amy Zhang as the last loose end for Blake Sten to tie off.

On the other hand, if I didn't find the evidence, the Alphabet Soup guys would go back to Washington empty-handed. And that might make *me* feel good but it would change nothing for Blake Sten.

Amy would still be a loose end worth tying off.

But . . . if I could find the evidence and get it to Holborn, and if Holborn could use it to bring down Hawk River, then Amy would get into Witness Protection. Holborn was willing to turn a blind eye to the Alphabet Soup guys' involvement, and they would go home unhappy but unexposed.

It was not an ideal solution, but it was a solution that kept Amy breathing and allowed Theresa to grow up with the one parent she had left.

I sat in my office drinking coffee and thinking about the different ways it could play out and how long it would be until the guys in the lobby came up for a visit. I thought about what I would say when they arrived.

I thought about calling Jill's apartment and leaving a message on her machine, and what a stupid idea that was. I thought about the bond we'd forged in bed the night before.

The sex had been primal, the connection between us transcendent.

How do you *unring* that bell?

I told myself to stop thinking about Jill and then I thought about her some more.

Two large figures appeared behind the frosted glass window of my office door. I unholstered my gun and put it on the desk blotter in front of me.

A knock on the door. Polite.

"Come in,"

They did. Holborn's description was perfect; these guys lifted heavy things for fun. They stepped to either side of the door and back-stepped once, putting the wall behind them. They scanned the room. It wasn't a particularly large room but they took their time with it.

The one who held his hand closer to his belt said, "That cop who was up here, he gone?" So Holborn had avoided the lobby on his way out, just to put these guys off balance. Nice of him. "Well?"

"No," I said. "He's hiding in the coat closet."

The other one looked in the coat closet. Careful. Then he stepped back to his previous position.

The talker said, "Show me your hands."

I lifted my hands, placed them on the desktop.

"With one finger, push your gun forward twelve inches, then lock your fingers together behind your head."

I hit the foot switch under my desk. The video camera hidden in my bookshelf started recording.

"I don't think so," I said. "The gun stays where it is, my hands stay on the desktop. If I go for it, you'll see. If you guys go for yours, I'll see. Most likely, we'll just have a conversation and everyone's hands will stay where they are."

We looked at each other for a while. The talker gave a sharp nod and his partner stepped out into the hallway.

Blake Sten and Joseph Grant entered the room. Sten carried what looked like a large black leather doctor's bag. He put the bag down on the corner of my desk, with a heavy thud. He opened the bag, looked into it for a few seconds, closed the bag.

Joseph Grant stepped forward, said, "When my father started Hawk River, do you know what we did for the U.S. military?" Nothing in his tone suggested stress.

"Laundry and Latrine," I said.

"That's right. L&L, they used to call it. Then he added dishwashing and peeling potatoes. All the grunt chores that even grunts shouldn't be wasting their time with in a war zone."

"Some people would argue that those grunt chores teach discipline and foster a sense of interdependence among the troops," I said.

"Stateside," said Joseph Grant. "During basic training. But if you haven't learned discipline and interdependence by the time you're in the shit, halfway round the world in some piss-ant country full of savages who want to kill you, then you are well and truly fucked. A soldier in-country should not be wasting his time on latrine duty. His time, and the taxpayer's money, are better spent killing the enemy and training to get better at killing the enemy."

"It's a good speech," I said. "Good sales pitch to lay on politicians and Pentagon brass."

"You bet it is. And it's true. You were never in the army, I don't expect you to know."

*I was in the KISS Army when I was a kid, does that count?* But of course I didn't give it voice. Then I auditioned, *You seem to be confusing me with someone who gives a shit.* Not much better.

I said, "I don't really care if your company peels potatoes and washes dishes for the military."

"But you don't think we should be carrying guns and engaging the enemy."

It wasn't exactly a question, so I didn't answer.

"Seriously," said Grant, "I want to know." Blake Sten and the talker stood watching my hands.

"What do you care what I think?"

"I'm curious to know how your mind works." He didn't say anything more, seemed willing to wait for an answer.

"All right, you got me," I said. "I don't really dig what you guys do. I think it drains skilled manpower and money from the military, and worse, it destroys accountability and subverts congressional oversight. I think, in the end, it makes our soldiers less safe and less effective. But it makes you rich and it makes a lot of politicians and generals rich. I get it. And I'm not trying to change it. So why are we having this conversation?"

Blake Sten stepped forward and dropped a newspaper on the desk, folded to reveal Delwood Crawley's "Chicago After Dark" column.

"Don't even pretend you weren't the source for this," said Grant.

"I wasn't the source for this," I said.

"Please . . ."

"But I think I know who was."

"That's pathetic."

"The guy who attacked me in the mall," I said. "I think he was the source. More accurately, his superiors in Washington."

I paused to give Grant an opening but he didn't speak. Just stood looking at me like I wasn't there.

"Your clients in Washington are unhappy with your ham-fisted efforts to stop Joan Richmond from testifying to Congress. They believe you've acted in a way that has increased their risk of exposure. And they've decided to shut you down, cauterize this whole thing and stop the information bleed." I watched Grant closely as I planted the seed. He was very good, but something in his eyes and something about his stillness told me that the seed was landing on fertile ground. I had to be careful. Such a seed is a fragile thing; if I pushed it too far, I'd crush it. And the pinkish color of Blake Sten's burn scar was deepening as I trashed the quality of his work.

I figured I'd said enough.

I closed with, "It had to be them. Why the hell else would they send someone to kill me?"

Grant's face changed subtly, "Nice try." He put on a smile, but the seed had now been planted. I could only hope that it would germinate later. He glanced at Blake Sten and they sat in the client chairs across the desk.

"Blake communicated our position to you quite clearly," said Grant, "but we obviously underestimated your persistence. Or overestimated your intelligence. Either way," a glance at the newspaper on the desk, "you will now hand over the evidence you've found."

"Mr. Grant, if I were the source of that story—which I'm not— wouldn't the evidence already be in the hands of the congressional OGR committee?"

"We have friends on the committee. If they'd received anything, we'd know. So that leaves you." Ever the pro, Grant gave away nothing by his tone or expression.

"Okay, so they haven't received anything. But I haven't found anything, either. Whatever you're looking for, I don't have it and I haven't had it."

"Bad news for you then." A quick nod to Blake Sten, who pulled a notebook from his pocket and began reading.

"Terry Green. Reporter at the *Chronicle*. Lives at 1725 West Winnemac. Wife named Angela . . ." He flipped the page. "Vince Cosimo, former driver for Johnny Grieco, now works for you part-time. Lives at 3794 North Lakewood. Divorced, no kids. Drives a blue Ford Escort . . ." Flipped the page again. I could see where this was heading and felt the muscles in my neck tightening.

"Your grandfather, Willis Dudgeon. Widower. Runs a charter fishing boat out of Golden Isles Marina. Lives at 23 Austin Avenue, Saint Simons Island, Georgia. Drives a GMC pickup . . ." He flipped the page. My heart was now beating loud and fast.

"Your girlfriend, Jill Browning. ER nurse at Rush. Lives at 540 West Belmont, apartment 3 . . ."

*In one smooth action, I can shoot Joseph Grant in the face . . . maybe also get to Sten before the guy at the back of the room blows my brains out . . . or maybe not.*

". . . Jill has a younger sister, Grace, housewife, husband named Peter Edwards. Lives in England, 287 Cranbrook Road, Bristol. Two kids, Jennifer and Danny." Sten looked up from his notebook. "Want to know where they go to kindergarten?"

I struggled to find my voice and to make it sound calm. I could hear a tremor in it when I said, "Your information is out of date. Jill and I broke up last December."

Sten shrugged. "Oh, you broke up. My mistake. Then I guess you won't mind if I slit her throat and set her on fire."

I kept my hands on the desktop. I could feel blood rush to my face. My arms started to twitch and tremble. I tried to still them, pressed my hands down harder, but they just kept twitching.

Blake Sten seemed amused.

"Jesus," he said, "don't have a fuckin' seizure."

Grant nodded at him, said, "I think he gets the message." Then to me, "You do get the message, don't you? I don't have to ask Blake to go through Terry Green's brothers and nephews and nieces, Angela Green's parents, Vince Cosimo's sisters, Grampa Dudgeon's fishing buddies . . ."

I didn't answer. Couldn't speak. Just sat in place, trying to control my shaking hands.

"Good. Here's how it will work. You will call Blake before the end of the business day tomorrow and you will tell him that you are ready to hand over what you've found. I don't imagine you keep it here but that should give you plenty of time to get it. When you call, Blake will tell you where to go and what time to arrive. And you will deliver. If you don't, the people on Blake's list will start dying. Clear?"

"I really don't have it," I said. My vocal cords were tight and the voice that came out of me sounded higher than my own. Like a much smaller version of me.

"As I said, bad news for you then." Grant stood. "If you really don't have it, you'd better find it. The deadline will not change, and neither will the consequences of failure. Good-bye."

He left the office without looking back. Blake Sten stood, tore a sheet out of his notebook, and put it in front of me. A phone number.

"I'll answer the phone until 5:00 P.M. tomorrow. After that, I won't answer the phone." He lifted the heavy doctor's bag from the edge of my desk. "In the meantime, you can occupy your mind trying to guess which one of your people will be the first to die."

# PART III

Then stand to your glasses steady
And drink to your comrade's eyes
Here's a toast to the dead already
And hurrah for the next who dies.

—DRINKING SONG POPULARIZED IN THE 1890s
BY CHICAGO NEWSPAPER REPORTERS

SOME SING IT STILL.

# CHAPTER THIRTY-SIX

**They were gone a full minute** before I could even move. I got up and locked the office door and returned to the desk and hit the foot switch to shut off the video camera.

*I've got you on tape, you bastards.*

I was still shaky as hell and my hands were hard to control. After dropping a cigarette on the floor trying to coax it from the pack, I moved to the center of the room, did a hundred Hindu squats to burn off some of the adrenaline. That helped some.

I slid the hollow dictionary from my bookshelf, unplugged the wires. Placed the book on my desk, opened the cover, and pulled out the digital video camera. Flipped the screen open, set the camera to playback mode, turned up the volume, and hit Play.

The video was just electronically generated noise. A high-pitched squeal tone filled the audio track. My heart sank.

The doctor's bag. Blake Sten had brought along an electronic signal generator, hooked to a powerful transmitter.

A jammer.

I had nothing on tape. Nothing at all.

* * *

Behind the bar at Rossi's, there's a sign, old and yellowed by years of nicotine residue. Not much lighting in the place but if you squint you can read the sign by the red glow coming from the neon beer logos in the wire-covered window.

*A bartender is just a pharmacist with a limited vocabulary.*

Terry sat facing the sign, drinking scotch. And smoking a cigarette. But Terry quit cigarettes ten years ago. My eyes adjusted to the gloom as I took the battered stool next to him. His expression was grim, his eyes a little unfocused. The smoke rose from his cigarette like ghost worms in the still air of the bar.

"Angela's not going to be happy," I said.

"Angela's not going to know," said Terry. "Angela is staying at her mom's tonight. And I'm not taking it up again."

"All evidence to the contrary."

"I'm not an addict like you. I'll smoke today, forget about it tomorrow."

The bartender came by and I nodded at Terry's drink.

"Same," I said.

"He's on my tab," said Terry, then pointed at his glass. "And hit me again."

I wondered how many Terry had already downed; this was clearly not just his second.

The drinks were poured and the bartender moved out of earshot.

"Taking the rest of the day off?" I said.

"Yep."

"Want to tell me about it?"

"Nope."

"Tell me anyway," I said.

Terry blew a stream of smoke at the burn-scarred bartop. "Sure," he said. "My editor's sending me to Springfield for a week, maybe two. I leave in the morning. Angela is royally pissed. I promised to be there for the amnio on Tuesday. Now I'm gonna miss it."

"And she's staying at her mom's tonight to register her disapproval."

"Oh, it's been registered, believe me. What's going on with you?"

Where to start? "Jill and I got back together last night," I said. "Lasted 'til she saw the news this morning." Easier to start with that than the fact that Joseph Grant had just threatened Angela's life.

"It would take a special kind of woman to see that and stick around. Honestly, made me a little nervous myself. It was brutal, dude."

"I don't get it. Didn't you see me try to catch the guy?"

"That what you were doing?" Terry sipped his drink. "Didn't look like it. The angle they showed, it looked like you were trying to give the guy an extra shove."

*Fuck.*

"Crawley told me it didn't look good," I said.

"You dealing with that asshole again? I warned you about him."

"I know. You see his column this morning?"

"I don't read his shit," said Terry. "Bad enough I gotta work at the same paper."

Instead of telling him about Joseph Grant, I said, "What's so important in Springfield?"

"Nothing. State budget. They asked real nice, like I was doing them a big favor, all the while making it clear I didn't have a choice. Even with staff cutbacks, it's total crap. I graduated from beat reporter a long time ago."

"Nothing to do with cutbacks," I said. "They're sending you away until the congressional hearings are over, keeping you off the Hawk River story."

"You know this for a fact, or is this just your usual paranoid rant?"

"I met with Isaac Richmond last night. He told me that you were no longer working the story."

"Goddamnit. I suspected as much."

"Hey, it's not the first time and it won't be the last. Thought you'd be used to it by now."

Terry swallowed some more scotch. "Don't start. I'm not in the mood."

"What?"

"You ever listen to yourself? You come on with all that sanctimonious bullshit. Sure, you're better than the rest of us. You quit, I stayed. Therefore, I sold out."

"Whoa. I never said that."

"You say it all the time. You say it every time you sneer about the state of the news business. Every time you talk about how you couldn't handle the compromises, like you're admitting some personal failing, but what you're really saying is plenty clear. Let me tell you something: quitting doesn't make you morally superior. I'm still in the trenches, busting my ass. And once in a while, I get a good story out there."

"Terry . . ."

"Yeah, I've been drinking. Doesn't mean it isn't true."

I fished my smokes from a pocket and lit one. Drank some scotch. I didn't want to deal with this right now. But it had obviously been brewing awhile and now it was out in the open and I couldn't pretend he hadn't said it.

And I couldn't escape the feeling that our friendship was hanging in the balance.

"Okay, Terry. Maybe it is true, a little bit. No, a lot. It is true. But if I sometimes act superior, I don't feel it. Tell me, how many people have you killed?" I dragged on my cigarette, forced myself to continue. "You want the truth? Truth is, I'm jealous."

"Nothing stopping you from going back to journalism," said Terry. "Hell, I've tried to bring you back, how many times?"

"That's not what I mean. I'm jealous of your entire life."

"Seriously?"

"Yeah, seriously. You've found a way to make it work for you. You've got a great wife, a nice home. I don't even know how to do that."

Terry looked at me for a long and uncomfortable moment. "Damn. Sorry."

"Don't be. And don't get the wrong idea—I still think the news business is a cesspool. I just don't think I'm better than you for not working in that particular cesspool. I've got one of my own."

Terry lifted his glass, said, "Here's a toast to the dead already, and hurrah for the next who dies."

"Here's to our respective cesspools," I said, clinked my glass against his.

And with that, our friendship was back on solid ground. But the exchange left me feeling naked. I was suddenly eager to change the subject, even if it meant telling him the bad news.

"Joseph Grant came to my office today."

"Jesus, he *must* be worried."

"Brought Blake Sten and a couple of soldiers with him."

"Sounds like a bad scene." Terry stubbed out his cigarette.

"It was a very bad scene. And you're not gonna like this but listen up. Because it involves you. And Angela."

The sun had set three hours earlier and now the sky was about as dark as it gets in the big city. Five months since I'd moved back to Chicago and I still missed the black velvet blanket, punctured by countless white pinholes, that drapes itself over south Georgia at night.

In Chicago, you sometimes have to take the existence of stars as an article of faith.

I was parked down the block from Blake Sten's Bridgeport home. Despite what you see on television, you really can't go unnoticed in a fancy sports car, so the car was a rental and my Shelby was parked back at the office.

For the sake of poetic symmetry, I'd rented a Malibu.

Sten was home when I arrived, almost an hour ago. I was waiting for him to go out and starting to think I was wasting my time. I didn't have time to waste, but there wasn't much else to do.

I'd called Vince earlier and also spoken briefly with Amy. They were getting along fine and the area around her house remained quiet. Amy had agreed to meet with Special Agent Holborn and I was now waiting for him to call me back with a meeting time. I'd left a message on his cell detailing the events following his visit to my office and suggesting that the meeting take place sooner rather than later. I figured Joseph Grant's detailed threats would get his attention.

But my phone had remained silent, except for calls from television reporters seeking my response to the mall video. Other than repeating *no comment* a half-dozen times, I hadn't said much since my meeting with Terry.

He'd taken the news better than I'd expected. He was a grown-up. Even if he'd warned me about Hawk River, he'd wanted in on the story. Now he had to deal with the consequences. I promised to call him by the five o'clock deadline tomorrow and let him know the score. And I gave him the number of John Stone at Stone Security, suggested he hire an armed bodyguard for Angela while he was in Springfield, and maybe one for himself. Joseph Grant's private army could get by a bodyguard easily enough, but they'd probably just move to another name on the list when they saw that Angela had one.

Or not.

Now I was hoping I could get into Sten's place, maybe find something I could take to Holborn. Anything. The lights were still on in Sten's window but I had the feeling he was settled in for the night. I looked at my watch: 10:25.

My cell rang and I picked it up and said, "Ray Dudgeon."

"Jesus Christ," said a voice I didn't recognize. "Hold on." Then, away from the mouthpiece, "Lieutenant, it's Ray Dudgeon."

A new voice on the line said, "I can't believe this. Ray? It's Angelo."

"What's going on, Mike?"

"Got a fresh stiff in Boystown. Need you to come make an ID."

*Boystown.* Jill lived near Boystown.

"Man or woman?"

"Man."

I resumed breathing. "Why me?"

"Your number on his cell. Guess he didn't have time to hit Send before someone caved in his skull. You keep the wrong company, my man."

A lot of people telling me that lately.

"How'd this fall to you?" I said. "Boystown's not Area 4."

"Watch commander called me for a favor. Crazy night in 3. Buncha suburban frat boys out gay-bashing, got some dude stabbed a cabbie on Addison, homeless woman under the wheels of a bus, an OD at Punkin' Donuts. Plus all the usual crap. Must be a full moon." He gave me the address.

"Be there in thirty minutes," I said.

# CHAPTER THIRTY-SEVEN

**I** **pulled to a stop behind an unmarked cruiser** and two blue-and-whites with their roof lights flashing. A kid in a police uniform strode toward me, his hand held up like a traffic cop.

"You can't park there." Blond wisps of hair sprouted from his upper lip, petitioning for a promotion to the rank of mustache.

"Lieutenant Angelo called me in. I'm Ray Dudgeon," I said.

"Oh, right." A flicker of uncertainty as he tried to remember where he'd seen my face before. "Come this way." Still uncertain.

The kid led me behind yellow crime scene tape and through the door of a storefront bar that was stripped bare, midrenovation. The carved mahogany bar had been sanded down and was waiting for varnish. The walls were painted a light green but the electrical outlets still hung from holes in the drywall, waiting for new switch plates. Drop cloths covered the floor. The smell of sanded wood and fresh paint wasn't quite strong enough to block out another smell. A sweet and sickening smell.

"In here," called Mike Angelo from behind a purple wall of plastic beads that hung down from the ceiling. We made our way through the beads and into the back room. Mike stood with two detectives, all three of them smoking. A forensics guy fiddled with his box of exotic tools. The body lay on the floor, covered by a blue tarpaulin. The smell was stifling.

Angelo looked from me to Policeboy and thrust his cigarette in my direction and said, "Who the hell is this?"

"He said he was Ray Dudgeon, sir."

"He said. But you didn't check his ID." Mike glanced at me and almost smiled but kept it straight.

"No, sir." The kid's pale cheeks turned red and he looked at his shiny shoes.

"Okay then. Lesson learned, I hope. Get back to your post." Then to me, "You're late." The kid muttered apologies and retreated outside.

"Traffic," I said.

Mike said, "Detective Samuels, Detective Furnandiz," and they each nodded at me in turn without speaking or offering to shake hands. "I hope you didn't eat in the last hour, Ray."

Furnandiz dropped his cigarette into an empty Coke bottle and said, "If you did, I hope you saved room for dessert. Somebody made crème brûlée outta this guy's face with a fuckin' blowtorch."

Mike waved his cigarette at the tarpaulin and said, "Gerry."

The forensics guy peeled back the tarp. I almost puked. A sharp spasm of the diaphragm but nothing came up.

Samuels said, "Try not to hurl on the vic, Dudgeon." I recognized his voice from the phone call earlier.

"I gotta let fly, I'll be sure to aim your way," I said.

"A little focus, please," said Mike.

I turned my attention back to the mess on the floor. Started with the part easiest to look at. The dead man wore black leather oxfords, black pants, a navy double-breasted blazer, and a white shirt.

The hands and wrists were burned right down to the bone.

If the man had had hair, it was now gone. His entire head and neck were burned through the skin and down to the level of muscle and tendon and bone. Burned all the way to his scorched shirt collar and half-melted bow tie. No visible skin remained. Lips were gone. No eyes, either.

My stomach did another somersault. I stepped back and managed not to vomit.

"Hey, Dudgeon, check out the eyeholes, maybe you know the guy." Samuels laughed. "Sorry, Lieutenant." *Asshole.*

I turned away from the body, braced my hands against my thighs, and drew a few deep breaths, until the roiling in my stomach stopped.

Mike offered me his cigarettes and I took one and lit it and inhaled smoke, which helped deaden the stench a bit.

Gerry the forensics guy said, "For what it's worth, he was dead before he was broiled." It wasn't worth much.

"How long ago?" I asked.

"Four hours, give or take."

"Well?" said Mike.

"That's Delwood Crawley." My stomach clenched again, but not as strong and it passed quickly.

"No shit?" said Furnandiz. He cocked his head to the side like a spaniel and looked at the corpse. "Looks kinda like him, now that you say the name."

"Right neighborhood for him," said Samuels.

"Let's not get ahead of ourselves," said Mike.

Samuels stepped forward to plead his case. "All due respect, Lieutenant, this thing looks pretty obvious. I mean, it's beyond brutal and you know how these guys get when they kill each other. And Crawley was a fudgepacker for sure." Samuels was working in the wrong district station.

"You know that?" said Mike. "For sure? I mean, the guy was from England. They all seem a little that way."

"I'm not gonna get ahead of myself. I'm just saying, once the binder's full, this thing's gonna go down as a fag divorce."

"What about it, Ray?" said Mike. "You knew the guy."

"I have no idea if he was gay or not. He was a bit theatrical, but that doesn't mean anything." I didn't look at Samuels and resisted the urge to use the word *bigot*. "I think he was married once."

"Lotta fags are married," said Samuels.

"Can we discuss this someplace that smells better?" I said. "I don't know about you guys, but I could use a drink. I'm buying."

"Good idea," said Mike Angelo.

We met up again a few blocks away, at a little shoebox on Broadway called Reflections. The place smelled like cigarettes, cheap beer, and Pine-Sol. A big improvement over burned flesh. On the downside, the jukebox was playing *Foreigner's Greatest Hits*.

A large fish tank dominated the wall behind the bar and strings of multicolored Christmas tree lights covered much of the ceiling. The lights were dusty but the fish tank was clean and its inhabitants looked healthy enough. Freebie promotional crap from beer distributors covered the walls and there was a basketball game on the television over the bar.

Most of the customers were professional drunks, middle-aged and older, of both sexes. The rest were young gay men who enjoyed slumming with professional drunks.

Samuels and Furnandiz came in behind me and headed to the back of the room, where they flashed their tin and commandeered a table from some fat drunks decked out in ill-fitting Bears jerseys and ball caps.

I caught the bartender's eye, ordered four bottles of Old Style. Mike came in and stood beside me while I waited for the beer.

"Just got a call from Sergeant Warren. He's tied up with an armed robbery over on Racine." He shook his head. "Some night."

"Not a full moon," I said. "I checked."

"Whatever. This is his case; I'm just here as an observer. Samuels is the lead detective on this."

"What aren't you telling me?" I said.

Mike glanced toward the cops at the back of the room. Our beer arrived and he picked up three of the bottles. "Sergeant Warren was a detective until recently. He's new to Area 3." He held my eyes. "Understand?"

"Yeah. He was one of your dicks who—"

"Right. Now don't fuck around with these guys. They don't know about Warren, but this case is a heater—Crawley wasn't just any old citizen and they're gonna be all over his life by morning. They'll have his Day-Timer, notes, e-mails, everything. If there's a connection to you, they'll find it. So play it straight."

Mike headed to the table while I paid for the beer.

When I joined them at the back, Samuels said, "Okay, Dudgeon. Somebody tries to off you on the Mag Mile and a couple days later Crawley gets dead while dialing your number. God don't make coincidences that big, so don't even bother. What's the connection?"

"I don't know that there is one," I said. He started to object but I held up my hand. "I'm not saying there isn't, I'm just saying I don't know, because I don't know who the guy in the mall was or why he came at me. Look, Mike'll tell you I'm a cooperative guy. I'll give you whatever I know."

"Forget about the mall then," said Samuels. "Tell us about Crawley."

"Sure. I think Blake Sten killed him."

That stunned them. Samuels seemed almost disappointed that he wasn't going to have the chance to play *bad cop* with me.

He said, "And who is Blake Sten, if you don't mind."

"I don't mind a bit. Sten is vice president of corporate security for a military contracting firm called Hawk River, based in Aurora." Furnandiz wrote down everything I said in his little notebook.

I glanced at Mike. His look said: *Are you insane?*

My look back said: *You told me to play it straight.*

"Your next question is why do I think it was Sten," I said. "When we're done here, take a look at Crawley's column in this morning's *Chronicle*. I was his source for the lead item." They were going to find out anyway. "I think that item is what triggered the murder. Congress is investigating the billing practices of military contractors . . ."

"Congress . . . as in, Washington."

"Yeah. Anyway, I was looking into it—"

"Who's your client?" said Samuels.

"Not just yet."

"Listen—"

"We'll get to my client in a minute," I said. But of course I had no intention of ever getting to my client. "I went out to Aurora a couple weeks ago, asked Joseph Grant—he's the CEO—some questions. He introduced me to Sten, and Sten threatened me off the case."

"Threatened you how? Like, *I'm gonna kill you?*"

"Not quite that directly. But get this—he asked me if I knew what the best weapon in the world is. He told me that, to him, the best weapon in the world is fire, because it scares people."

"Really?"

"Yeah. He's a vet—Gulf War One—and he's got a nasty burn scar himself. You ask me, he's a sociopath. I were you, I'd pick him up for questioning pretty quick. Looks like he's gone off the rails."

"What're you, a psychiatrist?"

"Hey. You wanted to know what I think. I'm telling you. But if you guys tell Sten you got this from me, I'm gonna end up like Crawley."

"Don't worry about it," said Samuels. I stared at him until he added, "If we question Sten, we'll tell him we got everything from Crawley's notes. For now."

My cell phone started vibrating in my pocket.

"I gotta hit the can," I said. "Be right back."

In the men's room, I flipped the phone open. There was a text message from Holborn. It read: *Under the Bean—2 A.M. Bring Zhang.*

I replied with: *In trouble, need help. With CPD @ Reflections on B'way. Come get me—stat.*

Then I speed-dialed Vince. When he answered, I told him to bring Amy to the Bean at two o'clock. Told him I didn't have time to explain. Hung up.

I passed by the table, said, "I'll get us another round," and kept walking to the bar. The bartender was busy. Good. It would eat up some time.

Three glam boys in bright silk and shiny leather came chattering into the bar, called out for Jägerbombs, and descended upon the juke-box. I hadn't thought the music could get worse, but they proved me wrong. First up was Madonna. As I paid for the beer and returned to the table, Madonna finished threatening to dress me up in her love and Cher began to assure me that "Love Hurts."

Don't I know it, sister.

I put the beer bottles on the table, took a swig of mine, and said, "I bet if you check, you'll find a connection between the murder scene and Blake Sten. I mean, the place would've been locked, right? These military contractor guys make a lot of money, maybe Sten is part owner of the building or the bar that was going in, or maybe the company doing the renovations. Something like that. So he'd have keys and he could make sure they'd be alone." It didn't mean anything. I was just talking, burning up minutes.

"Let's get back to Crawley," said Samuels. "You fed him a story about your investigation."

"Basically. Crawley's always looking for gossip . . ."

"Was," said Mike Angelo.

"Yeah, was. And he wanted to know what I was working on. He mostly does—did—society and celebrity, but he also liked thumbing his nose at politicians."

"So you basically got him killed," said Furnandiz.

"Check his voice mail at the *Chronicle*," I said. "Also his e-mails. I left him a message last night, told him not to run it, and this morning he sent me an e-mail saying he couldn't resist the story." I drank some beer. "So don't look at me; I tried to talk him out of it."

"But you gave him the story to begin with." He wasn't wrong. I did basically get Crawley killed. But I didn't want to face that right now.

"I already said that, yeah."

"So you give him the story, change your mind and ask him not to run it," said Samuels.

"Yes."

"And he runs it anyway, lets you know by e-mail."

"Right."

"Then he goes to meet with Sten at a bar that's closed for renovation."

"Presumably," I said. "I have no knowledge of how he ended up at the bar, or if he went willingly, or if he knew he was meeting Sten. I don't know anything after his e-mail to me this morning."

"And then Crawley calls you from the bar . . ."

Now the girls of Sister Sledge were declaring themselves a family. The glam boys sang along with the chorus, camping it up and making a few of the older drunks slightly uncomfortable. The bartender asked them to tone it down a bit, but he asked nicely and they complied with playful pouts, returned to their conversation.

I turned back to Samuels. "Sorry, what?"

"Crawley tries to call you from the bar . . ."

"I'm taking your word for that," I said. "I never got the call. You say he dialed my number and I believe you. But I don't have any idea why, unless he suddenly felt bad about running the item and wanted to apologize."

"Delwood Crawley?" said Mike Angelo.

"Nah, I don't really think so, either," I said. "Not his style."

Just as I was trying to think of another tangent to take us on, Special Agent Holborn came into the bar. The cops at the table were all looking at me and didn't notice him until he was standing over us.

In his most official *FBI Special Agent* voice, Holborn said, "Lieutenant Angelo, nice to see you again." He nodded at the detectives, "Gentlemen."

Mike fixed me with a slow burn. I tried to look like I was just as surprised as he, but I don't think he bought it.

"Agent Holborn," said Mike. "What's going on?"

Holborn put his hand on my shoulder. "I'm here to take my witness." He gave me a quick upward nod. "Get up."

I stood.

Mike said, "Wait a sec, the FBI is taking over the Crawley murder?"

Holborn shook his head. "Unrelated case," he said.

Samuels got tough, said, "Then wait your turn; we're in the middle of a murder here. You can have him when we're done with him."

"You're done with him now," said Holborn. "You have a problem with that, you can take it up with my SAC in the morning."

I shrugged at the detectives. "Sorry, guys. Call me tomorrow if you have any more questions." I added a friendly smile. "I'm always happy to cooperate."

# CHAPTER THIRTY-EIGHT

**I** **left my rental car at the meter** and rode down to Millennium Park with Holborn. Along the way, I told him about Crawley's death and gave him the details on Grant's visit to my office.

"So Sten broiled Crawley to send you a message. He figured you'd start picturing the same thing happening to the people you love. Extra motivation. That how you see it?"

"Partly," I said. "He also had to find out how much Crawley knew. And I'd denied being Crawley's source. Don't think they believed me but they'd need to be sure."

"I'm sure he told them before he died," said Holborn.

"I'm sure he did."

"You think it's your fault?" The very question I'd been avoiding for the last couple hours.

"Of course it's my fault. I mean I can spin it—they'd have done Crawley to find out how much he knew, even if I hadn't denied being his source. And I told him not to run the piece. But . . ."

"But you fed it to him in the first place," said Holborn.

"Yup. I did that."

We rode in silence for a while. Holborn and me and my guilt, all crowded into his Grand Marquis. Yes, Delwood Crawley was a scumbag. Yes, I'd told him not to run the piece. And yes, Blake Sten was the man ultimately responsible for his death. None of that mattered. None of that washed my hands clean.

*All the perfumes of Arabia . . .*

This was something I'd be carrying for a very long time. There was no way to rationalize it. There would be no thinking it away.

"I've been meeting with resistance up the line on this," said Holborn.

"Big surprise," I said.

"Not what you think. We're moving forward, cautiously. But I'm expending some personal capital on this within the Bureau." He took the ramp off Lake Shore Drive and hung a right on Randolph. "We'll see what Amy Zhang has to say. But you don't actually have any evidence to back her up, do you, Ray?"

"Um . . ." I said.

"I thought not." Holborn smiled at his little victory. "Told you I'm not an idiot."

"So why are you—"

"Because if I don't, civilians are gonna start dropping like flies." He pulled a U-turn, stopped in front of the park entrance. "Because if I don't, Grant and Sten are gonna get away clean." He shut off the ignition. "Right now I've got nothing to stop them with. Like you said, they've got heavy influence in very high places. If I move too soon, we'll lose them forever. So you need to be prepared, because I suspect some bodies are going to drop before we have enough on them."

Bodies. A minute ago, Holborn had called them *the people you love.* Now they were bodies.

"Those aren't just bodies," I said.

"I know. But until I can present some hard evidence, I'm flying solo on this." He looked at his watch. "It's time, let's go."

\* \* \*

The Bean is a polished stainless steel sculpture that measures sixty-six feet long and thirty-three feet high and resembles, well, a bean. Or a blob of liquid mercury. Anish Kapoor insisted that people call his creation Cloud Gate, but he'd taken too long deciding on the name and by the time he got around to announcing it, Chicagoans had already given it the nickname that everyone used. Nobody called it Cloud Gate.

Because of its shape, you can walk directly under the Bean, and that's where Amy and Vince were waiting when we arrived. Amy looked nervous, which was to be expected. I guess Vince was nervous, too, because he shook my hand unnecessarily when I said hello. I introduced them to Holborn and told Amy that she could trust him and she should tell him everything. She just nodded.

Holborn didn't want me there while they talked. He wanted her story untainted by my presence. I didn't like it, but I understood. So Vince and I stayed put, while Holborn took Amy for a walk in the park. I watched as they disappeared across the winding Frank Gehry walking bridge, then I leaned back against a low wall with Michigan Avenue behind me. From this spot, the Bean reflected the entire Chicago skyline. It was one of the most beautiful views in the city.

The Bean was new, but the Michigan Avenue skyline was the one great constant in my life, and it still filled me with awe. Like the Bean itself, the skyline provided convincing testament that humans aspire to beauty. Despite everything.

Chicago was Trigger City, but not all the triggers were bad.

Vince propped himself against the wall beside me and listened as I told him all about this case, taking it from my first visit to Isaac Richmond all the way to Delwood Crawley's death. His life was in danger now and I owed him the whole story.

I finished with an apology. I should've told him everything sooner. Should've given him the information he needed so he could've chosen to bail out before things got to this point.

When I was done, Vince said, "You ever try to go down on a chick in a Ford Escort?"

"What?"

"Happened to me a few weeks ago. Met this wild chick at a bar. We were dancing, you know, and things got pretty hot 'n' heavy and we ended up in my car."

"Uh-huh."

"And I broke the condom trying to get it on. Only condom I had. So we went oral. When it came my turn to give, man, it was a hell of a thing, trying to find a good position for her. I'm gonna have to get a bigger car."

"Vince, did you listen to a word I just said? They mean to kill you."

"I heard you," said Vince. "Thing is, when I used to drive for Johnny Greico, my life was in danger, but for what? For nothing. Few weeks ago, I was doing your shit jobs, following Romeo around, serving papers on losers. Better than driving for the Outfit, but still . . . the biggest thing in my life was getting head from some chick I met in a bar. You see?"

"I see."

"Amy's a real nice lady," said Vince.

"Yes, she is."

"And I'm helping you keep her alive." He let out a broad smile. "And that's fuckin' awesome. Greatest thing I've ever done."

Holborn and Amy returned in just under an hour. Vince took Amy home and Holborn gave me a ride back to my car.

He said, "She told me everything you've done for her."

"Uh-huh."

"I like her story, and I believe her, but . . ." He shrugged. "I'll do what I can. I'll try to sell it to the desk in Washington but getting her into the program may take a little time, if I can get her in at all."

"They're gonna start killing people at five o'clock tomorrow," I said.

Holborn didn't answer. We drove in silence for a while and I looked out the side window at Lake Michigan. Moonlight reflected off the calm black water, glittered like false hope.

"She's a brave woman," Holborn said.

"She is," I said.

"I can't help but think . . . the whole time she and her husband were setting up those Web sites and smuggling news into China, American search engines were helping the Chinese government censor the news and American ISPs were turning over the names of political dissidents to the MSS."

"Welcome to the new ethos," I said. "Whatever it takes to make Wall Street happy. China's a big market."

"You sound like a radical."

"Hell, no, I'm a capitalist," I said. "But we both know that isn't the system we've got. It's a rigged game, and it's been rigged so long we don't even see it anymore. People like Amy know what freedom means. We've forgotten."

After a few seconds, Holborn said, "You must be a lot of fun at parties."

I put my soapbox away, said, "You should see me limbo."

He pulled the car to a stop across the street from where I'd parked my rental.

"Come to my office at ten," he said as I opened the passenger door. "I'll have an answer on Amy by then. The rest of it, I don't know. We'll see what answer I get from National."


I wasn't going to get more than a few hours' sleep and I knew if I went to Joan Richmond's place, the sheets would smell of Jill and I wouldn't sleep at all. So I went home.

There was a message on my machine. I pressed Play. My grandfather's voice said, "Ray, it's Pop. Had a visit today from an old friend of yours, by the name of Tim Dellitt. Nice young man, former navy. Said you two went to PI school together. I'm taking him out fishing tomorrow. Guess you're not home, so call when you get a chance. Bye."

I snatched up the receiver and dialed, listened to the phone ring in my ear.

No answer. But my grandfather was a heavy sleeper. I let it ring on. Finally he picked up and croaked a groggy hello.

"Pop, it's Ray. Sorry to wake you."

"What time is it?"

I looked at my watch. "Almost five. Almost six, your time. Listen: I need you to wake up, this is important. You need to be alert." I heard the rustling of bedsheets through the phone as my grandfather sat up.

"All right, all right. I'm up. What's the trouble?"

"The man who came to see you."

"Yes, Tim. Nice fella . . ."

"No, Pop, he's not a nice fella. He's the furthest thing from a nice fella you ever met. And he never went to PI school with me."

"Well, then he played this old man for a sucker. What's going on?"

"I don't have time to explain. You still have your service pistol?"

" 'Course I do."

"Get it, load it, keep it with you. If Dellitt comes back, he means to kill you. Don't let him anywhere near the house."

After a few seconds of silence, my grandfather said, "I'm supposed to meet him at the marina this afternoon."

"You stay put. And call Sheriff Grayson."

"Sheriff Grayson retired."

"Then call whoever the hell replaced him, I don't care. This is serious—"

"All right, calm down, son. I'll take care of it."

"You promise. You're not going to the marina."

"I'm not going to the marina. I'll get my gun, I'll call the sheriff. Don't worry about me. You just take care of whatever this mess is you've got yourself into."

"I will."

"And you call me when you can."

I fought to get the lump out of my throat. "Sorry about this, Pop."

"All right. You be careful now." He hung up without saying good-bye.

I took a quick shower, set my alarm for eight-thirty, and was asleep in minutes.

# CHAPTER THIRTY-NINE

**I woke with a start, sat bolt upright** with my heart pounding and Sister Sledge singing in my head.

*We are family, I got all my sisters with me . . .*

I leapt from the bed, threw on a pair of jeans, T-shirt. Slapped on some deodorant. Grabbed my gun and threaded the holster on my belt. Ran a toothbrush around my mouth, slipped into a leather jacket, and was out the door in two minutes. Didn't stop to shave or comb my hair; just jammed a ball cap on my head as I flew out the door.

*We are family, I got all my sisters with me . . .*

Broke every conceivable traffic law getting past the morning congestion to Joan Richmond's condo. Parked at a fire hydrant in front. Jumped from the car and sprinted up Joan's front steps. Unlocked the door and was inside.

*We are a family, get up everybody and sing!*

Snatched the disco albums from Joan's CD collection. Flipped through to the ABBA CD, took a deep breath, held it, opened the jewel case.

It was *ABBA's Greatest Hits*. But it was too thick; there was another disc behind it. I pulled off the ABBA CD, and there it was. Not a music CD, but a computer CD-ROM. Written in Sharpie on the face was: *Joan Richmond #1.*

I flipped through the other disco and Europop albums. They all had CD-ROMs under the CDs. *Joan Richmond #2, Joan Richmond #3, Joan Richmond #4, Joan Richmond #5.*

I stuck the first one into Joan's computer. The files were password protected. I didn't even bother to try to guess a password. The FBI had guys who could get into it without breaking a sweat.

On the way to FBI headquarters, it occurred to me that my big mistake had been my hatred of disco. In the past few weeks I'd listened to most of Joan Richmond's music collection, but I hadn't even touched these discs.

And Steven Zhang had tried to tell me. The soundtrack to his suicide had been his final message to the world. He'd put *ABBA's Greatest Hits* on the stereo when he shot himself.

Amy had told me that Steven hadn't given the computer files to Joan, but she was wrong. He had given them to her, *after* he killed her. He knew he wouldn't have time to hide them after the gunshots shattered the calm of a Saturday afternoon in Lincoln Park, so he'd hidden them in plain sight.

I got Special Agent Holborn on the phone, told him I was coming in hot, and he said he'd clear the decks for my arrival.

And he did. I pulled into the visitor's parking lot on Roosevelt and one of the armed security guards was waiting for me. I hopped out of the car and he walked me into the security hut.

The older guard behind the counter said, "Gun, sir," and I handed him my pistol. We didn't bother with ID this time, and didn't need to.

Holborn stood on the other side of the metal detector. He said, "I'll vouch."

I walked through, set off the alarm, and the younger guard passed the wand over me and it beeped at my belt buckle and keys and watch and pocket change and Zippo. He held out his hand and I gave him the lighter.

"Got 'em?" said Holborn. I held up the CD cases and he took them from me. He was wearing latex gloves. "Let's go."

We walked briskly from the security hut to the main building, the escort guard trailing behind, passed through the main doors, and then to the reception desk. I passed my driver's license under the bullet-proof glass.

"Come on," said Holborn, "you can pick it up on your way out."

I left my driver's license with the receptionist and followed him through the inner doors. We walked down the long hallway but turned before the elevators. Down another narrow hallway, then another, to a set of steel double doors. The sign on the door said ERT.

"Evidence Response Team," said Holborn. "This is where we do all the stuff you see on CSI, minus all the bullshit you see on CSI."

"Never watched it," I said.

We passed through the doors and into a large, brightly lit room with a stainless steel counter running around the perimeter. On the counter there were computers, scanners, printers, microscopes, and a whole bunch of machines unfamiliar to me. There was a large stainless steel table in the center of the room.

An evidence technician in a white lab coat, latex gloves, and a hair-net greeted us and Holborn said, "Dan, I need these processed fast."

Dan took the CDs over to what looked like a large steel armoire with glass doors. Inside was a pole with some empty hangers on it, and a wire mesh shelf. He carefully removed the CDs from the jewel cases and put them on the mesh shelf, took the liner notes and put them on the shelf, disassembled the cases, and added each piece to the shelf. Then closed the doors and pressed a button on an electronic keypad next to the doors. A red light came on above the doors and the room filled with a whirring sound.

"It's basically a giant vacuum cleaner," said Holborn. "It'll collect any fibers, stray hairs, flakes of skin. It would be nice to have some DNA to positively link them to Steven Zhang."

After a minute or two, the whirring stopped and the red light switched to green. Dan took the CDs out of the unit and brought them to the counter, where he sprayed them with something from a can and stuck them under a viewer.

He turned to me, said, "We've got prints, I assume some of them are yours."

Holborn said, "Dudgeon's prints are on file from his gun permit."

"Okay," said Dan. "Should be easy enough. Give me twenty minutes and I'll get them to the computer guys."

"Thanks," said Holborn. He peeled off the latex gloves and tossed them in the trash on the way out the door.

Down the hall to another room, this one full of computer stations. Holborn leaned through the door, said, "Emmett, Dan's sending you some CDs. I need you to open them and see what we got, bring it up to the meeting room. Soon as you can. Thanks."

"Okay, there's a lot to go through," said Special Agent Emmett Sanders, "but let's start with a quick overview of what we know so far."

We sat in the boardroom where Holborn and I had met before. Sanders tapped on his laptop computer and the big screen on the far wall lit up with two spreadsheets, side by side.

"The first three discs are all spreadsheets," said Sanders. "What it looks like is the classic scam, keeping two sets of books. Hawk River charges the military obscene amounts of money for everything. Forty-five dollars for a can of soda? These guys make a five-thousand-dollar hammer look like a bargain. What they do is, they elevate all their costs to keep their profits looking less obscene on the false set of books for the auditors. Worth prosecuting of course, and just the sort of thing the congressional committee is looking for. But not earth-shattering." As he talked, the screen showed page after page of double spreadsheets. "Everywhere you look, they're doing it. Travel costs, equipment costs, materials, everything. Of course, we'll know more when the forensic accounting guys get to it, but that's what it looks like so far. Here, I'll show you some examples . . ."

I caught Holborn's eye and tapped on my watch. *Time's wasting.*

"Okay, fine. Next," said Holborn.

Sanders gave a little shrug of annoyance, tapped on his computer keyboard, and the screen changed to a list of names, with dollar figures and what looked like bank account numbers.

He said, "Next is hotter stuff. Disc number four. Details of kickbacks to military procurement officers."

"Damn," said Holborn. The phone on the boardroom table rang and he picked it up. "Holborn . . . yeah . . . great, thanks." He hung up the phone, smiled at me. "The only prints on the CD cases, other than yours, belong to one Steven Zhang."

Sanders cleared his throat, reclaiming the spotlight. "As I was saying, we've got the kickbacks. And that's not all." He tapped his keyboard again. The screen showed another spreadsheet, less complicated than the ones we looked at earlier and containing more text within its cells and fewer numbers. "These guys cut a lot of corners. Now this is all preliminary, and we'll know more once we've had time to go through it, but I think I've got an idea what's going on here . . ."

"Stop," I said. Then to Holborn, "It's two o'clock. I have to make a phone call by five or people start dying. We can't be sitting here going through spreadsheets all day."

Holborn said, "Emmett, forget the computer. We can't read the screen from here, anyway. Just tell us the big items. In a nutshell, please."

Agent Sanders put the computer aside, sighed. "In a nutshell, disc four tells us three things. One—Hawk River was bribing military procurement officers. Two—they cut corners by hiring a lot of third party nationals, who didn't receive anywhere near the training that their American employees got, and cut more corners by sending the TPNs into theater with inferior equipment. Three—the mortality rate of the TPNs is *seven times* that of their American employees. And they were keeping false records to cover that up."

"So Steven Zhang found the records on the computers, realized that they didn't match the official records that Joan Richmond had, and told her about it," I said.

"Possible," said Holborn. Then, to Sanders, "What's on disc five?"

Sanders smiled. "Disc five is the grand slam. Again we've got two sets of records, but this time, we're talking about deployment. Hawk River has contractors deployed in seventeen countries. Officially. Mostly on contract to governments, some to corporations. Oil companies and mining—gold, uranium, diamonds—mostly in Africa and the Middle East but also South and Central America. There are four more countries where they've got soldiers on a classified basis—Colombia, El Salvador, Chile, and the Congo. They're not officially there, but they're there. So those *black contracts* appear in the records, but the country names are coded."

"Where's the grand slam?" said Holborn.

"The grand slam is Sudan."

"Darfur?" I said.

"Exactly. See, the Western world has largely pulled out of Sudan because of the political pressure. Genocide is hard to explain at a public shareholders' meeting, so even the big Western oil companies pulled out."

"Oh, crap," I said. "China."

"Right. China is by far the biggest consumer of Sudanese oil. China also supplies the Sudanese government with the weapons they use to slaughter their citizens. The other investors in the oil industry in Sudan include Kuwait, Saudi Arabia, India, and Pakistan, but even they do it through partnership with China's petroleum giants. Really, it's China's game. And Hawk River has been playing in Darfur, working for a shell corporation that is supposed to be Kuwaiti but is really China." Sanders leaned back in his chair and smiled. "Like I said, grand slam."

Holborn and I stared at each other for a long time. Finally Holborn said, "Oh my God. Hawk River is working for the Chinese government."

"Explains a lot."

"It's fucking treason."

"Maybe. Or it's something that Typhon the Multiheaded Beast knows all about and wants to keep under wraps. Alphabet Soup."

# CHAPTER FORTY

**The implications were massive.** Holborn had to admit that my concern about his investigation being scuttled by higher-ups now didn't seem like such a paranoid fantasy.

With something this big, it would take time to get the machinery of the FBI into gear. Time to go through all the files and be sure that they really proved what Agent Sanders surmised. Time to prepare reports and action plans and time to send them up the chain of command and time to have them reviewed and approved. Time to assemble teams.

And during all that time, Holborn would be waiting for the other shoe to drop. Waiting for the phone call from National Headquarters that told him to stop and forget everything he had learned.

We both hoped that call would never come, but hope is a fragile thing and Typhon the Multiheaded Beast would have a say in the final decision. On that we agreed.

It would all play out in time. But time was not on our side.

It was Emmett Sanders, bless him, who came up with a short-term plan. Sanders took all the files and compressed them using a zip program so they could fit on one disc. He burned two copies of this disc.

He assured me that there would be no way to know that these were not the originals. The files showed the same *created on, modified on,* and *last opened* dates as the originals. All the metadata was identical.

Agent Dan in the ERT even transferred Steven Zhang's fingerprints onto the copies.

My part in the plan was simple. Deliver the copies to Isaac Richmond and Joseph Grant. Simple but not easy, because I had to make them believe that these were the originals and that I didn't know what was on them.

And my head was swimming with what was on them.

Agent Sanders told me that he'd encrypted the files far better than Steven Zhang had. It would probably take Grant's people a few days to break the passwords. In the meantime, if all went well, Holborn would get the go-ahead from National.

And if he didn't . . .

If he didn't, we'd have to leap off that bridge when we got to it.


Now it was four-thirty. I called Blake Sten and told him that I'd found the files on a CD-ROM hidden in Joan Richmond's music collection. He gave me an address in Winnetka—Joseph Grant's house. Told me to bring the disc and be there at nine, sharp. Told me to park my car beside the house and go to the servants' entrance at the back.

I told him I'd be there and closed the phone.


Isaac Richmond led me down the stairs to his basement den. From the gun range on the other side of the wall came the *pap-pap-pap-pap-pap* of pistol fire. I'd have preferred the sound of bowling pins crashing around.

"Have a seat," said Richmond and went through the door to the funhouse. The sound of gunfire stopped. He returned with the two Alphabet Soup guys and they sat, the taller man on the arm of the couch, the shorter one in a chair.

Richmond remained standing. He said, "What have you learned?"

"You wanted to know the truth of your daughter's death."

"Yes."

"I found it."

"And what about the evidence?"

"They're one and the same, aren't they?"

Richmond's mouth twitched. "Yes, I suppose they are."

I pulled the CD-ROM from my briefcase, dropped it on the table. "There you go."

"What's on it?"

"Don't know. Password protected. I couldn't get into it. I'm sure you guys can."

"Okay," said Richmond. "Good work." He moved to see me out.

"Wait a second," I said. "You know what happened to Delwood Crawley."

"Yes, we heard about that."

The taller man said, "You shouldn't have confided in him."

"That's true," I said. "I shouldn't have. But that's beside the point. Point is, Blake Sten has run amok."

"You sure it was Sten?" he said.

"Unless it was you guys."

"Don't be an asshole, Dudgeon. We don't operate like that."

"Then it was Sten. I've heard his sermon on the use of fire."

"All right," said Richmond, "we'll look into it."

"Not good enough," I said. "I've done what you asked, and now you're gonna leave me hanging out to dry." Then I told him about the visit by Sten and Grant, the list they had of everyone in my life, the threat to kill them one by one until I turned over the disc. The only thing I changed was the deadline. Told them it was five o'clock tomorrow. "But since I brought the disc to you, I can't give it to Grant tomorrow. Now I need you guys to put a stop to this."

The taller man said, "You're telling us that Joseph Grant was in the room when Sten made these threats?"

"No, I'm telling you that Grant himself made the threats. Sten just read the list of names."

He made eye contact with Richmond, and something was communicated between them. Richmond nodded at him and said, "Go ahead."

He said, "Sir, it looks like these guys are way out of control."

We were all quiet while Richmond thought things over.

Finally I said, "Joseph Grant is going to kill everyone who matters to me. My grandfather, my closest friends . . . the woman I'm in love with. These people are *civilians*—they didn't choose to get involved in this. Don't let them be collateral damage, Colonel."

Richmond still didn't speak.

"If you really are that grieving father," I said, "you won't let it go down like this."

I saw myself out and left him with a decision to make. A decision upon which my life probably depended.

# CHAPTER FORTY-ONE

*One down and one to go . . .*

I pulled to a stop in Joseph Grant's side driveway, looked up at the Georgian mansion at the top of the circular main drive to my right. It must've been eight thousand square feet, with clean white columns on either side of the front door and fifteen tall windows on the front wall and a slate roof with six chimneys. Flames flickered in gas lamps on either side of the front door and on poles lining the main driveway.

The driveway was full of cars and there was a uniformed valet standing by the front door. I took note of a couple of tricked-out Hummers, an Aston Martin, a Maybach, and more than a few Mercedeses.

That I was out of the rental and back in my own car made me feel a little better. A '68 Shelby has nothing to apologize for, even in company such as this. True, I hadn't actually bought the car and couldn't afford it but it was mine, at least for now.

At the back of the side driveway was a four-car garage. I could see two black Lincoln Navigators at the ready; the other two doors were closed. The servants' entrance led into a mudroom, beyond which I couldn't see.

My finger stopped on the way to the doorbell and I was gripped with the desire to get back in my car and drive away. Fast. But I knew that I wouldn't and I went ahead and rang the bell. What I didn't know was if I'd ever get out of this house alive.

Blake Sten opened the door, grunted at me, and led me through the mudroom and into a hallway. He wore a tuxedo, which looked about as natural on him as a tutu on a bear.

We passed the kitchen, which was bigger than my whole apartment. Three women in black-and-white uniforms buzzed around with dishes and trays. A little farther down the hall, Sten pointed at a door on the right.

"Go through there, down the hall. There's a door at the end. Knock on it."

It was a tight hallway with a low ceiling, more of a hidden passage, which led past the dining room to the front of the house. A way for servants to get around without spoiling the guests' view. I got to the end of the passage, knocked on the door.

Blake Sten opened the door. I guess he wanted to make the point that he had the run of the place. We were in a large study, decorated with heavy wood and leather furniture, antique Oriental rugs, Tiffany stained-glass lamps. Oil paintings of Revolutionary War battle scenes and English hunting dogs hung on the walls. In an antique mahogany cabinet, behind glass, a display of handguns throughout the ages. A giant buffalo head mounted on a plaque hung between the windows. A full suit of armor stood in the corner.

For a second I wondered if Grant might be inside it.

Crazy thought.

"Nice digs," I said.

"Sure," said Blake Sten.

And that was the extent of our conversation. We stood, we waited. I silently admired the nice digs some more, thinking *Sten seems different today*. It was possible that, having seen what he did to Delwood Crawley, I was just looking at him through different eyes.

*No, it's more than that. He's changed. No swagger. Sullen.* Then it hit me all at once: *Sten is depressed. He loved doing what he did to Crawley. He got to play with the demon again . . . he's upset that you came through with the evidence, because now he has to put the demon back in its cage. He was hoping you'd fail, so he could play with the demon some more . . . with Terry, with Angela . . . with Jill.*

After a few minutes, the double doors to the main hallway opened and Joseph Grant stepped into the room, looking like he was born in a tux.

"Mr. Dudgeon," he said, closing the doors behind him. "I'd offer you a drink, but I don't like you and I'd prefer to get our business concluded as quickly as possible so you can go away." He said it with a pleasant smile.

"You mean I'll be allowed to leave."

"Not only allowed, but encouraged. In fact, I'll insist on it." He stood in front of me with his hand out. "Give." I handed him the CD jewel case and he walked over to his massive carved oak desk, slid the disc into the slot on his computer. "I'm off to Washington in the morning and I'd hate to have this weighing on my mind. I'm glad you found it." Conversational.

"I'm glad I found it, too," I said.

"Bet you are." After a few seconds, he clicked the mouse. Then looked at me. "Did you look at it?"

"Couldn't get by the password."

"Good thing for you. Why'd you even try?"

"Curious, I guess."

"*Dumb* is the word you're looking for," he said. But as usual there was no discernible stress or edge in his voice. He tapped on the keyboard and hit Enter. Did it again. And again. Nodded to himself. "Okay, Mr. Dudgeon. You may go."

"Just like that?"

"Just like that."

"And you're just going to forget about me, about the people on Blake's list."

"No. I'm not going to forget about you." He clicked the mouse again and the computer ejected the CD-ROM and he put it back in the case. "I'll have my people crack this and see what's in it. If everything checks out, I'll start to forget about you. As the years pass and you don't resurface in any of my affairs, I may even forget about you entirely. As for the people on Blake's list, it will be *your* actions that determine their fate. Only you can get them killed, and only you can keep them safe. Your silence will keep them alive." He put the disc in a desk drawer, locked the drawer with a key, and put the key in the watch pocket of his vest.

As Joseph Grant left the room, I caught a glimpse through the open door of the party across the hallway. Women in floor-length silk gowns, diamonds draped around necks and dangling from earlobes. Men in tailored tuxedos, smoking fat cigars, gold watches on their wrists and power in their pockets.

And the other men, those in their *dress blues* with stars on the shoulders, ribbons and medals pinned to their chests, perfect posture, and a gravy train to catch.


I cruised down Sheridan Road, then Lake Shore Drive, wondering why Grant had allowed me to leave. He had the disc, so killing me was now a minimal risk. Even if it drew some attention, with the evidence now secured he was safe enough. And with me dead, Sten would be free to finish things with Amy, tie off the final loose end in their cover-up.

As I drove back into the city, I allowed myself to think the thoughts I'd suppressed on the way into Grant's home. I'd been prepared to trade my life for the lives of the people on Blake Sten's list. I really hadn't expected to make it out alive. It didn't make me happy, but I'd been willing.

I came up from my thoughts, realized I hadn't actually seen the traffic for miles. I was on autopilot, driving fast, jumping from lane to lane, passing slower cars. And I was already south of Lakeview. My forehead was damp and clammy, my hands shaking again. I cracked the window and lit a cigarette, changed lanes and checked my mirrors, slowed to a reasonable speed, checked my mirrors again.

*At least nobody's following me . . .*

But I was wrong.

When they tag-team you, when they've put a GPS tracker on your car, you don't know until it's too late.

For me, it was too late just south of Fullerton.

By that time I was back in the passing lane, with the concrete barrier to my left and the northbound lanes on the other side.

The first to show itself was a GMC passenger van directly in front of me. The van slowed down as a big Chevy Suburban slid over from the right lane and a black Lincoln Navigator came up fast from behind, completing the box.

In an instant, I was trapped.

There wasn't a damn thing I could do. They dictated our speed and they were so perfectly synchronized that no opening offered itself.

I slowed and the Navigator didn't. Our bumpers touched and I sped up again, got back in my box. They weren't going to let me bull my way out.

The Suburban to my right beeped its horn and I glanced over. I didn't recognize the tuxedoed driver but beyond him, leaning forward and grinning at me, was Blake Sten.

He held a small remote control unit in his right hand. He held it up to show me. Then he pressed the button.

*Whump!* Something blew in my left front wheel well and the steering wheel jerked violently to the left and the Suburban gave my right front quarter panel a gentle nudge.

And that's all it took. I bounced off the barrier to my left and the Suburban nudged harder and I felt the world start to turn over on its side.

It's funny how the mind works. Everything was in slow motion now, and just as the world turned past its tipping point and I knew I was going over, I thought:

*This is going to lower the resale value . . .*

※   ※   ※

*Strong hands, dragging me . . . car horns blaring, lights passing . . . am I dreaming? . . . a man with a bow tie . . . not Crawley . . . bow tie . . . tuxedo . . . a syringe . . . paramedic in a tuxedo . . . not a paramedic . . . syringe . . . bow tie . . . tuxedo . . . Grant's party . . . tuxedo . . . the Suburban driver . . . NOT A PARAMEDIC!*

I grabbed for my gun, stuck the barrel against the hand holding the syringe, pulled the trigger.

# CHAPTER FORTY-TWO

**I woke up in a hospital room.** Warm afternoon light streamed through the windows. A handsome nurse with long silver hair stood at my bedside.

"Hello," she said.

"Hello." My voice came out sounding scratchy.

She passed me a large Styrofoam cup and I sucked water through the bendy straw. There was an IV line in the back of my right hand. My left arm below the elbow was in a cast.

"Tell me your name and date of birth," she said.

I did.

"Good. Do you know what day this is?"

"Thursday, unless I've been unconscious longer than I think."

She nodded. "Do you remember what happened?"

"Car accident."

"Very good."

I squinted her nametag: Dr. Martin. Not a nurse. Sexist assumption.

The nametag also said: Rush Medical Center.

*Damn.*

I swallowed. "Is Jill Browning on duty?"

Dr. Martin pressed a button and the top of the bed began to rise, putting me in a slightly reclined sitting position.

"She was. But she became distressed, we had to send her home." She glanced at the bedside monitor, wrote something on a clipboard. "Apparently she's very fond of you. We've given her a few days off."

"So what's the damage?" I said.

"To your body? Not too bad, all things considered. Moderate concussion, you may experience headaches, perhaps mood swings for a few days. Simple fracture of the left wrist—it'll heal. Some bruising from the seat belt, some kidney bruising, and you may pass blood in your urine for a day or two. You'll have aches and pains for a while, but you'll be all right."

My head felt fuzzy. I said, "My head feels fuzzy."

"That'll pass."

"When do I get out of here?"

"Now, actually." She pulled the tape off of my hand and removed the IV needle, taped a small square of gauze over the hole. "There are a couple of policemen waiting to see you. After you're done with them, press your call button and a nurse will help you with your clothes."

"Thanks."

She started for the door, stopped. "Mr. Dudgeon, Jill has many friends at this hospital. We don't like to see her in pain."

"I don't, either."

"Then take better care of yourself."

She left the room.

A minute later, the door opened and two cops came in, approached the bed. I blinked at them, brought them into focus.

Not cops.

"Alphabet Soup," I said.

"What?" said the taller one. The one who always did the talking.

"You guys have names?" I said. "Because I'm sick of thinking of you as *the taller one* and *the shorter one*. You're practically the same height. It's confusing, and my head is fuzzy. They don't even have to be real names, just—"

"I'm Dave," said the taller one. "This is Anthony."

"Thanks," I said.

"We're going to take you home."

"What about the cops? Don't they need to speak with me?"

Dave smiled. "There won't be any cops," he said. "It's all taken care of."


But they didn't take me home. Not right away.

They took me to Chinatown.

We rode there in silence, pulled to a stop in front of a fire hydrant on Cermak Road. Dave and Anthony got out of the car. Anthony opened the back door and helped me out and I walked gingerly with them to the entrance of a Chinese restaurant.

The sign in the door said CLOSED and the blinds were drawn shut. Dave held a cell phone to his mouth and pressed a button and it beeped like a walkie-talkie.

"We're here," he said.

The door opened and we stepped inside the dimly lit restaurant. Along the left wall was a row of booths, tables to the right.

The man who let us in closed the door and locked it and stood in place.

We walked forward. Amy and Theresa Zhang sat at the back of the room. Vince sat with them. There was a woman standing like a sentry next to the table.

In a booth near the front of the room, Special Agent Holborn sat with a sour look on his face. Dave and Anthony walked me to the booth and I sat with Holborn. They went back and stood with the guy by the front door.

"Hello, Ray," said Holborn. Subdued. "Glad you didn't die."

"Me, too," I said. "Want to tell me what's going on?"

Holborn blew out a breath. "It's complicated."

"Of course it is," I said.

He fixed me with a look that held as much weariness as anger. "Don't say *I told you so*."

"I won't."

"There are . . ." He glanced at the Alphabet Soup guys without any affection, looked back at me. "There are issues of national security involved here."

"Of course there are," I said.

"My hands are tied."

"Not the call you were hoping for."

"No. But I got Amy and her daughter into the program. That's something."

"That's a lot," I said.

"Because of you, they're going to live."

"Because of you, too," I said.

"But that's all. There won't be any investigation."

"Typhon, the Multiheaded Beast," I said.

Holborn nodded, "I'm afraid so."

"Well, thanks for telling me."

"I did my best."

"I know you did."

Dave stepped to the booth, said, "Time to wrap it up."

"You want to say good-bye to Amy?" said Holborn.

I walked to the back of the room. Amy stood from the table and we took a long look at each other. I put my arms around her. She hugged me back, hugged me as tight as she could, pressed her face against my chest.

"Thank you, Ray. Thank you," was all she said. Then she started to cry.

I kissed the top of her head and stroked her hair and held her tight.

And I realized that I was crying, too.

# CHAPTER FORTY-THREE

**D**ave and Anthony drove me home, walked me up to my apartment, and saw me safely inside.

"What now?" I said.

"Nothing," said Dave. "It never happened."

"Grant and Sten."

He shook his head. "Read the paper tomorrow."

"So that's it?"

"That's it. Get some sleep, forget all about it. Like I said, it never happened."

They were out the door thirty seconds when I grabbed the phone, dialed my grandfather's number in Georgia.

He answered on the second ring.

"Pop, you okay?"

"Surely am." There was a pause on the line. "Your friend Tim Dellitt came back. I took him fishing."

"What?"

"Yup. Terrible thing, though. We were about five miles out. He slipped on the gunwale, hit his head, went overboard. Never came up again."

"You're kidding."

"Nope. First time I lost a customer in forty years. Just a tragic accident."

"Wow."

"Your old grandpa didn't forget everything he learned in Korea. Question is, how are you?"

"I'm fine, Pop. Thanks. Just . . . tired."

"Get you some sleep then. We'll talk later."

I slept for a long time, without dreaming. Woke up around noon the next day. Put on a pot of coffee and opened the newspaper.

And there it was.

Joseph Grant, CEO of Hawk River, suffered a massive heart attack in his hotel room in Washington, D.C., yesterday afternoon. The hotel doctor pronounced him dead at the scene.

Last night, Chicago police responded to a 911 call from a Bridgeport home. The caller identified himself as Blake Sten and told the dispatcher he was going to kill himself. When officers arrived at the scene, they forced the door and found Sten dead of a self-inflicted gunshot. There was a note indicating that he was despondent over the earlier death of his longtime friend and mentor, Joseph Grant.

Typhon strikes again.

I watched Chicago streak by and felt the same rush of anticipation that I'd always felt as a kid riding the El to Wrigley. I listened to the train's rumble-rattle music and realized that I was feeling better about myself than I had in a while.

I'd been hired to find the truth of Joan Richmond's death and I'd found it. It was a bad truth, and it was a truth I was powerless to change. But I'd found it.

Of course you never really know the whole truth. I'd never know what happened to the missing pages of Joan's diary, or what was on them. I'd never know how complicit our government had been with China's involvement in Darfur.

And I was only able to stand by and watch as Typhon the Multiheaded Beast swept in to protect the status quo, and swept the evidence back into the darkest corners of the intelligence community. *Like it never happened*.

But I hadn't set out to change the world.

And along the way, I'd met a remarkable woman who was in deep trouble—and I'd helped her out of it. Helped her start a new life with her daughter.

That was enough for me. It had to be.


I got off the El at Belmont, walked a few blocks east, and stood in front of the yellow brick apartment building with two stone lions at the courtyard entrance.

Dr. Martin's words echoed in my head.

She said, "Take better care of yourself."

I would.

Inside my pocket was a little blue box and inside the box was my grandmother's engagement ring. My grandfather had given it to me when I moved to Chicago to go to college.

He said, "When you meet the right girl, you'll know."

I knew.